#1 *New York Times* Bestselling Author
JOHANNA LINDSEY

"One of the most reliable authors around.
Her books are well-paced and well-written,
filled with strong characters, humor,
interesting plots — and, of course, romance."
Cincinnati Enquirer

"Johanna Lindsey transports us. . . . We have no
choice but to respond to the humor and the intensity."
San Diego Union-Tribune

"First rate romance."
New York Daily News

"Johanna Lindsey has a sure touch
where historical romance is concerned."
Newport News Daily Press

"She manages to etch memorable characters
in every novel she writes."
Chicago Sun-Times

"The charm and appeal of her characters
are infectious."
Publishers Weekly

"Long may she continue to write."
CompuServe Romance Reviews

JOHANNA LINDSEY

GLORIOUS ANGEL

AVON BOOKS
An Imprint of HarperCollinsPublishers

AVON BOOKS
An Imprint of HarperCollins*Publishers*
10 East 53rd Street
New York, New York 10022-5299

Copyright © 1982 by Johanna Lindsey
Excerpt from *The Pursuit* copyright © 2002 by Johanna Lindsey
ISBN: 0-380-79202-8
www.avonromance.com

First Avon Books paperback printing: February 1982

Avon Trademark Reg. U.S. Pat Off. and in Other Countries, Marca Registrada, Hecho en U.S.A.
HarperCollins ® is a registered trademark of HarperCollins Publishers Inc.

Printed in the U.S.A.

OPM 40 39

For my mother,
whose love and encouragement are priceless

GLORIOUS
ANGEL

One

Angela Sherrington tossed another log on the hearth. "Damn myself, anyhow!" she cursed as she glared at the sparks shooting out onto the floor.

If only she hadn't been so foolish as to waste matches! Now she was forced to keep the fire burning all day and all night. Since the matches had run out last week, the shack Angela called home had been hell to live in.

Angela cast another glowering look at the fire and then she walked out onto the narrow porch in front of the little one-room shack. She was hoping for a breeze, but it was at least eighty degrees. She cursed herself again. In this sorry year of 1862, matches were scarce. The war had made every necessity scarce, and she would just have to be more careful.

The Sherrington farm, if it could be considered

1

a farm at all, was less than a quarter mile from the Mobile River, and about a half day's ride from Mobile, Alabama's largest city. The fields surrounding the farm were newly bare, as was the harvest shed, with its rotting walls and leaky roof. The house had once been whitewashed, but now it was necessary to strain to see the few patches of remaining paint. Two wicker chairs in deplorable condition and a wooden crate that sufficed for a table were on the porch.

Reluctantly, Angela went back inside the house and began kneading dough at the kitchen table. The heat was wearing her down, what with the fire blazing behind her and the sun pouring in through the windows in front of her. But equally wearing was the worry over her father. He had gone to Mobile yesterday to sell the last of their corn crop. He should have returned yesterday afternoon, but for the fourth time in her life, Angela had spent the night by herself. It was a sad fact that all four times had happened since the war.

With a heavy sigh, Angela gazed out the cracked window to the red field. The field should have been plowed that morning to make it ready for the new crop of peas and lima beans. She would have begun the task herself if they owned more than one mule. But they didn't, and her father had old Sarah hitched to the wagon. Damn his old leather hide, where *was* he?

Angela had been up since well before dawn. That was the time she liked to clean house, the only time of day in summer when it was cool enough. Her home wasn't much, but nobody could say it wasn't clean.

Angela wiped at the sweat on her face. She tried to stop worrying, but she just couldn't. The other three times he had stayed away all night had been when he was too drunk to make it back to his wagon. She hoped he was only drunk, and that he hadn't gotten into a fight.

Angela could take care of herself. She wasn't worried about that. Even when her father was home, he was often drunk and lying in bed. She hated it, but there was nothing she could do to stop his drinking. William Sherrington was a drunk.

Of necessity, she had learned how to hunt game. Otherwise she might have starved waiting for him to come out of his stupors. She could kill a moving rabbit in only one shot.

Yes, she could take care of herself, but that didn't stop her from being uneasy whenever her father was away.

Awhile later the sound of an approaching wagon made Angela's spirits rise. It was about time! And now that her anxiety was over, her anger surfaced. Her father would get an earful this time.

But it was not old Sarah who came loping

around the tall cedars. Two gray mares were pulling a dusty, mud-splattered carriage. And the last person she wanted to see was driving that carriage.

Two

Billy Anderson slowed his mares. He had ridden as if an army of Yankees were hot on his tail. The chance he had been waiting for had come unexpectedly this morning, with the knowledge that William Sherrington was passed out drunk in the street, leaving his daughter alone. Billy grinned, recalling the day.

The morning had begun as any other, with the hot summer sun quickly melting any traces of the cool night. It would be another fiercely hot day, a day to fray everyone's nerves, a day to make tempers flare. Billy stretched lazily and wiped the sleep from his eyes. Before opening his father's store for business, he gazed out into the street where hawkers were crying their wares, servants were hurrying to market, children were playing while they had the chance to, before the heat sent everyone scurrying home to hide in their shaded houses.

It wasn't too different from before, Billy thought. At least Alabama was not like other southern states, where battles were being fought. The Union army had been kept out of Alabama. To many people here, the war was not quite real.

Billy snorted. Yankees were cowards—anyone with sense knew that. It was only a matter of time before the Confederacy won the war. Things would be normal again. And Billy's father would be out of debt.

A long sigh escaped him and Billy stretched, trying to shake the sleep from his lanky body. He moved over to the large table covered with bolts of material and fingered the dull cottons resting protectively on top of the more expensive cloths. It had been a long time since anyone had bought even the cheap cottons.

These were hard times for everyone. But that wouldn't last much longer—it couldn't. And one day this store would be Billy's. He didn't have the heart for merchandising, though. He didn't have the heart for much of anything—except whoring.

Billy grinned, his brown eyes crinkling. He sauntered over to the long counter where the money box was kept and sat down heavily on a three-legged stool behind it. Running his hands roughly through his reddish-brown hair, he tilted the stool until his back rested against the shelves behind him, and propped his feet up on the counter.

Sam Anderson would take a fit if he found his son like this, but Sam Anderson wouldn't be down for another hour or so, having had a late night with his cronies. Billy's father liked cards and dice, and anything else he could wager on, and Billy just managed to keep quiet every time his father said, "Just one big win, and we'll be out of debt." But Sam Anderson's luck wasn't with him, not the way it had been before the war. He continued to lose and borrow, lose and borrow more.

Billy snapped to attention when the tiny bells above the door jingled. His eyes widened with surprise when two young women entered, their frilly parasols swinging from their wrists, and he recognized nineteen-year-old Crystal Lonsdale, high and mighty princess of The Shadows plantation, and her friend, Candise Taylor. Billy assessed them thoroughly. Crystal was stunning, with wide blue eyes and shimmering blond hair. A trifle skinny for his taste, but certainly a beauty, and one of the most sought-after females in Mobile County.

Candise Taylor was a few years older than Crystal, with raven-black hair tucked neatly under her blue bonnet, and startling blue eyes the color of early dawn. She was the daughter of Jacob Maitland's closest friend, here for a visit from

England. She was as lovely as Crystal, with a softer face and gentle manner.

Billy came around the counter and approached the two fashionably dressed young women, the one in pink and the other in blue. He wished that he were not so poorly dressed.

"Can I be of service, ladies?" he asked in his most sophisticated voice, a charming smile on his thin lips. Crystal glanced at him briefly, then turned away. "I hardly think so. I can't imagine why Candise wanted to come in here."

"It never hurts to shop wisely, Crystal," Candise replied shyly.

Candise looked quite embarrassed, though not nearly as much as Billy as he watched them walk away from him and heard Crystal's annoyed drawl. "Really, Candise! Your daddy's as rich as mine is. Why, when Mr. Maitland asked me to accompany you shoppin', I never dreamed you'd want to come to a place like this!"

Billy bristled. The snobby little bitch! He'd love to throw Crystal Lonsdale out on the street. But he knew his father would horsewhip him if he so much as looked at her funny. She was too close to the Maitland family. Jacob Maitland was a very wealthy man. He was also a man to whom Sam Anderson was deeply indebted.

Billy stalked back to the counter and plopped down on the stool again. He watched the two young women furtively, his freckles noticeable now because his face was pale with anger.

Billy would have given anything to be as rich as Jacob Maitland. Billy had always envied the Maitlands. He could still remember the day they arrived in Mobile, fifteen years before. He had gone to the docks with his father to pick up a shipment of goods for the store. A large ship had just docked and there were Jacob and his wife and their two sons, the only passengers on that fine ship. Billy was awed by their rich clothes, the magnificent carriage awaiting them, the crate after crate after crate of Maitland belongings.

It was currently rumored that Jacob Maitland's business interests were so many that he was one of the richest men in the world. He had properties and businesses, mines, railroads, and countless other investments all over the world. Billy didn't know, but Maitland was surely one of the richest men in Alabama.

There was a man who didn't have to stay in the South while the war was going on, who could be living anywhere in the world. Yet he was a southern gentleman now, and had elected to stay and support the South. And support it he did, with money, and with his younger son Zachary, who had joined the army, leaving the older son, Bradford, to handle the family interests. Now, there was a fellow Billy envied—Bradford Maitland. He had all that money, lived as he pleased, and traveled all over the world.

What luck to be a Maitland! How Billy wished he were one of Jacob Maitland's sons. How often he had dreamed of being part of that family. He didn't have those silly dreams anymore, but the envy was still there.

Billy's attention was abruptly drawn.

"Why, even trash like the Sherringtons come in here," Crystal was sneering.

"You mean that poor man you pointed out to me? The one lying in the alley?"

"That disgusting wretch we saw lying drunk in the alley. Yes, William Sherrington. Did you know they live only a mile away from Golden Oaks?" Crystal asked her friend disdainfully. "I can't imagine why Jacob Maitland lets a man like that farm his land."

"I think it's a shame," Candise ventured.

"Heavens, Candise! You'd pity anyone. Now let's leave this place before someone sees us here."

A smirk formed on Billy's lips as he watched the two girls leave the store. Yes, run little princess, before any of your fancy friends finds you slumming. Bitch!

His blood had quickened as he listened to them discussing Angela Sherrington's father. That wild, fiery-tempered hellion had been his obsession for a long time. Although she had only just turned fourteen, she had filled out nicely recently. She was the prettiest piece of white trash he'd ever seen.

Billy had hardly recognized her when she came into the store a few months back. No longer a skinny little brat with stringy brown curls, she had started showing curves. And her face had changed. Angela Sherrington was downright pretty. Her eyes were deep violet pools hidden by thick, sooty lashes. Billy had never before seen eyes that color. They could catch and hold attention as if casting a spell.

After that day, Billy had started going out to the Sherrington farm and hiding in the crop of cedars that formed a thick wall in front of the Sherrington shack. He watched her working in the fields with her father. She wore tight breeches and a cotton shirt with rolled-up sleeves. Billy couldn't take his eyes off her.

Billy waited impatiently for his father to come down so he could leave. And when he left the store, he made sure that William Sherrington was just where Crystal had said he was.

Now Billy's time was at hand. Just thinking about Angela being all alone in that shack caused an ache in his loins. Now he would have her! He could just feel her wiggling beneath him. He would be the first, too, and that counted for a lot. Lord, but he couldn't wait!

Billy halted the mares and leaped down from his father's carriage.

"That's far enough, Billy Anderson."

Billy smiled. She was going to put up a fight, and that just might be even more fun.

"Now, is that any kind of greetin', Angela?" he asked indignantly.

He stared at the rifle she held pointed at him but then his eyes moved to her slim hips, outlined by breeches, then up to the tight shirt. Her breasts pressed hard against the rough material. Obviously, she wore nothing beneath it.

"What're you doin' here, Billy?"

He looked at her face now, smudged with dirt and flour, but still pretty, and then he caught and held her eyes. What he saw surprised him. Was it humor? Was she laughing at him?

"I just came for a visit," Billy said, running a hand nervously through his hair. "Anythin' wrong with that?"

"Since when you come visitin'? I thought you was the kind that just hid behind trees, too damn scared to come forward," she replied.

"So you know about that?" he asked smoothly, though his blush betrayed him.

"Yeah, I know. I seen you plenty times, hidin' over there," she said, nodding toward the cedars. "What you been spyin' on me for?"

"Don't you know?"

Her eyes widened and seemed to turn a few shades darker, a striking violet-blue. Now there was no trace of humor. "You get, Billy! Get!"

"You sure ain't bein' very neighborly, Angela," he said warily, his dark brown eyes on the rifle held firmly in her hands.

"You ain't my neighbor, and I got no call to be neighborly to the likes of you."

"I only came to visit—sit down and talk a spell. Why don't you put down that rifle and—"

"You admitted why you came, Billy, so don't be

tellin' me lies now," she said coldly. "And this here rifle ain't leavin' my hands, so why don't you get your skinny ass on back to the city where you belong."

"You're a foul-mouthed little bitch, ain't you?" he sneered.

She smiled, showing gleaming white teeth. "Why, thank you, Billy Anderson. If that ain't the nicest compliment I ever did get."

He decided on a different approach.

"All right. You know why I came, so why are you bein' so disagreeable? I'm not just out for a little fun. I'll take care of you. I'll set you up in a house in the city. You can leave this little farm and live a life of ease."

"And what would I have to do in return for this life of ease?" she asked.

"You know the answer to that."

"Yeah, I know," she returned. "And my answer is no."

"What the hell are you savin' yourself for?" Billy asked, his freckled face showing his irritation and bewilderment.

"Not for the likes of you, that's for sure."

"The only thing you got to look forward to is marryin' another dirt farmer and livin' just as you are now for the rest of your life. Is that what you want?"

"I got no complaints," she replied defensively.

"You're lyin'!" he snapped and started toward her.

"Don't you come no closer, Billy!" Her voice rose to a high pitch. She stared straight into his angry eyes. "I'm gonna tell you honest that I'll shoot you without battin' an eye. I'm sick'n tired of you boys thinkin' you can have me just for the askin'. Hell, most of you don't even ask—you just grab. I've had it, do you hear? I ain't got the strength for no more fightin'. But this here rifle's got strength. It's got the strength to blow your conceited head off. So you better get before that's just what happens!"

He backed away, the fury in her voice warning him that she meant what she said. Damn!

"I'll have you yet, Angela, just remember that!" he called as he climbed back in the carriage, his mouth set in a tight line. "You're dealin' with a man now, not a boy!"

She laughed. "I ain't never shot no man, but I reckon there's a first time for everythin'. Don't come back, Billy, or you'll be the first."

"I'll be back," he promised. "And I'll *be* the first, only not the way you mean. I will have you, Angela Sherrington, I promise you that."

Billy Anderson drove away recklessly, taking his fury out on the two hapless gray mares.

Three

Angela slammed the door with a bang and threw the bolt, then collapsed against it, her heart pounding painfully. Icy rage gripped her, as it did every time she was confronted by boys like Billy. What did they think she was, a whore? Of course they did. Why else were they forever grabbing her?

Angela sighed impatiently. She realized she had no one to blame but herself. She used to enjoy whipping any boy who dared to tease her. And that was all they used to do—just tease. It had been a show of strength then. But now it was getting harder and harder to win those fights. The same boys she used to send away with bloodied noses were now almost men.

Angela had always felt awkward around girls, having been raised without a woman. She had run with boys instead, until their constant teasing became unbearable. Soon, girls her own age would have nothing to do with her. And colored girls shied away from her because she was white. The only friend she had was Hannah, kind-hearted Hannah.

A knock made Angela start and she clutched the rifle tightly. Had Billy come back already?

"It's me, child. That boy done gone."

Hearing Hannah's voice, Angela threw the door open eagerly and stomped out on the porch.

"That sorry son ov a pig had the nerve to—"

"I knows, Missy. I knows." Hannah soothed, startled by Angela's fury. "That boy passed me on the road and I seen him turnin' to come here, so's I snuck 'round the trees and was hidin' behind the house, waitin' to see iffen you'd need help. O Lordy, Master Maitland sure ain't gonna like this, he sure ain't," Hannah mumbled to herself.

"What?"

"Nothin', Missy, nothin'," Hannah said quickly. She put her arm around Angela and urged her to sit on the porch steps. "I guess you's just growin' up. Yessum, you sure is."

Angela wondered briefly why Hannah would mention Jacob Maitland, but Angela wasn't sure she'd heard correctly, so she let it pass.

Angela had first met Hannah on the day, five years before, when the older woman had emerged from the forest of cedars between Golden Oaks and the Sherringtons' little farm, saying she was lost and close to fainting from the heat. Angela insisted she come inside and rest. Later, Angela showed Hannah the way back to Golden Oaks.

Angela just couldn't understand how a servant from Golden Oaks could have gotten lost. All she had to do was go down to the river and follow it. The plantation was only a little ways back from the rolling Mobile River, and clearly visible from the river's edge. Or else she could have gone along the river road until she came to the long lane of giant live oaks that led to the mansion where the Maitlands lived.

To Angela's surprise, Hannah returned a week after that with a sack of flour and a basket of eggs. She said they were payment for Angela's having saved her life. And no matter how Angela protested, Hannah insisted she had a debt to repay. William Sherrington thought the whole thing was funny, and he saw no reason not to accept the goods. Food was food, and the Sherringtons never had too much of it.

"The gal thinks she has a debt to repay, so who are we to say no?" William had laughed. "It ain't as if we was takin' charity."

Hannah came once a month after that, always bringing something with her. First it was food, but since the war had started, she brought pins, salt, matches, and fabric. Most poor people were now doing without those things.

Everything Hannah brought she stole from the Maitland household, swearing to the good Lord that the goods would never be missed. Each month, Angela made her promise not to steal any more, but Hannah continued to break her promise every month.

Angela had a special affection for Hannah, her only woman acquaintance. It didn't matter that the color of their skin was different. They were just two women, a young girl and a plump woman three times as old who just sat and talked.

Charissa Sherrington had run off a year after Angela was born. Her mother had tried to take her with her, but her father had found them and brought Angela back, perhaps hoping to force Charissa to return. But she hadn't.

Angela sometimes wondered what it would have been like if her father had not found them. And she often wondered where her mother was now. Her father had raised her by himself, which accounted for her unfeminine habits.

So Angela confided to Hannah most of the girlish things she might have told a mother, things she wouldn't dream of speaking to her father about. And one of those things was that she fancied herself in love with Bradford Maitland. But of course, that had been last year, before Hannah told her the terrible truth about Jacob Maitland's oldest son.

"That boy, he the only one to bother you?" Hannah was asking her now.

"Billy's the only one who's ever come here, but he ain't the only one who's insulted me."

The whites of Hannah's eyes grew rounder. "What you mean, child?"

Angela had always been too embarrassed to mention to Hannah about the scraps she got into with boys. But after the shock today, embarrassment didn't matter.

"I've been defendin' myself for a long time now against them young jackasses who want to grab me all the time."

"Lordy, Miss Angela!" Hannah cried. "Why ain't you told me 'bout this sooner?"

"It only happens when I go to the city. And so far I can still take care of myself. But I ain't gonna do no fightin' no more. I'm gonna use this!" Angela said hotly, holding up her father's rifle.

"Who them boys been botherin' you?"

"Just boys I've known since as far back as I can remember."

"But their names?" Hannah persisted.

Angela's brow creased in thought. "Judd Holt and Sammy Sumpter," she said, then added, "and the Wilcox brothers and Bobo Deleron too. Those are the ones I've been obliged to whip occasionally."

Hannah shook her head. "And that one come here today? What's his name, Missy?"

"Billy Anderson. But why're you askin' me about all this?" Angela questioned, her temper ebbing now.

"Just wonderin'," Hannah said evasively.

"Where's your pa? Why weren't he out here runnin' that Billy Anderson off?"

"He stayed in the city last night and hasn't been home since."

"You mean he left you all alone?"

"Yes, but—"

"O' Lordy!" Hannah exclaimed and hoisted herself to her feet. "I gots to go!"

"Wait, Hannah! Did you by chance bring any matches?" Angela called after her.

"Yessum, they's in the basket on the porch," Hannah replied, already hurrying back to Golden Oaks.

Angela shook her head. What had got into Hannah? She seemed more upset about Billy's coming here than Angela was.

Billy Anderson tore into the gray mares with his short whip, taking his anger out on them all the way back to Mobile. He would never forgive Angela for making a fool of him. He couldn't remember ever being this enraged before, except maybe last year when his father had locked him in his room to keep him from volunteering, and him seventeen years old then and wanting more than anything to get in on the fighting and be a hero.

This was even worse. Angela had made him look like a coward. If she so much as breathed a word about running him off at riflepoint, he'd kill her. He should have taken that rifle away from her and given her a good thrashing. Then he could have thrown her down and gotten what he came for.

In his reckless race away from the scene of his humiliation, Billy almost careened into a passing carriage. He cursed aloud, then flushed when he saw who was in the carriage. Crystal Lonsdale and Candise Taylor barely glanced at him as they went by. Seeing them brought back the morning clearly.

Now Angela was probably laughing at him, just like that Crystal. But she wouldn't be for long. He'd have Angela yet. She'd never make a fool of him again.

Four

 Hannah went the full mile back to Golden Oaks, almost running. She didn't bother with the back entrance, but walked right through the front door and made straight for the master's study. Lord, but Master Jacob was going to raise the roof.

Hannah could hear Candise Taylor and Crystal Lonsdale playing backgammon in the drawing room. Candise and her father had been honored guests at Golden Oaks for two weeks now, but they would soon be going back to England. Crystal Lonsdale had been a regular visitor to Golden Oaks for quite a few years now, and her brother Robert even longer. Robert had joined the Alabama troops along with Zachary, Jacob's younger son, when the war first broke out. Under Braxton Bragg, they defended the coast between Pensacola and Mobile. Robert had stayed to guard Mobile Bay, but Zachary had gone with Bragg when he took command of the Army of Tennessee. Lord, protect them, Hannah thought, as she had so many times.

Hannah knocked softly on the study door and entered when Jacob Maitland bid her. She stood before the desk where Jacob was poring through the ledger, as he did every afternoon. He hadn't looked up yet to see who had come into the room, so Hannah stood patiently.

She knew Jacob was going to be upset and that was bad. He had had a mild stroke a few years before and was supposed to take it easy. He left most of his business interests to others now.

Hannah would die if anything happened to Jacob Maitland. She remembered all too well what life had been like before he came to Golden Oaks, buying the land and mansion as well as all the slaves. Those had been days of constant fear, fear of having family members sold away, fear of the whip.

Now the slaves no longer felt like slaves, and it was all Jacob Maitland's doing. Hannah knew there wasn't anything she wouldn't do for Jacob Maitland. He had given her new life, self-respect. Most important, he had given back her firstborn, her son taken from her and sold eighteen years ago, when he was four. Jacob found the boy and brought him back to Hannah.

She knew where Jacob's convictions lay, that he would have set all his people free if it weren't necessary to give the impression of conforming to southern standards in order to live here. But, in this war, he actually supported the North.

Of course, Jacob was unaware that Hannah knew all these things and more. Only she and her family knew, for her husband, Luke, was Jacob's manservant, and overheard Jacob talking in his sleep. But her family guarded those secrets. Hannah had once slipped and revealed a fact to Angela that no one was supposed to know. But Angela was a good girl. She knew the tragedies that would result if she told anyone the secret. Hannah was certain Angela wouldn't.

Jacob still hadn't looked up from his ledgers, but Hannah stood patiently, her brown eyes resting on him fondly as she waited. He was a fine-looking man of forty-eight, with only a slight shading of gray at his temples. The rest of his hair was still so black it sometimes looked blue. But his eyes! Lord, that man had scary eyes. If the devil ever came up and showed himself, Hannah was sure he would have eyes just like Jacob Maitland's. They were a light golden brown, except when he was angry. And for all his goodness, this man sure had a temper. And when that temper rose, those eyes would change to pure gold-yellow flames, ready to burn into whomever they lit on.

Of Jacob Maitland's two children, only Bradford looked exactly like his father. Zachary was the same height as his older brother and his father, just an inch under six feet, but Zachary took his mother's eyes and temperament. He was certainly not as adventurous as his brother.

Jacob Maitland looked up now and frowned slightly. "What are you doing back so soon? She *was* at home, wasn't she?"

Hannah always liked to listen to Jacob Maitland talk. He had such a fine, precise way of speaking. She'd tried to copy his way of talking years ago, but her family made such fun of her that she gave it up.

"Yessuh, she's home."

"Well then, how is she? Is she still making you promise not to steal from me?" Jacob chuckled.

"I left 'fore she had a chance to," Hannah said, still squeezing her hands nervously.

"Is something wrong, Hannah?" Jacob questioned, his eyes narrowing. "Out with it."

"Maybe we should go out to the stables, Master Jacob, 'cause I gots this feelin' you's gonna be raisin' your voice, and the young ladies is back from the city and in the drawin' room. They's gonna hear you."

"Out with it!"

Hannah took a deep breath and shivered slightly, seeing those gold-brown eyes already lighting up with flame.

"Missy Angela almost got herself raped this mornin'," Hannah blurted out, her eyes wide, waiting for the storm to break.

"*She what?*" he demanded, jumping instantly to

his feet. "How could that happen with her father there?"

"He weren't there."

"Was—was Angela hurt?"

"Oh, no, sir. She held that young buck off with her rifle. But he was sure wantin' her. He done threatened he'd get her yet. But she weren't scared none, only madder than a wet hen."

"What kind of boy would try to rape a child?" Jacob asked as he sat down wearily in his chair again. "I don't understand it."

"I tried to tell you she done started to grow," Hannah reminded him reproachfully.

"She's still only fourteen years old. Hell, she's still just a baby."

Hannah didn't remind him that "babies" Angela's age get married and have babies of their own. "You ain't seen her ever since you and her pa had that bad fight. The little Missy is turnin' out right pretty."

Jacob didn't seem to hear her. "What's this boy's name? By God, he's going to wish he were dead!"

"Billy Anderson."

"You mean Sam Anderson's son?" Jacob looked astonished.

"Yessuh."

"Have there been any others who have tried to bother Angela?" Jacob asked.

"Yessuh. And that worries me no end, 'cause that poor little Missy's been havin' to spend nights all by herself out there."

"Why?"

Hannah lowered her eyes and spoke in a whisper. "Her papa's been leavin' her all alone while he spends the night in Mobile. At least that's what he did last night."

"That son of a bitch!" Jacob came to his feet again, this time toppling his chair to the floor. There was a raging fire in the depth of his eyes. "Tell Zeke to take my horse and go to the city. He is to bring back Sam Anderson *and* William Sherrington. And tell him to ride like the devil is on his tail! You got that, Hannah?"

"Yessuh." She smiled for the first time.

"Well, get going! And then come back here and tell me the rest of it."

It was nearly dusk when William Sherrington barged into Jacob's study unannounced. His clothes were dirt-stained and wrinkled, with a few patches on his baggy pants. His bright red hair was parted in the middle, and plastered to his head with a foul-smelling oil. The whites of his eyes were veined with streaks of red as bright as his hair. He had a crumpled old hat in one hand, which he pointed at Jacob.

"Just what the hell you think you're doin' sendin' your nigger to fetch me?" William Sherrington stormed. "I warned you five years ago that I'd—"

"Shut up, Sherrington, and sit down!" Jacob growled. "Five years ago you blackmailed me,

threatened to go to my sons and tell them about
Charissa and me if I didn't leave you to raise An-
gela to your liking. I backed down then, fool that
I was, but Angela wasn't in danger at that time."

"What danger?"

Jacob rose from his chair, his face a thunderous
mask. "Do you think you can just leave her un-
chaperoned and go off on your drunken binges
and that nothing will happen? I should have sent
the law after you, not Zeke!"

William Sherrington paled under his sunburned skin. "What happened?"

"Nothing—this time, no thanks to you. But Angela was nearly raped by that young pup Billy
Anderson. Raped, by God! It's the last straw,
Sherrington. Before—you threatened. Now—I
promise. If you ever leave that girl alone again,
you'll find yourself rotting in a Union prison.
And don't think I can't arrange it."

"Now see here—"

Jacob raised his brow and William fell silent.
"Are you going to tell me I'm wrong? That you
haven't left Angela alone to fend for herself?"

William Sherrington stared down at his feet uncomfortably. "Well, maybe I been a bit lax, but the
girl can take care of herself."

"My God, she's only fourteen! She shouldn't
have to take care of herself! You're unfit to raise
her and you know it as well as I!"

"You ain't takin' her away from me. I need—I

want her with me. She's all I got since her ma ran off like she did," William said in a pathetic voice.

"I offered to send her to school. The offer is still open. It would be the best place for her," Jacob said, although he knew his offer would be refused.

"We ain't acceptin' charity, Maitland. I told you that time and again. Angela don't need no schoolin'. It'd only make her discontent with what she's got."

"You are a fool, man!" Jacob exclaimed angrily. "A pigheaded fool!"

"Maybe, but Angie stays with me, and there'll be a mighty stink raised if you try to take her away from me."

Jacob sighed. "You've heard my warning, Sherrington. If anything should happen to Angela, I'll have your hide."

Jacob watched William Sherrington stomp out of the room. Jacob's anger rose again a few minutes later when Hannah announced Sam Anderson.

Five

The sun had set by the time Angela reached the city. She had walked all afternoon, staying close to the river so she wouldn't run into anyone. She loved the river. It had taken her and her father all the way to Montgomery last year in February to see Jefferson Davis sworn in as the first Confederate President. Angela had never been so far from home before. It was so exciting. But that marked the beginning of her father's unhappiness.

William Sherrington was a true Southerner, born and raised, and he wanted more than anything to fight for his homeland. But he was too old. And he was a drunk. The army didn't want him.

He began to drink more and more after the refusal, and to curse the Yankees with a vengeance. He had never cottoned to Northerners, but now he hated them passionately. Angela felt she had to hate them too, though she didn't quite know why. She couldn't understand how people who used to be friends could now kill each other. It just didn't make any sense.

Angela hated the war. She didn't care why it had started and was still going on, she only knew that because of the war, she no longer loved Bradford Maitland. She hated him now. What else could she do but hate him? Hannah had let the truth slip out—that Bradford was not in Europe as everyone supposed, but was actually fighting for the Union! How upset Hannah had been until Angela swore she would keep the secret. After all, it wouldn't hurt Bradford if she told anyone, for he wasn't here. It would hurt Jacob, and she couldn't do that. But she hated Bradford now. And she hated even more the fact that she had to hate Bradford Maitland at all.

As she entered the city, Angela realized that her father might be home by now. But then again, he might not. And after what had happened today, she didn't want to spend the night at home alone. She would not mind walking back along the river at night, not as long as she had her rifle.

The sky was a dark purple now, and the street lamps were already lit. Angela had a pretty good idea where she could find her father. There were certain barrelhouses that he liked and a certain brothel he visited whenever he came to the city.

She headed for the waterfront. She was wear-

ing her newest dress, a light yellow cotton, for
Hannah had impressed on her that young women
did not go about in public in breeches. The dress
was already too small—tight across her breasts
and too short—but she didn't much care.

Angela started combing the streets for the sight
of her father's wagon and old Sarah. She hid in
darkened alleys, staying out of the way of drunks
and riffraff. An hour passed and then, slowly, another.

She was exhausted by the time she reached a
deserted part of the docks, her last hope. There
was a brothel in this area that she knew her father
had been to before. Down the street, she saw
what looked like his wagon, but she wasn't quite
sure. She started to run toward the wagon, beginning to hope. But Angela was pulled to a jerking
stop when a strong hand grabbed hold of her
arm.

The rifle fell out of her hand and she started to
scream. But she clamped her mouth shut when
she saw Bobo Deleron. She hadn't seen Bobo
since last winter. He had grown. He now towered well above her small height. There was a
stubble of whiskers on his square chin, and his
dark gray eyes under thin brows regarded her
with humor.

"Where you off to so fast, Angie? Did you go
and shoot someone with that there rifle?"

Bobo was not alone and Angela groaned as an

older, burly youth bent down and seized her weapon.

"This rifle ain't been fired, Bobo," the boy said. "But it sure is a pretty piece." He looked up then and grinned as his eyes raked over Angela. "So's she."

"Yeah, I reckon she is that," Bobo said almost grudgingly. "This here's Angie Sherrington." As he said her name, his strong fingers dug into her arm, making her wince. "Angie comes from folks like you and me, Seth, but she thinks she's better'n us. Ain't that right, Angie?"

"I never said that, Bobo Deleron, and you know it."

"No, but that's sure the way you act."

Bobo's tone had turned angry, making Angela uneasy. She had smelled liquor on his breath, and she remembered the last time she tangled with him. She had had to kick him squarely between the legs to get away from him that time, and he swore he'd get even with her.

Now she became increasingly aware that it was dark and no one else was near.

"I—I'm goin' to meet my pa, Bobo," Angela said in a voice that sounded like a mere squeak. "So you better let loose of me right now."

"Where is your pa?"

"Over yonder."

She pointed her free arm to the wagon she had been running to, but she was closer to it now, and she now realized that it wasn't her father's wagon after all.

"Looks to me like your pa's in Nina's place, and he'll most likely be busy for a while." The older boy chuckled. "Why don't you stay and keep us company, gal?"

"If it's all the same to you, I'll be gettin' my pa and headin' home." Angela tried for a level voice, but she knew she sounded as scared as she felt.

Bobo had just grown too much. He must be at least seventeen now. Bobo was angry—and he was not alone.

She had to get away. "Can I have my rifle back now? I really have to go."

She started to reach for the rifle, but Bobo jerked her back. "What do you think, Seth?" His friend grinned.

"I think," Seth said, "a weapon as fine as this should be workin' for the Cause, and I'll be joinin' up soon. Yes, sir, it's only right that I keep it."

Angela's eyes widened in fear. "You can't do that! Papa and I would starve without it!"

Seth chuckled. "Now ain't you exaggeratin' a bit, little girl? If you got a pa who can afford Nina's, then you ain't gonna starve."

Angela turned to Bobo with pleading eyes. "Bobo, please! Tell him we can't live without that rifle. There ain't no money to buy a new rifle."

But Bobo was more than a little drunk. "Shut up, Angie. He can have your damn rifle and he can have you too, just as soon as I'm finished with you."

But all was not lost. Bobo held her, and Bobo was drunk. She waited until he started to move and then, in a quick motion, she jerked her arm free and broke into a run. But Bobo was fast. His fingers dug into her hair, and he pulled her back painfully.

"Lemme go!" she yelled, her temper finally coming to the surface. "Lemme go, you damn yellow-gutted coward! I'll—"

Bobo's laughter cut her short. "Now if that ain't the old fire-spittin' Angie I'm used to. Didn't recognize that gal who was beggin' a moment ago."

"You sorry son ov a pig! Let go my hair!" Angela shouted, and when that didn't work, she swung a closed fist at him.

But Bobo caught her hand and twisted her arm behind her back. "You ain't gonna bloody my nose again, Angie." He pulled her hair back and forced her to look at him. "You ain't gonna do nothin' 'cept get yourself screwed nice and proper. It should've happened last winter, but you managed to get away from me then, didn't you?"

Angela started to scream, but Bobo released her hair and clamped his hand over her mouth. Just then, Seth came up behind her and raised her skirt, running a sweaty hand up between her thighs.

"Are we gonna stand here and talk about it, or

are we gonna get down to business?" Seth asked.

"Get away from her, Seth," Bobo warned coldly. "I've got a score to settle with her first. You can have whatever's left."

Seth stepped back. "Now look here, Bobo. Are you sure there'll be anythin' left of the gal that's worth havin'?"

"She may be messed up a bit, but she'll still be kickin'. Angie here has spunk." Bobo chuckled then and pressed her close to him. "She ain't gonna lay down and spread her legs for us. She's gonna fight to the end. But in the fightin', she's gonna get what's comin' to her."

"I don't know, Bobo." Seth shook his head. "I don't hold with beatin' up a gal who ain't done me no wrong."

Bobo turned Angela around in his arms so that she faced Seth, but he kept his hand securely over her mouth. And now his other hand covered one of her small breasts and squeezed painfully, making her squirm.

"Look at her," Bobo demanded. "You want her, don't you? And you won't be the one that hurts her—I will. You ain't been around long enough to know what a bitch this gal is. There'll be a lot of boys around here who'll be glad to know she finally lost a fight."

He dragged her into a narrow alley only a few feet away, and Angela tried one last time to free herself. She opened her mouth and clamped her teeth down on the soft part of Bobo's hand. He

cried out in pain and released her, and her feet
carried her back out into the street, right into the
arms of Seth. She struggled fiercely to get out of
the strong arms that held her.

"Hold on, girl. I'm not going to hurt you."

It was not Seth's voice. Through tear-blurred
eyes, Angela saw that the man who held her was
wearing fine clothes, certainly not the old overalls
Seth had been wearing. Here was help after all!
She burst into fresh tears and buried her face
against the man's broad chest, collapsing.

"Hey, mister. I want to thank you for stopping
this little gal, but I'll take her off your hands
now," Bobo called.

"What is she so frightened of?" the man questioned calmly. One arm held Angela protectively,
the other stroked her hair to soothe her, for she
had begun to tremble when she heard Bobo's
voice.

"Ah, hell. We was just havin' a little fun, and
then she went and bit me!"

"Why?"

Angela stepped back and looked up at the face
of her rescuer, ready to explain. But the words
stuck in her throat as she stared up into the bright
golden-brown eyes regarding her quizzically.
Dark though it was, she still knew those eyes.

"You look scared to death, girl. You're safe now.
No one is going to hurt you."

Angela couldn't speak. This was as close as she
had ever come to Bradford Maitland.

Bradford smiled. "What was the trouble here? Did you really bite this boy?"

Angela managed to utter, "I had to. It was the only way I could get away from him."

"Don't you be tellin' no lies now," Bobo warned in a menacing tone.

Angela swung around to face him, her eyes shooting sparks of rage. "You shut your mouth, Bobo Deleron! You ain't got me at your mercy no more and I don't tell lies like you do." She turned back to Bradford, and his look of concern dissolved her anger. She started crying again. "He—he was gonna rape me. Both of them was. And the other one was gonna keep my pa's rifle. We'll starve without it."

Bradford pulled Angela back against him, but at the same time he reached inside his coat and withdrew a handgun. He pointed this at Seth, whose eyes bulged in fright.

"Drop the rifle," Bradford said in a soft but deadly voice. "And then move away from it."

Seth did as he was told, but Bobo was more angry than intimidated. "You shouldn't be buttin' in here, mister. The girl's nothin' but white trash and no concern of yours. Besides, she's lyin'. We wasn't gonna hurt her none."

"Maybe we ought to let the sheriff decide," Bradford suggested smoothly.

"Now, there ain't no call for that." Bobo backed off quickly. "Ain't no harm been done."

"I think the girl disagrees," Bradford replied.

"What do you say, honey? Shall we talk to the sheriff?"

Angela whispered against his chest, "I don't want to cause you any more trouble." But then she added forcefully, "But you can tell Bobo if he ever comes near me again, I'll blow his head off!"

Bradford burst out laughing, much to Bobo and Seth's chagrin.

"You heard her, boys." Bradford chuckled. "I suggest you move along quickly before she realizes her rifle is within easy reach and she starts to regret letting you off so easy this time for what you"—he paused before ending—"didn't do."

It didn't take Bobo more than a second to take off, and Seth quickly followed.

Angela wasn't thinking about revenge. With Bobo and Seth gone, the street seemed awfully quiet. The only sound she could hear was her heart beating. Or was it his? She felt so utterly comfortable she wanted just to stand here and lean against the tall frame of Bradford Maitland all night. But she knew she couldn't do that.

She stepped back, ready to express her gratitude, but Bradford was regarding her with a mixture of amusement and curiosity, and she found herself tongue-tied once again.

"It's not my habit to rescue females in distress," he remarked thoughtfully. "Usually they have to be rescued from me. So why don't you thank me for saving you from a fate worse than death? You *are* a virgin, aren't you?" he asked frankly.

His question shocked her out of her silence. "Yes—and I—do thank you."

"That's better. What is your name?"

"Angela," she replied slowly, still finding it difficult to talk to him.

"Well, Angela, don't you know better than to be out alone, especially in this part of town?"

"I—I had to find my pa."

"And did you?"

"No, I reckon he's gone home by now," Angela answered more easily now.

"Well, I think you should do the same, don't you?" he said, and retrieved her rifle for her. "It has been a delight and a pleasure, Angela."

There was nothing she could do but turn and start back to the river. But before long he caught up to her.

"I'll walk you home," he offered in a rather irritable voice, as if he felt he had to, but didn't really want to.

"I can manage, Mr. Maitland," Angela replied, her chin tilted proudly.

Bradford grinned. "I'm sure you can, Angel," he said in a lighter tone. "But I feel responsible for you now."

"My—my name is Angela," she stated in a strangely quiet voice.

"Yes, I know. Now, where do you live?" he asked her patiently, his eyes warm.

Her heart soared. He'd called her Angel on purpose!

"I live on the other side of Golden Oaks."

"For heaven's sake, why didn't you tell me that to begin with? Come on." He took her arm and led her back up the street to his carriage. "I was on my way to Golden Oaks before you—ran into me."

Bradford Maitland didn't speak again until they had left the city and were traveling along the river road at a moderate pace. The road was deserted. The moon was hidden by dark gray clouds threatening rain. Blackness surrounded them as they rode along.

"You were going to walk all this way?" Bradford inquired in a disbelieving voice.

"It's not that far."

"I know how far it is, Angela. I have walked it before, and it takes most of the day to do so. You probably wouldn't have reached home until morning."

"I would've managed."

He laughed heartily at her confident reply, then asked, "How did you know my name?"

"Why, you must have introduced yourself," she replied nervously.

"No, I didn't. You know me, don't you?"

"Yeah," she answered in a whisper, then added heedlessly, "How come you're here in Alabama? You're not spyin' for the North, are you?"

She was nearly unseated as Bradford jerked the carriage to an abrupt halt. Then he grabbed both her arms and turned her in the seat to face him.

"Spying? Where did you get a notion like that, girl?"

He sounded so angry that Angela was too frightened to speak. She could have cut out her tongue right then and there for making him angry.

"Answer me!" he demanded now. "Why do you question my loyalty?"

"I don't question your loyalty, Mr. Maitland," Angela said weakly. "I know you joined the Union Army last year." She felt him stiffen and quickly added, "I thought it was a terrible thing when I heard, but now I don't care anymore."

"Who did you hear this from?"

"Hannah told me. She didn't mean to, but it just slipped out."

"Hannah?"

"From Golden Oaks. Hannah's about the closest friend I got. You won't be mad at her none for tellin' me, will you? It's not as if I told anyone. And I never will. I mean, I got no call to. This here war is crazy if you ask me. You fightin' on one side and your brother on the other—it's crazy. But you helped me tonight and I wouldn't hurt you for the world. I won't tell no one you're a Yankee soldier—I swear."

"When you start talking, you talk a mile a minute, don't you, Angela?" His tone was lighter now and he released her arms.

"I just want you to know your secret is safe

with me. You do believe me, don't you?" she pleaded.

He flicked the reins and they began moving again. "I guess I'll have to. I suppose you think I'm a traitor?"

"I don't see why you had to go and join them Bluecoats," she said sternly, then her face turned a bright pink. Luckily, it was too dark for him to see her embarrassment. "But I guess that's your business."

Bradford's amusement returned. "It's quite simple, really. I'm not a Southerner. My family has only lived in the South for the last fifteen years. I lived up North before then, and for a while out West. Even after my father surprised us by buying Golden Oaks, and moved the family down here, I still spent most of these last years up North, in school, and on business. I don't believe in slavery. More importantly, I don't believe in a divided nation. If states are allowed to secede and form new nations, what is to stop all the states from doing so? We would end up another Europe. No, my loyalty is with the North and the Union."

"But your brother joined the Confederacy," Angela reminded him.

"Zachary is a hypocrite," Bradford replied, his voice suddenly cold. "He joined the Confederacy for God only knows what reason, but it has nothing to do with loyalty."

"How long have you been back? I mean—"

Bradford chuckled. "You're determined to know why I'm here, aren't you?" he said, his tone more congenial. "Well, it's no big military secret. I came in on one of the blockade runners today, all aboveboard, mind you. At present, I am no longer in the army. I was wounded during the Seven Days' Battle in Virginia and discharged because of it."

"But you're all right now?" she asked anxiously.

"Yes. I took a chest wound and it was assumed I wouldn't recover. But as you can see, I made fools of those army doctors."

Angela giggled. "I'm glad to hear it."

"But," he added as an afterthought, "I will be joining up again, just as soon as my old commander is replaced. We never saw eye to eye. In fact, he caused me more frustration than the enemy. In the meantime, you could say I'm on furlough. Hell, I'm telling you more than I should. You have a way of drawing me out, Angel."

She was in love with Bradford Maitland all over again. This was the happiest day of her life.

"I've talked enough about myself," Bradford said now. "What about your family?"

"My family? It's just me and my pa."

"Who is?"

"William Sherrington."

Angela couldn't see the frown that crossed

Bradford's brow. "Then your mother was Charissa Stewart?"

"That was her name before she married my pa," Angela answered with surprise. "But how'd you know that?"

"So you are Charissa Stewart's daughter," he remarked oldly, ignoring her question.

"Did you know my mother?"

"No, fortunately I never met the—woman," Bradford returned and then fell silent.

Angela stared at his tall frame silhouetted in the dark beside her. What did he mean, "fortunately"? Had she really heard anger in his tone? No, surely it was her imagination.

Angela closed her eyes, swaying with the bounce of the carriage, and reflected on the first time she ever set eyes on Bradford Maitland. It was three years ago. She was just eleven, and Bradford was twenty then, home from school for the summer. She had gone to the city with her father to sell the corn crop, but she got tired of waiting around the marketplace and decided to go on home. It had rained heavily the night before, and as she ran along the river road, she made a game of dodging mud puddles.

And then he charged by on a swift black stallion, on the way to the city. He looked like some avenging angel, dressed all in white, riding tall on that giant black beast. When he passed her, his horse splashed red mud all over the front of her yellow dress. Bradford pulled up his horse and trotted back to her. He tossed her a gold coin, apologized, and told her to buy a new dress, then galloped away.

From the moment she stared up into his hand-some face, she was in love. She told herself many times that it was silly to think she was in love, for she knew nothing about that. Maybe she just worshiped him. But whatever it was, it was easier to call it love.

She still had that gold coin. She had worked a small hole in it and begged her father to buy her a long chain so she could wear it as a necklace. It was around her neck now, as it had been for three years, resting between the two small hills of her breasts. She had continued to wear it even after she decided she hated Bradford Maitland for join-ing the Union. But she didn't hate him anymore. She could never hate him again.

They reached her home all too soon. After she watched Bradford drive away, she stood on the porch for a long time, remembering his parting words.

"Take care of yourself, Angel. You're getting too old to traipse about by yourself." Flicking the reins, he drove off.

"Is that you, gal?"

Angela frowned when William Sherrington came to the front door.

"It's me, Pa."

"Where you been?"

"Out lookin' for you!" she snapped angrily, though she was more than relieved to find him home. "And if you'd come home last night, then I wouldn't have had to."

"I'm right sorry 'bout that, Angie," he replied in a voice that sounded a bit frightened. "It won't happen again. Was that Billy Anderson who brung you home?"

"Lord, no!" she exclaimed. "It was Bradford Maitland."

"Well, that was kind of him. And I promise, Angie, I won't never leave you alone again. If I go to the city, then you're comin' with me. I know I ain't been a good pa to you lately, but I will be from now on. I promise."

He was close to tears, and all the anger left her. "Get on with you, Pa. You know I wouldn't want no other pa but you." She came over to him and hugged him soundly. "Now get yourself to sleep. We got a field to plow come mornin'."

Six

Instead of going to Golden Oaks, Bradford drove farther up the river road to The Shadows plantation and his fiancée, Crystal Lonsdale.

Crystal was blissfully unaware of his activities during the last year and a half—or so he assumed. After his conversation with Angela Sherrington, he wasn't sure of his secret any longer.

Well, if Crystal didn't know, then she soon would, for besides wanting to see his father, his reason for coming home was to make a clean breast of it with Crystal. Better now than after the war. It would give Crystal time to get used to his stand. Then, when he returned to her after the war, there would be nothing to prevent their immediate marriage.

Bradford turned onto the gravel drive leading to

The Shadows. It was not a proper hour of night to call, but he had chosen this time in hopes of avoiding Crystal's father, and Robert too. It was one thing to tell Crystal where his loyalties lay. She was the woman who loved him and would never betray him. But to face the rest of the family might be suicide. He could even find himself shot as a spy, as the Sherrington girl had suggested he might be.

He was not a spy, nor could he ever be. Bradford was too honest for that.

Lights were still burning in the lower half of the house, and as Bradford approached the entrance, he could hear the soft notes of a piano. He frowned slightly, wondering if Crystal were entertaining guests.

Old Rueben, the Lonsdales' Negro butler, answered Bradford's knock, stepping back in surprise.

"Is that really you, Mr. Brad? Lord, Miss Crystal will sure be glad to see you!"

"I hope so, Rueben." Bradford grinned. "Is she in the drawing room?"

"Yessuh. An' you can go right on in. I don't reckon you'll be wantin' a chaperon for this reunion." Rueben grinned. "Nor will she."

"She's alone then?"

"She is."

Bradford crossed the center hall and paused only for a moment before he opened the double doors to the drawing room. Crystal was seated at the piano, dressed in pink and white silk.

She was playing a haunting piece that he didn't recognize. Everything about the room transported him into the past, including Crystal. She hadn't changed at all. She was still the most beautiful woman he had ever known.

She was so completely absorbed in her music that she was unaware of his presence. And when she finished, a long sigh escaped her.

"I hope that sigh is for me," he said softly.

Crystal stood up. It was a few moments before she cried his name and ran into his arms.

Bradford kissed her lingeringly. She returned his kiss, but not for nearly as long as he would have liked. She never would let him hold her for very long. Yet she was remarkably contradictory in that she would have taken him to her bed had he even insinuated as much. He had been the one to hold back.

He was quite the proper gentleman before the war, much to his regret now. Had he taken her before, she would be more pliant now, and more likely to see his point of view.

"Oh, Brad." She pushed away from him and looked up reproachfully. "Why didn't you answer any of my letters? I wrote so many I lost count long ago."

"I haven't received any letters."

"Your father said you probably didn't, what with the blockade and all, but I was still hopin' you had," she replied. Then her eyes narrowed and her hands went to her slim hips and she said sternly,

"So where were you, Bradford Maitland, when I came to England on my tour? I waited and waited for you to show up, but you never did. Two years, Brad—I haven't seen you for two years!"

"The business takes me all over, Crystal. And there is a war going on," Bradford reminded her gently.

"You think I don't know that? Robby went an' joined up with all the other youngbloods from around here. He stayed here to guard Fort Morgan, but I still hardly ever see him anymore. An' your brother joined too. But did you? No, your business is more important to you." He started to speak, but she went on. "It has been such an embarrassment, not bein' able to tell my friends that my fiancé is fightin' for our cause along with the rest of our brave men."

Bradford took her shoulders and set her away from him. "Is that so important to you, Crystal, what your friends think?" he asked sharply.

"Well, of course it's important. I can't have my husband known as a coward, can I?"

Bradford felt his temper rising. "What about a husband who is a Union sympathizer? Is that worse than a coward in your opinion?"

"A *Yankee!*" She gasped in horror. "Don't be silly, Brad. You're a Southerner, same as I. It's not funny when you make jokes like that."

"And if I'm not joking?"

"Stop it, Bradford. You're frightenin' me."

He grabbed her arm to stop her from backing

away from him. He had had it all so well planned,
what he was going to say to her, something about
a divided nation, something sensible that Lincoln
had said, but Bradford couldn't remember any of
it now.

"I'm not a Southerner, Crystal. I never was and
I think you know that."

"No!" she cried, throwing her hands up over
her ears. "I'm not goin' to listen! I'm not!"

"Yes, you will, damnit!" He took her hands
down and then locked his arms around her so she
couldn't move. "Did you really expect me to fight
for something I don't believe in, to fight to up-
hold something I'm completely against? If my beliefs led me to take sides, Crystal, I would not
choose the South. You should respect that."

Bradford sighed. There was no way he could
tell her the complete truth now, that he had already fought with the Union and would again.
She might sound the alarm and he would never
leave Mobile alive. He wanted desperately to
make her understand.

"Crystal, if I didn't stand by my convictions,
then I would be less than a man. Can't you see
that?"

"No!" she retorted hotly, trying to move away
from him. "All I see is that I've gone and wasted
the best years of my life on—a Yankee sympathizer! You let go of me this minute, before I
scream!"

He released her instantly and she stumbled

back, then glared at him. "Our engagement is over. I would never—ever marry a man with such—such—oh! You may not be fightin' with the North, but you're still a Yankee. And I despise all Yankees!"

"Crystal, you're upset, but once you have time to think—"

"Get out of here!" she cut him off, her voice rising hysterically. "I hate you, Bradford! I never want to see you again. Never!"

He turned to leave, but stopped at the door. "It's not over between us, Crystal. You're still going to be my wife, and I'll return after the war to prove that."

He left before she could reply again. Oddly, he was thinking about the Sherrington girl. She had understood. She didn't condemn him. Yet the woman who had professed to love him did not understand.

But he was not yet through with Crystal Lonsdale. Someday he would return and make her understand.

Seven

Angela Sherrington sat in one of the two old wicker chairs on the narrow porch, staring pensively at the bare field in front of her house. In her mind's eye she could see the field full of corn as it had been only a week ago. Would she ever see it that way again? Would anything *ever* be the same again?

Bradford Maitland's gold coin was pressed hard in her palm. It somehow gave her comfort when she most needed it. And Angela needed it now more than ever.

She was still wearing the dark brown cotton dress that she had worn to the funeral that morning. She had wanted to wear black, but she didn't own a black dress.

This last week was like a bad dream come and gone. They were fortunate to have a fair corn crop this year, and it had taken three trips to the city to sell it all. Angela had gone with her father each time, for he had kept his promise of three years ago and never left her alone. Three long years ago. The time had passed so quickly, tragically for most, but uneventfully for Angela. The boys who used to tease and fight with her didn't bother her anymore, and Bobo had taken her warning to heart, never coming near her again. Her father even allowed her to go off by herself once more like she used to, instead of staying constantly within his sight. Yes, the years had been uneventful, until this year of 1865.

A year ago the Union had won an important victory in the Battle of Mobile Bay. The fighting had finally reached Alabama. Fort Gaines surrendered only a few days after the disastrous battle. And on Mobile Point, directly opposite, Fort Morgan surrendered after withstanding an eighteen-day siege. The Yankees finally had their foothold in Alabama.

Six months later, Fort Blakely and Spanish Fort were sieged. And then in April of this year, eight months after the Battle of Mobile Bay, the Union Army, commanded by General E. R. S. Canby, had defeated the Confederate land forces and occupied Mobile.

Miraculously, the Sherringtons' little farm had been passed by. During that terrifying time, her father boarded up their house and they waited, wondering whether they would be burned out.

Would they lose their crop? Or their lives? But the danger passed and Reconstruction began.

To Angela, losing the war held no major personal consequences. She had never owned a slave. She didn't own land, and so was not facing taxes she couldn't pay. Nor would the land they sharecropped be sold out from under them, for their landlord was financially stable.

And Angela was not shocked by poverty as many fine southern ladies were, for poverty was all she knew. She and her pa had always gotten by.

It was Frank Colman, an old friend and drinking buddy of her father's, who found her that day as she waited in the wagon for her pa. She had guessed right away that something terrible was wrong, for Frank wouldn't look her straight in the face. He told her about the fight her father had gotten into. Some barroom argument with a Yankee over the war, Frank said. A ruckus started— more men joined in—everybody fighting—her father fell—hit his head on a table—died right then.

She had run all the way to the bar and found William Sherrington lying on a sawdust floor, dirty and bloodied from the fight, dead.

As she fell down beside him in utter disbelief, all the times they had fought and argued over his drinking went through her mind, all the harsh words she had thrown at him over the years because of it.

She had burst into tears on the floor and the

men around her had moved back, shamefaced, as she poured out her grief and fury.

Her father had been buried this morning. She was alone in the world now, completely alone. What was she going to do? She had asked herself that question so many times already, but she had no answers.

She could always marry Clinton Pratt, she supposed. He had asked her many times this last year and she was sure he would ask her again. Clinton was a nice young man who worked a small farm farther up the river. He came often to visit and talk with her. She enjoyed his company, but she didn't want to marry him. She didn't love him.

A new flood of tears began. *Oh, Pa, why did you have to leave me? I don't want to be alone, Pa! I don't like being alone!*

She really wanted to stay right where she was. This was her home. She had old Sarah. She could work the farm by herself, she was sure she could. But of course, that wasn't up to her, it was up to Jacob Maitland. He might not let her stay on the farm, thinking she couldn't work it by herself.

But she would probably know today one way or the other, for Jacob Maitland had been at the funeral this morning to pay his respects, and he told her he would be out to see her later. She would have to convince him that she could make a go of it on her own. She would have to!

* * *

Jacob Maitland drew up in the handsomest carriage Angela had ever seen. It was new, with rich green velvet seats and shiny new black paint.

It was said that Jacob Maitland was so rich that the war hadn't even dented his fortune. He had never needed to depend on his plantation to support him. In fact, his land was hardly worked at all during the war. It made people wonder why he came to the South in the first place, and why he stayed at Golden Oaks during the war, instead of going to Europe, where most of his business interests were.

He had frequently come to their farm when she was a child, always bringing her candy, sometimes a little toy. Angela imagined the reason he came was to look after his interests. Then eight years ago, her father and Jacob had had heated words. Angela thought surely they would be evicted after that, but they weren't. But Jacob Maitland stopped coming to the farm then. She never discovered what they had argued about. And she missed his visits.

He was a good landlord, there was no denying that. Even when their crop wasn't a good one, he never complained. And during the war, he insisted on taking a lesser share. It had made Angela feel twice as guilty about taking the food Hannah stole from him.

But now Angela couldn't help but be afraid.

"Angela, my dear, you have my deepest sympathies for the loss of your father," Jacob Maitland began. "You must be feeling a great emptiness now."

"Yes, I am," Angela replied in a weak whisper, her eyes downcast.

"I knew your father for almost eighteen years," Jacob continued in a soft voice. "He was working this farm before I even came to Alabama."

"Then you knew my ma too?" Angela asked curiously, her eyes lighting up.

"Yes, yes, I did," Jacob returned, a faraway look in his eyes. "She should never have gone West by herself all those years ago. She—"

"West?" Angela broke in excitedly. "Is that where she went? Pa never told me."

"Yes, that's where she went," Jacob answered sadly. "Did you know that you are the exact image of your mother?"

"Pa always said I had her eyes and hair," Angela answered easily, relaxing now.

"It's much more than that, my dear. Your mother was the loveliest woman I ever knew. She had a grace about her, a fragility, and a most exquisite beauty. You are just like her."

"You're funnin' me, Mr. Maitland. I ain't graceful, and I sure ain't fragile."

"You could be, with the proper training," Jacob replied with a tender smile.

"Trainin'? Oh, you mean like schoolin'?" she

asked. "I ain't never had time for that. Pa needed me here to help work the farm."

"Yes. About this farm, Angela. Now that your father is—ah, no longer with us, I want—"

"Please, Mr. Maitland," Angela cut in, frightened of what he was going to say. "I can work this farm by myself. I've helped Pa since before I can remember. I'm stronger than I look, really I am."

"What on earth can you be thinking of, child? I can't let you stay on this farm by yourself," Jacob exclaimed in surprise, shaking his head.

"But I—"

Jacob held up his hand to stop her. "I will not hear another word about it. And don't look so miserable, my dear. I was going to tell you, before you interrupted me, that I want you to come and live at Golden Oaks."

A look of pure disbelief spread across Angela's features. "Why?"

Jacob Maitland laughed then. "Let's just say I feel responsible for you. After all, I've known you all your life, Angela. I waited with William Sherrington while your mother was giving birth to you. And I want to help you."

"But what about your family? And you got so many servants livin' in your house now."

"Nonsense," he replied. "The servants don't live in the house, child. And my family will welcome you. Have no fear about that."

"If you ain't the nicest man I ever did know!" Angela said, tears coming to her eyes again.

"Then it's settled, my dear. I'll leave you here to pack your belongings, and I'll send the carriage back for you in a couple of hours."

Eight

 Angela was sure she had dreamed her meeting with Jacob Maitland. But two hours later, the shiny new black carriage came for her, and she knew it was true. She was going to Golden Oaks.

The only thing she could think about on that short mile ride to her new home was that she would now be closer to Bradford Maitland. She had never outgrown her childhood infatuation. If anything, the seventeen-year-old Angela loved him more than she had at fourteen.

Hannah had told her that Bradford was no longer in the army, but he was still up North running Maitland Enterprises in New York. Zachary was home, though, sent back from the war late in '62 with a leg injury. He had promptly married Miss Crystal Lonsdale, and they were both living at Golden Oaks now.

Angela recalled the first time she had ever seen Golden Oaks, ten years ago, when Jacob Maitland's wife died. Her father had gone to pay his respects, and Angela tagged along. And then there were the many times when her father brought a share of his crop to the Maitlands' storage house, and in the recent years, she always went with him. But she had never before been inside the huge mansion. And now she would work there!

Angela didn't feel belittled by being a servant. Working in that fine house would be much easier than working a farm. Being a Maitland servant, she would see Bradford often when he came home. And even though he could never return her love, she would be near him, and that was all that mattered.

The carriage pulled up to the front of the house and Angela stared up at the eight huge Doric columns that lined the wide front gallery. But then her eyes were drawn to someone looking out of an upstairs window. The curtains were quickly drawn shut, making Angela feel uneasy. Who had been watching her arrival?

"Well, Angela, welcome to Golden Oaks," Jacob Maitland said as he came out to greet her.

"Thank you, sir," Angela returned with a shy smile, but then her violet eyes brightened and she relaxed when Hannah appeared on the gallery behind Jacob.

"Missy Angela, I is sure glad you agreed to

come here to live!" Hannah cried with her usual exuberance. "I was right sorry to hear 'bout your papa, but I's mighty relieved to know you gonna be taken care of."

"Mr. Maitland has been very kind."

"Angela, please, I want you to call me Jacob. After all, we're old friends."

"All right, sir—I mean, Jacob."

"That's much better." Jacob smiled warmly. "Hannah will show you to your room. And Hannah, don't you go tiring her out with your chattering. Angela has had a trying morning, and I want her to rest for the rest of the afternoon." He turned back to Angela. "We've already had lunch, my dear, but Hannah will have something sent to your room. And someone will call you when it's time for dinner. My son Zachary has developed the southern habit of napping after lunch, as his wife does, because of the heat. But you will meet them this evening."

"Come along, Missy," Hannah said as she held the door open. "I gots you a room on the cool side of the house all fixed up. It overlooks the river, and gets a real nice breeze when there's one to be had."

Angela followed Hannah into the entrance hall, hurrying to keep up as she headed for the large curving staircase at the end of the hall. Angela didn't have time to stop and look at the beautiful pictures that covered the white walls, or to have more than a glimpse through the open doors they passed.

At the top of the stairs was a long hallway that covered the length of the house, and on each end was a wide-open window, letting in daylight and what little breeze there was. There were eight doors off the hallway, four on each side. Hannah turned left at the top of the stairs and stood waiting in front of the last door at the back of the house.

Angela hurried on, glancing at the family portraits lining the hall. She stopped short when a pair of golden-brown eyes stared down at her from the wall. The picture held a remarkable likeness, the artist catching the proud, uplifted chin, the high cheekbones and straight, narrow nose, the firm, smiling lips, and the high forehead and thick, slightly curving black eyebrows that matched his wavy hair. It was an excellent portrait of Bradford Maitland.

"That's a real nice picture of Master Jacob. Always thought it should of gone in the study," Hannah said as she approached the portrait.

"But I thought it was Bradford."

"No, child, that's Master Jacob when he was younger. Master Bradford's picture's down the hall. If you puts them together, it looks like someone done painted two pictures of the same man—'cept for the eyes. Bradford got's a little more fire in his eyes, 'cause he didn't like havin' his picture done, and it shows. He wanted his picture far away from his room, which is on this side of the house."

"This side?"

"Yessum," Hannah chuckled gleefully. "Thought you might like havin' the room across from his—that is, if that boy ever decides to come home."

The fact that Angela was going to live inside the house, instead of with the other servants, struck her. She didn't understand it. Perhaps Jacob Maitland was just being very considerate, because she would be the only white servant.

Angela was shocked by the room that was going to be hers. This one room was bigger than the house she had lived in all her life. Painted in off-shades of lavender and rich, dark shades of purple and blue, it even smelled of lavender. She had never seen anything so richly beautiful. And this room was to be hers!

The floor was polished to such a high gloss that it actually reflected the fine, expensive furniture. The massive bed had four tall posts and a frilly canopy overhead, with a lavender and blue taffeta spread covering it. The drapes were a dark blue velvet, and were presently closed to keep out the afternoon heat. There was a comfortable chair in a corner, and a long sofa, tables, a dresser, and a tall, framed mirror. How ever could she get used to living in all this?

"Are you sure I'm supposed to have this

room?" Angela whispered, disbelief apparent on her lovely face.

Hannah laughed. "Master Jacob said I could choose any one of the empty rooms for you, and I chose this one. They's all about the same anyway. I know this ain't what you use to, Missy, but you's here now, and you just gonna have to gets use to it. There's nothin' to worry yourself about no more, and I sure is happy about that. Now you rest, like the master said." And Hannah left her there.

Rest? In the middle of the afternoon? How could she?

A sudden breeze stirred the heavy drapes, and Angela went to the window and moved the material aside. The river was within easy walking distance, and she imagined what it would be like to just sit here and watch the stately steamboats pass. A lovely garden was in the back of the house, and the fragrance of jasmine and magnolias drifted up to her.

There were beautiful rolling lawns on this side of the house and in the back, leading down to the river, lawns shaded by large oaks and bushy willows. The servants' quarters and the stable were to the right of the house in a well-shaded forest of cedars. It was a picture of breathtaking beauty.

There was a knock and a light-skinned Negro girl about the same age as Angela entered with a tray of food, which she set down on a table without saying a word. Angela smiled meekly at her as she left. She didn't know how she was supposed to act with the other servants, but she wanted to make friends. She hoped they wouldn't resent her being here.

Nine

 Angela spent the afternoon pacing restlessly about the large bedroom. She had tried to lie down on the big bed and rest but that was impossible for a girl who had never known idle time. With nothing to do, the minutes dragged by.

Why couldn't they have given her something to do? She wondered now just what her duties would be, for Mr. Maitland had failed to tell her. Would she be serving just one person? She hoped there would be enough work to keep her busy. Most of all, she didn't want Jacob Maitland to regret bringing her here.

This wasting of time, Angela thought, is ridiculous. There must be something she could do.

She opened the door and stepped into the hallway. The silence was eerie for a house supposedly full of family and servants. She walked a little

ways, then smiled up at the portrait of Jacob
Maitland. Curiosity drove her down the long
hallway until she came to Bradford's portrait. She
gasped when she came face to face with it. This
was not the Bradford Maitland she carried in her
memories. This Bradford, with his darkly tanned
face, his unruly black hair, and those angry eyes,
made Angela think of a brigand pirate, or even a
wild Indian, who could kill without mercy. This
Bradford was a dangerous man.

Angela shivered. This was a Bradford she had
never seen. Or had she? Did Bradford look like
this the night he rescued her from Bobo? She
shook her head. She didn't know.

Angela turned with a shudder and made her
way downstairs.

The dining room was the first room she came
to. It was very impressive, with a long table that
would seat ten, and high-backed chairs and cush-
ioned seats. There were two doors off the dining
room. One was open and showed a huge empty
room that ran nearly the length of the house. Angela opened the other door and found herself in a
red-brick kitchen, a recent extension of the house.
A woman of extremely large proportions was
rolling a thin dough on a large table. A young girl
was beside her peeling peaches, with a small boy
at her elbow, asking if he could have some.

"You must be the little girl Hannah told me
about," the large woman grinned when she noticed Angela. "What can I do for you, Missy?"

"Is there a rag I can use?" Angela asked.

The woman looked at her curiously, then pointed a flour-covered finger to another door. "There's lots of rags in that closet—from Miss Crystal's old dresses."

"Thank you," Angela replied shyly and opened the closet.

The little room was a storage area for the household cleaning items. There was a box of rags on the floor, but Angela was appalled by the scraps of material she found in it. Silks, velvets, taffeta, and other fine fabrics filled the box. How could such expensive materials find their way to a rag box? Taking a square of white cotton, she went to the dining room. It proved to be dust free, so Angela went to the room next to it. This was the morning room, she would learn later. It wasn't large, and held just enough furniture to accommodate the family. The walls, draperies, and furniture were all in shades of white and soft blues.

The floor was spotless, as were the tables, but Angela found dust on a large cabinet that held hundreds of little figurines, and she started to work on that. She was enchanted by the glassy little figures, and handled them with tender care as she moved them about. After a few minutes, she started humming, content she had found something to do.

"You see, Robby, I told you I heard someone in here."

Angela spun around quickly and met the contemptuous glare of Crystal Maitland. Her brother Robert was looking at Angela with a mixture of surprise and pleasure, his dark brown eyes scrutinizing her. Angela knew Crystal only from Hannah's descriptions, but she had seen Robert on occasion in the city. He was a lean man, about twenty-five, of medium height, with light blond hair like his sister, and strong, aristocratic features. Crystal's brother was also Zachary Maitland's closest friend, and he spent as much time at Golden Oaks as he did at his own plantation.

"Well, at least she's makin' herself useful," Crystal continued, as if Angela weren't in the room.

"Oh, I'm sure your esteemed father-in-law has something much more useful in mind for the little orphan," Robert said dryly.

"Now, Robby, I told you I didn't want to hear that kind of talk. Father Maitland wouldn't dare bring her here to be his mistress," Crystal replied tartly.

"Wouldn't he?" Robert asked with a raised brow. "Look at her. You can't deny she's pretty, and Lord knows this house doesn't need any more servants. Maybe the old man has become foolish enough to think we wouldn't guess his real reason for bringin' the girl here."

"Oh, stop it!" Crystal demanded. "If I were inclined to believe you, I'd throw her out on her ear. But I don't believe your silly notion. And I'll make sure she has plenty to do and earns her keep. Besides, it'll be right nice havin' a white servant girl in the house, as long as she's learned to be civil. She used to be quite wild, you know."

"She looks pretty tame to me," Robert returned, a grin coming to his lips as he boldly eyed Angela.

Angela's cheeks flamed. Didn't they care that she was standing right there?

"Your name's Angela, isn't it, girl?" Crystal questioned, her annoyance with her brother now directed at Angela.

"Yes."

"Well, Angela, go and fetch me a glass of lemonade and bring it to the drawin' room. And be quick about it."

Angela slipped passed them without a word and hurried to the kitchen, the color still high on her face. Hannah was there and she smiled a warm greeting when Angela came into the room.

"Tilda says you was here earlier, but you ain't been introduced proper like," Hannah said carefully. "This here's Tilda, the best cook there is hereabouts."

"I'm mighty pleased to meet you, Tilda," Angela said sincerely.

"So's I, Missy. It sure is gonna be nice havin' you here with us."

Angela wanted to stay and chat, but she was afraid to keep Crystal Maitland waiting. "Can I have a glass of lemonade?" she asked quickly.

"You can have anything you wants, Missy," Tilda answered jovially. "There's a pitcher right there on the counter. Let me just wipe my hands here and I'll gets you a glass."

Tilda moved to the counter and poured a large glass of the cold lemonade, making Angela thirsty. She took the glass, said her thanks, and hurried out of the room. She went straight to the front room on the right of the hall, the only other room with an open door, and found Crystal and Robert relaxed on a large green and white sofa.

Crystal took the glass of lemonade and tasted it, then made a face. "There ain't enough sugar in this, girl! Take it back and make sure it's sweet enough before you return."

Angela took the glass and left the room, but she stopped just outside the door when she heard Robert Lonsdale burst into laughter.

"Since when did you get a sweet tooth?" Robert asked, chuckling.

"I haven't. But I told you I'd make her earn her keep," Crystal answered, then giggled. "My, it's gonna be fun havin' that girl here after all."

"Yes. I think I might extend my visit," Robert said thoughtfully, then added, "To watch the fun, of course. I never realized you had such a cruel streak in you, sister. If the old man knew what—"

"Oh, hush up, Robert!" Crystal snapped, then smiled wickedly. "Father Maitland ain't gonna know."

Angela was close to tears as she hurried back to the kitchen. To be purposely cruel, just for sport!

"Can you make this a little sweeter?" she asked, trying not to show how upset she was.

"Tilda puts lots of sugar in her lemonade," Hannah answered, surprised. "If you wants more sugar, you's gonna get fat, Missy."

"Oh, it's not for me," Angela said quickly. "The lemonade is for Miss Crystal."

"Why you fetchin' for her?" Hannah asked, her brow creased.

"She told me to."

"Then she tell you it ain't sweet enough?"

"Yes."

"Lord, what's the gal think she's doin'?" Hannah exclaimed. "You wait here, Missy. Don't you do nothin' 'cept watch Tilda make her peach pie. I'll take Miss Crystal her lemonade. You wait about ten minutes, and then come to the master's study. He'll want to talk with you."

Ten minutes later, Hannah opened the door to the study and Angela walked in apprehensively. The room was large, and extended to the rear of the house, with the red-yellow rays of the setting sun steaming in the back windows. One wall was covered from floor to ceiling with books, another held a large gun case. There were stuffed animal heads mounted on wooden plaques, and pictures of wild horses and open plains on the walls. The floor-length draperies were dark brown, and the furniture was covered in black leather. This was definitely a man's study.

"Hannah, tell the others to wait in the dining room. I will be delayed for a few minutes," Jacob said.

"Yessuh," Hannah replied and closed the door, a knowing smile on her lips.

Jacob came around his desk and led Angela to a long sofa. "My dear, something has happened that I don't quite understand, and I think you can help me."

"I'd be mighty pleased to help, sir," Angela returned eagerly.

"Hannah tells me that you went to the kitchen for a glass of lemonade, and that you came back a few minutes later to make it sweeter. Is that correct?"

"Yes, sir."

"And that lemonade was for my daughter-in-law?"

"Yes, sir."

"Did she ask you to get her the lemonade, or did she tell you to get it?" Jacob questioned.

"It don't really make much difference, sir," Angela returned.

"Which was it, Angela?"

"Well, as I recall, she told me to get it," Angela answered meekly. What had she done wrong?

"And why did you do it?"

"Why did I? Oh, I know you told me to rest, and I didn't mean to disobey your wishes, but I just ain't used to restin', sir. I had to do somethin' and so I come downstairs to see if I could be helpful. I started dustin' furniture, and then Miss Crystal told me. I know you ain't said what my duties are yet, but I didn't see no harm in startin' work. I'm right sorry if I made you angry, Mr. Maitland."

"Oh, Angela, what am I going to do with you?" he laughed. "One more question, my dear: Did my daughter-in-law refer to you as a servant?"

"She did mention it when she was talkin' to her brother about me. But that's a silly question, Mr. Maitland. You must of told your family why you was bringin' me here."

"Yes, I did," he said with a sigh. "But apparently I didn't explain the situation well enough. Come along, we'll go into dinner now."

"Do you want me to serve the table?"

"No, you will dine with the family," Jacob said in a patient tone.

"But I can't do that!" Angela was becoming alarmed. "They won't like it!"

"I am the head of this household, Angela. My family may be stubborn and spoiled, but my word is law. And I thought we agreed you would call me Jacob," he reminded with a gentle smile.

When they appeared in the doorway, all eyes in the dining room turned to them. Angela felt her palms begin to sweat. She didn't understand what this was all about. Why did Jacob insist she dine with them tonight? There was bound to be

resentment. She saw it already, just because Jacob
had dared to bring her into the room with him.

"Are we having another guest for supper,
Father?"

It was Zachary Maitland who asked the question. Angela had never seen Zachary before, but
she wasn't surprised by the resemblance he bore
his father. He reminded her of Bradford, except
for his bright green eyes.

"Why do you ask?"

"There's been an extra plate set at the table,"
Crystal volunteered.

"The extra setting is for Angela," Jacob replied,
and looked at each person in the room to gauge
their reactions.

"You can't mean to let her eat with us just
'cause she's white!" Crystal exclaimed indignantly. "I've never heard of anything so preposterous!"

"This is absurd, Father," Zachary added.
"What will the other servants think!"

"That's enough!" Jacob pronounced. It was
such a commanding tone that it brought immediate silence.

"I intend to explain," Jacob went on in a calmer
tone. "But first, Robert, my boy, be so good as to
let Angela have your seat. I want her to sit next to
me."

Robert thought of Jacob Maitland as a second
father. He had done so ever since he and Zachary

became close friends twelve years before. But he did as he was asked without a word.

"You really are goin' too far, Father Maitland. How much more of this do you expect us to put up with?"

"You will put up with anything I desire, my dear. I believe my wishes are still law in this house."

Jacob brought Angela to the chair and pushed it in for her, then sat down at the head of the table. Angela fearfully kept her eyes lowered.

"Now I have quite a bit to say," Jacob began in a level voice. "I informed all of you yesterday that one of my renters had passed on, and had left his daughter an orphan. I told you that I felt responsible for Angela Sherrington, having known her father all these years, and that I was bringing her to Golden Oaks to live. I told Angela exactly the same thing. Now how on earth could all of you, including Angela, come to the conclusion that I brought her here to be a servant?"

"You mean that's not why she's here?" Zachary asked incredulously.

"It most certainly is not!"

"Oh, Lord! Then Robby was right!" Crystal gasped. "How do you dare bring your mistress here and flaunt her in front of us?"

"For God's sake!" Jacob stormed, his eyes suddenly alive with fire. "Where do you get these incredible notions? If I were going to be crude enough to bring my mistress into my house, then I would be crude enough to tell you about it. And since you have already opened this tasteless subject, I will tell you that I most certainly do have a mistress, who lives comfortably in the city. She is a lovely widow in her late thirties, who has no wish to remarry, though I have asked her. That you would think me lecherous enough to seduce a child Angela's age is unforgivable!"

"They why have you brought her here?" Crystal asked defiantly.

Jacob sighed. "Angela is to become a member of this family, and she is to be treated as such."

"You can't be serious?" Zachary laughed.

"I have never been more serious in my life. I have known Angela since she was born, and I've always been concerned for her welfare. I feel like a father to her, and if she will let me, I would like to be just that. A father to replace the one she lost."

By now, Angela had tears on her cheeks. All the questions she would have asked were asked by Crystal and Zachary and answered in turn. Was this really possible? How was it that fortune could shine on her so brightly?

"You must forgive me, Angela, for not telling you about this when we were in the study, but I wanted to say it only once," Jacob said tenderly, then continued. "And I'm sorry I wasn't more explicit when I talked to you after the funeral. But now that you know I want to take care of you, will you agree?"

"I would be a fool to refuse your kind offer, Mr. Maitland—I mean, Jacob," she managed without breaking down.

"Splendid!" He looked around the table, defying the others to say anything more. Then he smiled and called out in a booming voice, "Tilda, you can send in the food now."

Ten

The night was a long one, for Angela had a difficult time falling asleep. She spent hours remembering every word said at the dining-room table.

Crystal hated her, Angela had no doubts on that score. But Robert Lonsdale was a different story. He had been surprised at first, but then Angela detected amusement in him. He had eyed her all evening, as if she were a mare he was appraising for purchase. She would have to be wary of Robert, she was sure of that.

As the night wore on, Angela began worrying about Bradford. How would he react? It suddenly hit her that he might not like it any better than Zachary did.

She fell asleep thinking of her father. He had been gruff and took to the bottle a bit too much, but she had loved him. She had had a hard childhood, but she would give anything to be home with William Sherrington now. She cried herself to sleep.

"Mornin', Missy." Hannah came bustling into the room in a cheery mood. "Sun's been shinin' for some time now. You don't usually sleep this late, do you?"

Angela opened her eyes to find the room flooded in daylight. "What time is it?"

"A little past eight."

"Eight!" Angela quickly jumped from the bed and ran for the closet.

"What's your hurry, honey?"

Angela stopped short as she realized there was no hurry. She no longer had chores to do.

"I guess I forgot."

Hannah laughed in her cheerful way. "You'll get use to this easy life soon enough. All you got to worry about is if you wants your breakfast downstairs, or if you wants me to send up a tray for you."

"Will the others be goin' down to eat?" Angela asked apprehensively.

"Only Mr. Lonsdale. Master Jacob ate some time ago, and Miss Crystal eats in her room."

"And Zachary?"

"He went into the city this mornin'," Hannah replied. "He gots hisself a law office he's tryin' to build up again, now that the war is over."

"Then I guess I'll go down for breakfast, Hannah," Angela stated. As long as she didn't have to face Crystal or Zachary and their obvious dislike of her, there was no point in staying in her room. "I can't go gettin' lazy."

"Good girl. You gonna need all the exercise you can get, now you ain't got so much to do. And afterward, Master Jacob wants to see you in the study."

"Did I do something wrong again?"

"No, honeychild, he just wants to talk to you," Hannah replied quickly, setting Angela's mind at ease. "Now, I'll send Eulalia up to fix your hair and help you dress. She's gonna be your personal maid, 'lessen you don't like her?"

"But I don't—"

"You hush now." Hannah cut her off as she went to the door, knowing Angela's objections. "You gonna be a lady now, and ladies don't do *nothin'* for themselves. You got lots to get use to, child."

A while later, Angela was wearing a stiff green cotton dress, with an equally rough chemise under it. She would much rather be wearing her old beat-up breeches and cotton shirt. But Hannah had taken it upon herself to get rid of those old articles.

Angela had argued about it, but to no avail. She had also spent thirty minutes in battle with the young girl who was going to be her maid. Eulalia had received orders from Hannah to fix Angela's hair into a becoming coiffure. Her hair was a few inches below her shoulders, and she was used to wearing it in tight pigtails, or tied back with a ribbon. She had won that battle, and her auburn hair was neatly tied with a green ribbon.

When she walked nervously into the dining room, she found Robert still there, sipping black coffee.

"I was beginnin' to think you weren't comin' down," Robert said, a warm smile coming to his lips when he saw her. "I'm glad I waited."

"I'm sorry I took so long. Have you eaten already?" Angela asked uneasily. She wished he wouldn't stare so.

"Yes, and a pleasant meal it was. Tilda's artistry has drawn me to Golden Oaks for many a year— made this place a home away from home, you might say. But now I'll have to admit Golden Oaks has a much greater attraction," he added meaningfully.

Angela found herself blushing. "I really don't know what you mean," she said awkwardly. "But if you've finished your meal, don't let me keep you. Surely you must have something to do, other than keep me company."

He laughed heartily. "But my dear girl, I have nothin' but time on my hands, and I can think of no better way to spend it than with you."

Angela's face reddened and she sat down and busied herself with piling food on her plate. She could see that it would be easy to obtain Robert as an ally, but she was afraid the sacrifice expected of her would be too great.

"Don't you have a plantation to run, Mr. Lonsdale?" she asked pointedly.

"Not as long as my father's still livin'. He deplores my help, and frankly, I deplore givin' it. Even though the war greatly diminished his wealth, the old man was able to pay the back taxes on The Shadows and he's managin' quite well by himself. It's almost as if the war never was. I find things to do, to pass the time agreeably."

Angela was incensed by his laziness. "Drinkin' and gamblin', no doubt. All you planters' sons are alike."

"Not all of us," Robert came back with a grin. "Some are not as lucky as I."

She stared, aghast. He had taken her statement as a compliment, not as the sarcasm she intended. He really was insufferable. She had thought that the breed of men who lived each day only for pleasure, leaving work for others, had ended with the war. But apparently she was wrong. Robert Lonsdale was just such a man.

"Perhaps you would care for a ride this mornin'," Robert continued confidently. "To see The Shadows? Father has done considerable repair, and it's really quite beautiful once again. It went to ruin durin' the last years of the war, what with most of the slaves runnin' off when things started gettin' bad. But they came back soon enough, once they found the Yankees' idea of freedom was a lot worse than what they'd left."

Angela cooled her temper. Robert couldn't help being what he was, and she needed him as a friend, not an enemy. She held back the caustic words and instead gave him a radiant smile, grateful that she had an excuse to decline his offer.

"I'd love to see The Shadows with you, Mr. Lonsdale, but Jacob wants to see me after breakfast. Maybe another time though, if that's all right."

He frowned for just a moment, then smiled brightly once again. "There will certainly be another time. And no more 'Mr. Lonsdale,' Angela. You must call me Robert—I insist."

Eleven

Jacob Maitland took her to Mobile a little later. They traveled in a comfortable enclosed carriage that kept out the hot sun.

She hadn't realized the extent of Jacob Maitland's generosity. She had never dreamed that when he said he wanted to be like a father to her, he meant to bestow on her everything the rest of his family took for granted.

"Angela," he had begun that morning, "I know you told me yesterday that you never had time for schooling. Now that you no longer have to work, would you like to go to school?"

She sighed regretfully. "I'm too old for school now."

"Nonsense," Jacob returned with a smile. "You're never too old to learn. And I didn't mean a public school for children, my dear. I meant a private school for young women."

"But I can't even write my name."

"I will arrange for you to have a special tutor to teach you all the basics, and then you can go to classes with the other girls. The choice is entirely yours, of course. I'm not saying you have to go."

"But I'd love to go," she said quickly. "I've always wondered what folks found so interestin' in books."

"You can find that out for yourself now. And when you come home, you might like to help me with my ledgers."

"Oh, I'd love to help you any way I can, Mr.—Jacob."

"Good. Now we have to decide on the school. There are many to choose from, here and up North. There is a fine school in Massachusetts. One of the teachers there, Naomi Barkley, was a very good friend of your mother's. In fact, your mother attended that school when she was your age."

"My mother went to a northern school?"

"Yes. Massachusetts was her home until she came to Alabama and married your father."

Angela was dumbfounded. "I didn't know—I mean, Pa never told me. I always thought she was born here. How do you know this?"

Jacob hesitated before answering carefully, "I used to live in Massachusetts myself. I still have business interests there. My father was acquainted with Charissa's parents. They were well-to-do before the Depression of 1837. They died after that, and left your mother penniless. Charissa became a governess for a while, and then she came here."

"Why did she come here?"

"Well, I don't . . . When you are older, perhaps you will be able to understand."

He knew the reasons, but he didn't want to tell her. And she couldn't press him for answers. She just couldn't. But she wanted to know.

"Now, about the school," Jacob continued. "I am of the opinion that northern schools are the best. Both my sons went to school in the North. But you have a choice. I could send you to Europe, but I thought you might like to see your mother's home."

"Yes, I would!" Angela said with excitement. "The school in Massachusetts is my choice."

"You don't have a dislike for the North, then?"

"No. Bradford—I mean, your older son— fought for the North. I have nothing against Northerners."

Jacob was frowning at her now.

"How did you know Bradford fought for the Union?"

Angela paled. How could she have let that slip?

"I—I—" She couldn't think of an explanation.

Jacob saw how upset she was and quickly smiled to put her at ease. "It's all right, Angela. I was just surprised that you knew. It doesn't matter anymore who knows, now that the North has won." He dismissed the subject. "You will have to leave in about ten days, Angela, and that doesn't give us much time. We will go to the city today to have you fitted for clothes. I'm told seventeen dresses should be adequate for the school year. There isn't enough time to have that many made for you here, and the North will feature warmer materials anyway. So Miss Barkley, the woman I mentioned earlier, will help you complete your wardrobe once you are there."

Angela was shocked. "But I don't need—"

But he anticipated her objection. "I have asked that you let me think of you as a daughter, Angela," he interrupted her softly. "I would do no less for Zachary's wife, so please let me do as much for you. And if you are feeling shy about it, think of it as helping out some poor seamstress who needs the business."

So they were on their way to the city to choose dress styles and materials appropriate to a young lady of seventeen. Later, they bought all the accessories Jacob insisted she needed, in the very stores she had once looked in on so wistfully. Trunks were bought, and bonnets and shoes, toilet articles, warm jackets for the colder weather she would soon encounter. So much money changed hands that Angela was dazed. It was all really happening, and to Angela Sherrington!

Twelve

 After three winters in South Hadley, Massachusetts, Angela should have been used to cold weather, but she wasn't. She didn't think she ever would be. The other girls didn't seem to mind it, though, for most of them came from northern states.

Angela didn't have any friends in school, except for Naomi Barkley, who treated her more like a daughter than a pupil. Angela had long ago given up hope of finding a friend. It wasn't her fault. She had tried hard to be friendly. But the other students took an immediate dislike to her because of her southern accent, for many of them had lost brothers and fathers because of the war. As they blamed the South for the war, they blamed her.

Wishing it had been different, Angela managed to live with the hostility the first year, for she had

Naomi, and Angela lost herself in learning. But being the butt of practical jokes, she couldn't help losing her temper occasionally. She shocked the other girls with her knowledge of swear words. Angela would hurl expletives at them that turned their faces red. She enjoyed shocking them. It was the only relief she had.

One good thing was that, through Naomi, Angela came to know more about her own mother. She even learned about the things that Jacob Maitland had been reluctant to discuss, her mother's reason for leaving Springfield, Massachusetts.

Charissa had been thirteen when her parents' world crumbled in the Depression of 1837. But they managed to keep her in school, and she was kept in the dark about their poverty and mounting debts. She didn't discover the truth until they died in 1845. Since Charissa's family and the Maitlands had been good friends, Charissa became a companion to Jacob's mother. When Jacob's mother died, in '47, Charissa became a governess for a banking family.

Naomi saw her occasionally then, and Charissa confessed that she was in love with a married man, that it was impossible for him to leave his wife and children. She wouldn't say who the man was, but Naomi suspected it was the banker. Because of the hopelessness of her romance, Charissa left Springfield for Alabama.

Angela wondered why Jacob had been so reluctant to tell her the truth. She was certainly old enough to understand.

On one of the girls' frequent outings to Springfield, Angela huddled close to the entrance of a store, waiting for the other girls to finish with their purchases. She really shouldn't have come today, for she had a lot of studying to do. But she needed a little more blue yarn to finish a sweater she was making for Naomi.

Angela pulled the hood of her cape tighter about her face, feeling the fur lining cold against her skin. She wished the other girls would hurry.

Suddenly a commotion caught her attention. Down the street, on the opposite side, two little boys were having an argument. Angela watched with alarm as one boy pushed the other, and a fight began. But just then, a tall man approached and said something to the boys. They immediately stopped fighting and ran off in separate directions.

The man seemed vaguely familiar, and she watched him intently.

Angela gasped, drawing the attention of Jane and Sybil, who had come out of the store.

"Did you know that man, Angela?" Jane asked.

Angela turned around to look at them, the color gone from her face. It had been almost five and a half years since she last saw Bradford Maitland. For some mysterious reason that the family wouldn't talk about, he had not returned to

Golden Oaks since the summer of '62. What was he doing in Springfield?

Sybil giggled and whispered something to Jane, whose eyes opened wide. But Angela wasn't paying attention to them as she stared at the brown building across the street. She was lost in the past. In all these years, hardly a day passed that Angela didn't think about Bradford, and now she had seen him once again.

Jane shook Angela's arm. "Why don't you go in there and see him? You know you want to."

"I—I couldn't," Angela stammered.

"Of course you can," Jane said, a gleam in her eyes. "We will say that you met a lady friend who offered to take you back to school."

"But that's a lie."

"We'll keep your secret, Angela," Sybil offered encouragement. "And you can always hire a carriage to take you back to school if your friend won't. It's early in the afternoon. You won't be missed until dinner. Go on into the building."

Angela handed her small package to Jane and slowly crossed the street.

But when she reached the steps that led to the brown building, she suddenly had reservations about going on. It was an awfully brash thing to do, to go looking for a man. What would Bradford think of her?

Angela turned about quickly, suddenly ready to run back to the store. But the girls were gone.

Why not see it through? It seemed silly not to talk to Bradford.

Angela mounted the steps and knocked loudly on the door. A few moments later the door was opened by a tall man in rolled-up shirt sleeves and vest, a cigar stuck between his teeth, who waited for her to speak. When she didn't, he grabbed her arm and pulled her inside, closing the door behind her.

"Got to keep the cold out, honey," the man said in a gruff but friendly voice.

It took Angela a few seconds for her eyes to become adjusted to the dim lighting in the foyer, but she could see clearly into the room off the foyer that was brightly lit and filled with men and expensively dressed women sitting around large tables. This was a gambling house! Smoke floated out of the wide double doors, and the sound of laughter, groaning, shouting, and swearing mingled together. She saw that the foyer and the room beyond had dark red walls, with lewd pictures covering them.

The man behind Angela startled her when he began removing her cape. "Since you ain't escorted, you must be the new girl Henry promised to send over. Hey Peter!" he called out. "Go tell Maudie the new girl is here. You better give me your jacket too, honey. It's nice and warm in here and we don't want to hide the goods. You're sure a fancy dresser, but you ain't much for words. Come on, Maudie's waiting."

Angela was speechless. What new girl was she supposed to be? She should explain, but the man was pulling her along behind him. He entered a room across from where the gamblers were winning and losing fortunes, and left her without saying any more.

The room was large, and filled with women dressed in bright silks and satins, and lounging on plush velvet sofas. Even the walls were velvet. There was a fancy staircase in the back of the room, and here Angela saw Bradford on his way up the stairs, a pretty redhead on his arm. He saw her too and suddenly stopped. Her heart seemed to stop and her palms began to sweat. Did he recognize her after all this time?

"Hey, Maudie, I've changed my mind," Bradford said. "I'll take that new girl."

Maudie looked in Angela's direction and then smiled up at Bradford. "New is right, gent. That one will cost you extra."

"Hell!" Bradford grumbled. "I've already lost a damn fortune at your tables, so have a little pity."

"Sorry, gent, but that one is going to be in demand. She comes high."

"All right, how much?"

"Double," Maudie answered.

Maudie approached Angela as the redhead left Bradford's side and descended the stairs, a pouting expression on her heavily painted face. Angela realized now that all these women were prostitutes.

She would have a hard time explaining her way out of here. But maybe Bradford had recognized her and was saving her from an embarrassing situation. He would find a way to get her out of here, she was sure of it. She hurried over to him and he slipped his arm around her waist. As they started up the stairs, Angela smelled liquor fumes on him.

"Name's Bradford, my dear, and you damn well better be worth what I paid for you," he said, his yellow-brown eyes roving over her body.

She was afraid to say anything just yet, and allowed him to lead her to an upstairs room. Bradford closed the door. His next words made her gasp.

"You can shed your clothes while I fix us a drink. I see Maudie's got some bubbly on hand."

Maybe she had misunderstood. "You're *already* drunk, Bradford. Don't you think you've had enough?"

"Start shedding those pretty clothes. Don't know why I have to tell you how to do your job."

Angela was in shock. He *didn't* recognize her! He had no idea who she was! He thought she was a prostitute! What was she going to do?

"Bradford, you don't understand. I—"

She had started to gather her wits when he crossed to her in quick strides and tilted her face to his. Angela shrank back from him when she saw the yellow flames in his eyes. This was the Bradford from the portrait. She felt an unreasonable fear as he grabbed her shoulders.

"What the hell is the matter with you, girl? If this frightened act is supposed to excite your customers, you can stop it right now. It doesn't work for me. Now get your dress off."

"I—I can't," Angela stammered, her mind fogging over.

All of a sudden he laughed, lights dancing in his amber eyes.

"Why in blazes didn't you say so?"

He turned her around and started to unfasten her bindings. Angela realized that he had mistaken her refusal. He assumed that she couldn't remove her dress without help. She stood motionless while his fingers worked on her bindings. She was afraid to move. Now that she had let it go this far, would she be able to stop him? And then she realized with a sudden terrible jolt that she didn't *want* him to stop. Hundreds of times she had dreamed of a moment like this one, with the two of them alone together, making love.

This was the man she had loved all these years, and at this moment he wanted her, too. She wanted to feel his hands on her, to taste his kisses, if only for this one time.

Oh, God, why not? She could have this one time with him, to remember forever. She could give him her love, as she had always wanted to. She would give herself freely to him and pretend for a little while that he loved her too.

Bradford bent down and kissed the soft flesh of her neck, making her tremble with his nearness.

"I'm sorry I yelled at you earlier, honey, but you had me worried that you didn't want to go through with this."

"You mean you wouldn't force me if I didn't want to?" she asked as she turned around to face him.

"Hell no!" Bradford growled, insulted.

He surprised her by taking her in his arms and making her head spin with the forcefulness of his kiss. It was her first kiss, and given by the man she had always loved! She felt weak, yet exhilarated, and a strange fluttering moved through her.

Suddenly Bradford released her, leaving her breathless. "Damned if I don't feel like I'm in another place and time."

He gently removed her clothes, and the sight of her standing naked, with only a gold coin hanging between the generous mounds of her breasts, moved him deeply. He slowly took the pins from her hair, letting the soft brown curls fall gently about her shoulders. He kissed her eyes and her face, then gently brushed her lips before he picked her up and carried her to the bed.

Angela was afraid she wouldn't know what to do, but Bradford led her in everything. He was gentle as he introduced her body to the feel of his hands and his lips. She felt no shame as he explored her. She was soon able to caress and stroke him in return, and even to clasp his manhood and find elation in his groan of pleasure.

When he finally mounted her, Angela was prepared to experience the ultimate in pleasure, but she wasn't prepared for what followed. Pain burst like fire inside her. She clenched her teeth and only a gasp escaped her. But he looked down at her with a puzzled frown.

"Did I hurt you?"

"No," she quickly reassured him.

"Then why the nails in my back?" he grinned.

"I'm sorry. I didn't realize—"

"Don't apologize. It's not often I find a passionate woman. In fact, it's been my luck to pick the ice maidens of this world—until now."

He kissed her again and started to move in her once more. The pain was gone now. It felt so good having him inside her, meeting his body with each grinding plunge. All too soon he thrust deep in her and then stopped, leaving her regretting that it was over. She expected him to roll away, but he didn't. He just lay on her, breathing heavily, then started to move in her again.

She was delighted that it wasn't over yet, that he was still in her, loving her. And then a new sensation started to grow in her, one that was exquisitely different. It intensified, getting stronger and stronger until it burst forth in one giant throb of pleasure. She had entered a whole new world.

He kissed her gently, then whispered, "If I weren't so tired, I could make love to you all afternoon and on through the night. Next time."

He eased away with a heavy sigh and lay on

his stomach beside her on the bed. His eyes were closed and sleep caught up with him quickly. Angela stared at his muscular body, so lean and perfect, then at his face, relaxed in slumber.

It was all over now, and Angela knew she must leave this place quickly, before Maudie found another customer for her. She slipped out of bed slowly, trying not to disturb Bradford, then she saw the bloodstain on the satin sheet. She gasped at the evidence of her innocence, and hastily pulled the top sheet up to cover Bradford and the stain, then went to the bowl of water in the corner of the room and washed herself.

She took the time to pin her hair back up, leaving a few of her curls to hang in ringlets, for she had to look the same as she had when she left the school. Then she began to put her clothes back on, but soon realized she couldn't fasten the dress by herself. She had to have something to cover her unlaced back, and there was nothing in the room except his silver brocaded vest, or his white frilled shirt, or his coat. She put on the vest over her dress. Then it dawned on her that she would have to leave her own cape and jacket behind. She couldn't go back downstairs to get them. She prayed there was another way out of this building other than through the room where Maudie was.

Angela crossed to the bed for one last look at the man sleeping there. "I love you, Bradford Maitland, and I always will," she whispered.

"What?" he mumbled, without opening his golden-brown eyes.

Angela inhaled sharply. "Nothing, Bradford. Go back to sleep."

With a deep breath, she quickly left the room, closing the door quietly. Then she started toward the back of the building, praying desperately for a safe exit.

Thirteen

Angela returned to school late in the afternoon and went straight to her room without being noticed. She stayed there until dinner. So far, her joyous afternoon had gone undetected.

That night at dinner, Angela knew the girls were waiting for her outburst of temper over the trick they had played on her. But she surprised them with smiles and warm cheerful greetings. She knew they were dying of curiosity. Good!

Later that night, when Angela slowly drifted to sleep, miles away in Springfield, Bradford Maitland was rudely awakened from his slumber.

"This is a fine thing!" Maudie yelled as she burst into the room, startling him awake. "I go off to do some shopping and have a little dinner, and I come back to find you've had that girl up here all day." She stopped and looked about the room. "Where the hell is she?"

Bradford shrugged. "I asked her to stay, but I guess she got tired of watching me sleep. Isn't she downstairs?"

"Would I be here asking for her if she was?" Maudie said stiffly. "Now what the hell did you do to that girl to make her run off?"

"Shut up, woman, and give me a chance to wake up!" Bradford growled.

"I ain't leaving here till I get to the bottom of this." Maudie stood her ground at the foot of the bed.

"Well, get the hell out of here while I dress."

"No time for bashfulness, gent," she replied with a deep chuckle. "I've seen hundreds of men without their clothes on. You ain't no different."

Bradford cursed under his breath. He wasn't about to parade himself before the fat old bitch. Grabbing the top sheet, he wrapped it around his middle, crossed to the chair where he had thrown his clothes, then stood behind it to dress.

"What the hell is this?" Maudie shrieked suddenly. "I bet you weren't even going to tell me, were you? You were going to sneak out without paying the extra!"

"Extra for what?" Bradford sighed.

"She was a virgin—as if you didn't know! And the proof's right there on the bed."

Bradford stared at the stain and his eyes suddenly narrowed dangerously. "What are you try-

ing to pull, Maudie? The girl was a prostitute—
she knew what she was doing! You want to explain to me how the hell a girl can be a prostitute
and a virgin at the same time?"

Maudie stepped back a little, wary of the fire
that leaped in his eyes. But she wasn't about to be
cheated.

"Was the girl bleeding before you took her?"
Maudie asked quickly.

"No."

"Then how do you explain that bloodstain in
the middle of the bed, unless the girl was a virgin?"

Bradford looked at the stain again, his brow
wrinkled in thought. Was it possible? And then
he remembered the way the girl's body had suddenly stiffened, and her nails digging into his
back. And she had been frightened and nervous
to begin with.

"Good Lord!" he fumed. "What the hell was
she doing, throwing her virginity away like that?
And she didn't even get paid for it—you did!"

"That's right, gent. But not enough, not enough
for a virgin."

"I didn't ask for a virgin," he reminded her
acidly. "And I don't intend to pay just because
that little girl happened to be one."

"You better do the right thing, gent, or you ain't
going to be welcome in my club again," Maudie
pronounced indignantly.

"What was the girl doing in your house anyway, if you didn't know she was a virgin?" he demanded.

"I was expecting a new girl and I thought she was the one. She came in unescorted, and she didn't say anything when I gave her to you. She wanted it done. Lord knows why, but she wanted to be busted. And there's plenty men would have paid a fortune to bust her."

"So she wasn't even one of your girls, and yet you're trying to get more money out of me."

"She's going to be one of my girls, just as soon as I can find her. That girl's a little gold mine. She probably came to my place because she wants to get started in the business. But the point is," Maudie said, shaking a pudgy finger in the air, "she came here to have her first man, and anything that happened in my place I get paid for."

Bradford shook his head, but he took out his wallet and pulled out five one-hundred-dollar bills, dropping them on the chair seat. "Will that be sufficient?"

She came over and picked up the money while Bradford put his white frilled shirt on. "I suppose it will have to do," she retorted, and stuck the bills between her huge breasts. "Don't know why you put up such a fuss about it in the first place."

"You have already soaked me for over ten thousand at your tables. The girl should have been on the house."

"Hell, that's just a drop in the bucket for you. I hear you Maitlands can afford to lose that much every day."

"That's hardly the point, Maudie," Bradford said, reaching for his vest. "For Christ's sake!" He looked around to see if he was mistaken, but he wasn't. "The girl stole my vest!"

Maudie barked her laughter. "You just can't win for losing today, can you, gent?"

"Why would she take my vest and not my wallet? There's more than five thousand in it."

"Maybe you won the poor girl's heart, and she just wanted a keepsake. Or more likely, she just couldn't find your wallet, or was too stupid even to know where to look. Next time you're in town, gent, come see me again. That little girl is going to be very much in demand here, and if you think she's worth the high price I'm going to set for her, then you can have her again."

"Oh, she's worth it, Maudie, and I'll have her again," Bradford replied with a grin on his lips as he picked up his coat and started for the door. "But I won't be paying you for her. I'm going to find her before you do, Maudie, and that's a promise."

"You bastard!" she called out after him, but he was already running downstairs, his laughter drowning out her curses.

Bradford went straight to David Welk, his Springfield lawyer, getting the poor man out of bed, and gave David Angela's description. They made arrangements for the whole city to be searched. Welk even arranged for a man to be posted at Maudie's place, just in case the girl did go back there. It was imperative that Bradford return to New York tomorrow on business, or he would have stayed to help in the search. He wanted fast results.

Bradford hated mysteries. Why had the girl done what she did? She let him believe she was a whore, when in fact she had never been with a man before. And why take his vest and not his money?

He had to find her. He wanted answers.

But above all, he wanted her. Just thinking about her stirred him deeply. He was not finished with her. One way or another, he would have her again.

Fourteen

When Bradford returned to his home in New York, he found a telegram from David Welk and also a message from his fiancée, Candise Taylor. He ignored her message, and quickly opened David's telegram.

HAVE FOUND THE GIRL. NAME ANGELA.
HAVE REASON TO BELIEVE SHE WILL
LEAVE THE STATE SOON. ADVISE.

"Damn!" he swore aloud.

He couldn't return just yet, at least not for a few days. But what if the girl were gone by then? It was imperative that he not lose her.

Bradford quickly scribbled off instructions for David and sent them off with a servant. Bradford hoped he could trust David to carry out his orders. As he wrote, he exulted silently, *Angela . . . her name is Angela!*

David Welk stepped out of his carriage at the train depot and searched the crowds for the man who had urgently sent for him. After a few moments he finally saw him waving frantically from inside the station house and hurried over to him.

"Well? Where is she?" David asked.

"Right over there, sir, with that older woman in green," the man replied. "I didn't think you would get here in time. Her train leaves in about ten minutes."

"Is there a police officer around?"

"There is one by the entrance."

David sighed regretfully. "Go and get him."

When the man David had hired to watch Angela left to do as ordered, David pulled Bradford's telegram out of his pocket and read it once more.

KEEP GIRL UNDER SURVEILLANCE.
IF SHE ATTEMPTS TO LEAVE STATE,
STOP HER. ARREST HER IF NECESSARY.

David shook his head. This was deplorable. But Bradford had told him about the stolen vest. He did have cause. And he could think of no legal way to stop the girl except to arrest her.

* * *

Angela hugged Naomi Barkley good-bye. "Thank you for seeing me off."

"Well, don't forget to send me a wire and I'll meet you when you return."

"That isn't necessary, Naomi," Angela protested.

"Nonsense. I have nothing better to do. Are you sure you won't change your mind and spend your Christmas vacation with me? I would love to have you."

Angela grinned and shook her head. "You know me. I'll take every chance I have to get away from this cold, miserable weather."

"Then you had better hurry, dear. The porter is waiting to put your luggage on the train."

"Angela."

Angela turned around. She didn't recognize the man standing behind her. "Yes?"

"Is your name Angela?"

She stared at the man curiously. Two other men stood behind him. One was a police officer.

"Who are you?" she asked warily.

"I'm a lawyer, miss."

Angela's eyes widened. Oh, God, something had happened to Jacob—she just knew it.

"You have bad news?"

"Is your name Angela?" he persisted.

"Yes, yes," she said worriedly.

The lawyer turned to the policeman and summoned him forward. "Her name is the same and she fits the description. Arrest her."

Angela gasped.

At that moment, Naomi stepped in front of Angela and glowered at the policeman. "Don't you dare touch this girl! She is a student on her way home for Christmas vacation. This gentleman has obviously made a serious mistake."

"I'm afraid not, madam," David said uncomfortably. "The girl stole an article of clothing from a client of mine. My client is presently out of the state, but when he returns, he will decide whether or not to press charges."

"This is preposterous!"

"I quite agree, madam, and this is most unpleasant for me. But no mistake has been made."

Naomi turned to Angela, who was deathly white. "Angela?"

Angela thought surely she was going to faint. Bradford was going to put her in jail for stealing his vest!

"I—I did take something that didn't belong to me—I had to," Angela said in a frightened voice. "But I would have returned it if I knew where to reach—the gentleman. You can have it back."

"I'm afraid it's too late for that, miss," David Welk said. "A crime has been committed."

"But I'm not a thief!" Angela protested shrilly, her fear growing. "I didn't take the damn vest because I wanted it. I needed it that day to—to—"

Angela faltered. How could she explain? The lawyer must know the whole sordid story. But Naomi didn't know, and Angela couldn't possibly tell her.

The policeman took Angela's arm firmly and led her away. Naomi followed, calling out, "Angela, I will wire Jacob and he will get this all straightened out."

"No!" Angela cried, facing her. The policeman waited for Naomi to catch up to them. "No, Jacob must *not know* about this."

"But he can help, dear."

"No!"

"Jacob is an understanding man."

"He won't be this time. I can't explain it, but please—*don't* tell him."

Naomi shook her head. "I have to, Angela. He is your guardian."

Angela took a deep breath. She would have to tell Naomi now.

"Naomi, the vest I took belonged to Bradford Maitland, Jacob's son."

"*He* is the one responsible for this?"

"Yes. And Jacob would be furious if he found out. But more than that, he would demand an explanation, and that is something I cannot give him."

"But how could Bradford do this to you? You're a member of his family! And heavens, you have done nothing but talk about him since I've known you. I had the distinct impression that you were madly in love with him."

"It doesn't matter what I felt. Bradford didn't recognize me the day we met in Springfield. And even if he did recognize me, he doesn't know his father is my guardian. He hasn't been home in all the years since Jacob took me in."

"Why didn't you tell him who you were?"

"He thought—oh, Naomi, don't ask me about that day! I thought I wanted to remember it always, but now I wish it had never happened."

More than that, she wished she had never laid eyes on Bradford Maitland. God, why hadn't she told him who she was? She wouldn't be in this mess now if she had.

"I will have a talk with that lawyer," Naomi suggested, cutting into Angela's thoughts.

"No!"

"But he works for Bradford, and maybe for Jacob as well, so he must be told you are Jacob's ward."

"Then he will feel it's his duty to tell Jacob, and I would rather die than have Jacob know what I've done," Angela said miserably.

"Angela, you seem to be forgetting that Jacob is expecting you home for Christmas."

"You can tell him I got sick and can't make it, that I will be staying with you instead. Please, Naomi, do that for me. I'm sure I can get myself out of this mess before the holidays are over, so the school won't have to know anything, nor will Jacob. Bradford had no reason to do what he did and I'll make him see that when he comes back."

Naomi sighed. "Angela, I don't understand any of this, but I will cover for you. It's against my better judgment, but I'll do it."

Fifteen

Bradford rode to the jail with David Welk in a hired coach. Bradford had been delayed in New York longer than expected and this was the third day the girl had spent locked up. She was a student, and from a very exclusive girls' school. Bradford would never have believed it, but that was where David had found her and she admitted to the theft. Yes, this was the girl.

"I was really hoping it wouldn't come to this," Bradford said reflectively when they reached their destination. "But then again, it might just be to my advantage. She will undoubtedly be quite grateful when I have her released. You did find a house in the country?"

"Yes."

"A private, secluded house?"

"Yes, *yes*," David replied with a good deal of

116

annoyance. "And I have to tell you I don't approve of what you're planning, Bradford."

"Why? I will have the girl's consent. I won't be breaking any law, David."

"It's immoral."

Bradford laughed.

"Well, we're here," David said huffily. "You know, what I don't understand is why the girl's parents haven't been here."

"Has anyone been notified that she was arrested?" Bradford asked.

"I assumed the chaperon who was with the girl has taken care of that."

Bradford shrugged. "Perhaps her parents don't give a damn. At any rate, if they do come, they won't find her here now. And there's no need for you to wait, David. I can handle things from here." Then he added, "I assume the house you found is well stocked?"

"Yes," David replied. "And there's a carriage and a pair of matched bays in the stable. You will have to attend them yourself, though, since you specified no servants."

"You've done wonders, David, and in such a short time. Thank you."

"Don't thank me. You didn't need a lawyer for this. Any experienced madam would have done."

"Miss Smith."

Angela was staring fixedly at the ceiling, counting the cracks for the hundredth time as she lay stretched out on a narrow cot. She had never been so angry in her entire life. She was furious. She had had three days to feed that fury.

"Angela Smith!"

She gasped and sat up. She must remember that she had used the name Smith. She had impulsively lied about it and all the other information demanded of her, so she wouldn't involve the school in scandal.

She stood up quickly when the door opened and a guard stepped into the cell. "Well, don't just stand there, girl," he said impatiently. "Come along."

"Where?" she asked warily.

"You're being released. The man you robbed has decided not to press charges. All he wants is a few minutes of your time. He's waiting out front."

"Oh, he is, is he?" Angela said icily.

She picked up the one small suitcase she had kept with a few changes of clothes in it. Naomi had taken the rest of her luggage. And then Angela walked stiffly out of the cell and continued to the entrance, not waiting for anyone to tell her whether she could or not. She was stopped, but only to be handed her cape and jacket. She donned them quickly and left the building.

The bright morning sun blinded her when she walked out the door. That and the recently fallen snow made everything a white blur for a moment and she had to stop to get her bearings. But with squinting and shading her eyes with her hand, she finally saw him just a few yards from her, standing in front of a small coach.

She walked toward him, deliberately taking her time, her eyes riveted on his face. He was smiling, actually smiling! That was the last straw. She stopped only inches from him and then her hand snaked through the air and cracked against his cold cheek.

Bradford was genuinely surprised. "What was that for?"

"You dare to ask!" she shouted furiously. "If I had a gun right now I would shoot you. I would honest to God shoot you dead!"

"Lower your voice, damnit, or you will have the police out here to arrest you again."

"Yes, by all means, throw me in jail again!" she stormed. "You can say I assaulted you."

Bradford's eyes narrowed. "Get in the coach."

"I certainly will not!"

He grabbed her arm and shoved her roughly through the coach door, tossing her suitcase in after her. Quickly, he was inside and the driver started them off down the street.

Angela crawled up on the seat opposite him and glared at him murderously. "You stop this coach right now and let me out! I refuse to go anywhere with you!"

"Shut up, Miss Smith, and stop acting as if I wronged you. You stole from me, remember? I could have left you to rot in jail."

Angela felt a tight knot swell in her throat. Her

lower lip began to tremble and tears sprang to her eyes.

"You didn't have to be so cruel," she said in a tiny voice. "I offered to give your vest back, but your lawyer said that wasn't good enough. All along, it was your fault I took the vest to begin with."

"My fault? That's ridiculous."

"Is it?" Her body stiffened and her eyes glistened with anger again. "I needed you that day to fasten my dress, but you were passed out. That was why I needed your damn vest."

"So that's why you took it?" Bradford laughed. "My dear, there were any number of women below who would have been glad to assist you."

"I couldn't go down there and risk running into that horrible Maudie." Angela was aghast.

"So you fled, and fortunately left your jacket and cape behind."

"Fortunately?"

"That's how we found you. I had a man sent there in case you returned, and he discovered from the doorman that you had left the articles behind. It was lucky for you he swiped them before Maudie found them."

"I wouldn't call it lucky if it led you to me," Angela snapped.

"Would you rather Maudie found you? She was determined to, you know." He grinned when she remained silent. "I didn't think so. At any rate, there was a piece of note paper in the pocket

of your jacket, math notes written on school sta-
tionery. My man went to the school and you were
recognized from a description." When she still
did not speak, he sighed. "Angela, I didn't want
to have you arrested, I only wanted you to be
here when I returned."

It took all of Angela's willpower not to strike
him again. "Are you saying that I spent the last
three days in jail, not because I took your vest, but
because you wanted to make sure I would be here
when you returned? Of all the contemptible,
loathsome—"

"That's enough!" Bradford cut her short. "If
you want to talk about what is contemptible, let's
talk about you. You are a student in an exclusive
school, you obviously come from a good back-
ground, yet you went to a brothel to prostitute
yourself."

"I did not!" Angela gasped.

"Then what would you call it, Miss Smith?" he
asked her pointedly. "Do you deny I paid for
you? Or are you going to say I raped you?"

"What I did doesn't excuse what you did!"

"Miss Smith, I took something from you that
day that I didn't expect or ask for, yet it ended up
costing me another five hundred dollars."

"What are you talking about?"

"Your virginity."

Angela gasped.

"I think you owe me an explanation. What
were you doing in a place like that?"

Angela felt trapped now. "I saw you outside and I—thought I recognized you. I didn't know what kind of place that was. I just wanted to talk to you."

"Well, we certainly talked, didn't we?" he said sarcastically. "And here I wasn't even the man you thought you knew, was I?"

"No, you certainly aren't the man I thought you were," Angela replied with a meaning only she understood.

"So why didn't you make your excuses and leave as soon as you knew you had made a mistake?"

"I—" She couldn't go on, not without telling him the truth.

"What's the matter, Miss Smith?" he taunted her. "Are you ashamed to admit you were just looking for some fun and excitement? There are a lot of girls like you who want the best of both worlds, but not many as daring as you."

Angela blushed hotly. "You're wrong! I wasn't looking for fun and excitement."

"Then enlighten me. If you didn't just want to get rid of your virginity so you could enjoy a promiscuous life, why did you give yourself to me?"

Angela drew herself up. "I don't have to answer your question, Mr. Maitland."

Bradford frowned, then shrugged. "I suppose I can let it go for now. But I promise you, I *will* get the answers I want before I'm finished with you."

Before he was finished with her? What did that mean? It sounded like a threat.

She finally became aware of how much time had passed and, looking out the coach window, she recognized open country. "Where are you taking me?" she asked in alarm.

"You are going to be my guest for a while."

"I certainly am not!"

"Angela, settle down." Bradford shook his head. "I really should know better than to try to predict a woman's behavior."

"What are you talking about?"

"You, my dear. I was so sure that you would be grateful to me for not pressing charges, that you would be happy to comply with my suggestion that you spend the rest of the holidays with me. I even went so far as to procure a house in the country for us. We are going there now."

"*You* can go there, or drop dead, for all I care. I'm going to South Hadley and hope to God I can forget I ever met you," she said stiffly.

"What has happened to the girl who was so worried she wouldn't please me?" he asked her pointedly.

Angela blushed and looked out the window, unable to face him. "That girl spent three miserable days in jail and found out what a bastard you are."

"Let me make it up to you, Angel," Bradford said quietly.

Angela turned dark violet eyes on him. "Can't you understand that I despise you? You have no right to kidnap me. And to put me in jail—I hate you!"

"Angela, you don't know me well enough to hate me."

"Yes I do," she replied coldly.

He leaned forward in his seat and reached for her hand, but she quickly snatched it away. "Look, I am sorry for the way I've handled things thus far. I don't want to fight with you. I want you. That's why I'm here. That's why I've gone to all this trouble."

Angela didn't reply. Slowly, Bradford sat back and watched her. They remained silent for the rest of the journey.

Sixteen

Angela showed little interest in her surroundings. The huge bedroom was warm and cozy, with a fire burning in the grate and thick carpeting to sink her bare toes into. It was a luxurious room, but as far as she was concerned, it was just another jail.

It was utterly inconceivable that she was here, but she was. The door was locked from the other side, and the windows were two stories high—and Bradford would be joining her soon.

"You're going to be mine for a while, whether you like it or not," he had said after dragging her inside the large country house and carrying her upstairs. "I'll give you the afternoon to think it over and see that there is nothing you can do about it. For your own sake, I hope you're more congenial when I join you tonight."

The afternoon had dragged by while Angela

paced the floor in a rage and screamed her throat raw demanding release. And what made it worse, what made it so unbearably frustrating, was that just a few days ago she would have been ecstatic to be with Bradford.

She gathered every available weapon in the room—books, vases, a clock, two small iron statues—and piled them on the bed, ready to hurl them the moment the door opened. And if that didn't keep him out, then the iron poker from the fireplace would at least keep him away from her.

Bradford had spent most of the day downstairs, pacing. He knew he had no right to keep the girl here against her will, that he could very well end up in jail himself because of it. But he didn't care. Damned if he wasn't willing to pay that price.

He spent the latter part of the afternoon preparing dinner, then grimaced at the disaster he had made of the kitchen. Soon, he set a tray of food down on a table next to Angela's room, then moved to unlock her door. Locking her in had disturbed his conscience, but he could see no other way. All she needed, he reasoned, was time to calm down. After all, she had opened her arms to him before. She must have liked him.

There was no sound from inside the room. Bradford turned the key in the lock and opened the door. He gasped and stepped aside as an object sailed past his head and shattered in the corridor behind him. When he saw Angela on the other side of the bed with a book raised to throw, he quickly stepped out of the room and closed the door again.

He frowned. This was going to be difficult.

"Angela, this won't work," he called out to her. "I'm still coming in."

"You do and you'll be hurting in the morning."

"I brought food. You have to eat."

"I've gone without food. I don't want anything from you."

Bradford shook his head. Many people had gone without food during the war. It made him wonder where Angela Smith had spent those hard years. There were so many things about the girl that he wanted to know, and he was determined to learn everything. In the next few days he would come to know all about her.

He scanned the corridor for a shield, saw the tray of food and quickly removed everything from the tray. Holding it in front of him, he opened the door slowly and poked his head in. As soon as an object hit the door, he rushed inside. A vase struck the tray and a book bounced off his thigh before he reached the bed.

Angela stood rigidly with an iron poker in her hand and he laughed. "You don't give up, do you, Angel?"

"Don't call me that!" she shouted before she swung at him.

But his reflexes were well trained. He stepped out of the way and then grabbed her wrist before she could raise the poker again.

"Now what will you fight with?" he asked after he jerked the weapon out of her hand.

"This!" She raised her other hand to strike him, but he caught that too.

"And now what?" he chuckled.

He drew her to him and then fell with her across the bed, gazing down at her and grinning at the anger sparkling in her eyes, now a dark violet-blue.

"Don't be mad anymore, Angel. Don't fight me."

"You can't keep me here like this!" she hissed at him. Ignoring her words, he bent over her and buried his face against her neck. Angela gasped as his lips caused goose bumps to spread across her arms. She shivered as her legs were pressed hard against his. She tried to get her hands loose, but he held her tight and continued his onslaught against her sensitive skin.

"Stop it," she protested, but she heard the weakness in her voice. "Please!"

Bradford answered by claiming her lips. She felt his hunger, was overpowered by it, and then she felt her own hunger being drawn out. She tried desperately to remember that she hated him. She ought to be repelled by his touch, she told herself furiously. Instead, she was arching her back to get closer to him, damning the clothes that separated them.

"Love me, Angel," he whispered huskily as his lips moved along her throat. "Be mine, as you were mine before. I've never wanted anything as much as I want you."

"No," Angela moaned with the last of her resistance.

"Yes," he murmured.

"Yes," she sighed.

Seventeen

 After that first time, she rejoiced in the week they had together in the beautiful country house. He couldn't get enough of her, nor she of him. She quickly learned that she was quite passionate. All Bradford had to do was touch her and she wanted him.

And he learned soon enough that she would not talk about the past. The one time he did question her, she became upset and frightened. She was never going to tell him who she really was. It was too late for that now. He would be furious if he knew, and then she would lose him.

So Bradford did not question her again. They did talk, however, a great deal. He told her about the war and the battles he won and lost.

"The Potomac Army was the best," Bradford said as they sipped warm wine before the fire. "I rejoined in the summer of '63 when the army was commanded by General George Meade. Fighting with old George was an honor, Angel. You had to respect the man's courage. We engaged Lee near Gettysburg and forced the Rebs to retreat to Virginia. That was a day for celebration.

"But it was not all glorious victories—some were enough to turn any man's stomach. It was outright slaughter at Cemetery Ridge when we cut down nearly all of a Rebel division as they charged that accursed hill."

Bradford's expression turned hard as he remembered. He didn't talk any more of the war that afternoon, but the next day he concluded his story.

"After Cemetery Ridge, I rode under Little Phil with the cavalry until the end of the war."

"Was he a general too?"

"Major General Sheridan. He was a good man. There were many more decisive battles, and then in '65 we encountered Lee's army again. Hell, we knew the South was defeated, but they were too stubborn to admit it. We got Lee to surrender in April when we blocked his line of retreat."

"I wish the war had ended then," Angela remarked, remembering that it was after Lee's surrender that Canby occupied Mobile, and Wilson raided Alabama.

"It didn't take long after the victory at Appomattox for the remaining southern armies to be brought to heel. But why did you say that, Angel? You were safe up here in the North, weren't you?"

"Yes, of course," she lied quickly.

Angela had Naomi to thank for helping her to lose her southern accent. She was glad Bradford took it for granted she was from the North, though she didn't like lying to him. Omitting the truth was one thing, but an outright lie was different.

That day, Bradford explained how the war had changed him. It also explained his high-handed treatment of her.

"All that killing, seeing friends shot, seeing young boys dying, it made me realize how short life really is, and how uncertain. I decided about halfway through the war that if I came out of it alive, I was going to live the rest of my life to the fullest. No compromising, no second best. And I've done just that. Anything I've set my mind on, I've gone after and gotten. There's no reason to settle for less when you don't have to. I got you, didn't I?" He grinned.

Yes, he had gotten her, and she was willing to follow him to the ends of the earth. Only he didn't ask her to. He fully expected her to return to school, and he took her there himself when the holidays were over.

Angela was miserable that day, until he explained that he would return when school finished for the summer.

When the first flowers came to the school for Angela Smith, Angela was delighted. She couldn't claim the flowers herself, and they were sent away, but at least she knew they were from Bradford, that he hadn't forgotten. He sent flowers three more times, but they were turned away too. And then no more arrived. But she wasn't upset. She didn't expect him to keep sending flowers. After all, flowers were ridiculously expensive in the winter time.

But then summer arrived, and Bradford didn't.

Eighteen

Zachary Maitland knocked on the door to the study and then opened it without waiting for a reply. "Father, I would like a word with you, if you can spare me a minute."

"A minute is about all I can spare," Jacob replied from his position behind the desk. "I want to finish these accounts before it's time to leave to meet Angela."

"Well, Angela is the reason I want to talk to you, Father. It is time you realized what you are doing," Zachary said as he sat down in the leather chair by the desk.

"What I have come to realize is that one of my sons has turned into a snob, like his wife," Jacob replied with some irritation. "I thought I raised you better than that, Zachary."

"I resent your choice of words."

"I thought you might, but I believe 'snob' is the

134

right word indeed. It describes you and Crystal perfectly. It's a shame you can't be more like your brother-in-law—though I fear he changes his opinion of Angela only because he's in love with her."

"He's a besotted fool, but he'll get over it," Zachary replied drily.

"Really?" Jacob asked, closing his books for the day. "It seems to me that *you* were the fool when it came to love. You cast aside your convictions just so you could win Crystal over."

"I believe I have lived here long enough to give the South my loyalty," Zachary retorted with indignation. "It was a good cause to fight for. I didn't change loyalties for Crystal's sake."

"Who are you trying to convince, Zachary, me or yourself? Crystal and Robert were loyal to the South because the South is all they've ever known. But you no more believed in the southern cause than Bradford or I did. At least my oldest son had the guts to fight for his beliefs, even if it cost him dearly."

"Is it my fault Crystal broke their engagement and said she never wanted to see him again when she discovered he was sympathetic to the North? I could have told her, but I didn't!" Zachary shouted, to hide his deep fear of his older brother. He always felt uneasy when his father touched on this subject. "It was Bradford's fault he lost her, not mine!"

"Crystal made a hasty decision, but you didn't

give her time to reconsider it. You were after the girl from the moment you knew Bradford was with the Union. You joined the Confederacy and bided your time, knowing what would happen when she learned about his sympathies. Did it ever occur to you that she might have married you just to spite Bradford?"

"She loves me, Father, and I love her."

"I might believe that if I saw some grandchildren as proof. You've been married to that woman for six years now! But all I see is that this so-called love between you and Crystal is keeping Bradford away from his home."

"I'm not stopping him from coming home, and neither is Crystal. Bradford has stayed up North because he wants to," Zachary said stubbornly, but he couldn't quite meet his father's gaze.

"It's not because he wants to, Zachary," Jacob sighed. "It's because he's afraid if he came face to face with you, he might kill you. He loved Crystal enough to make her his wife. They had an argument and she called off the engagement. But time would have mended it. He was still determined to marry her when he came back, and you knew that. Do you think he will ever forgive you?"

No, Zachary thought to himself, he won't. And thank God he chose to stay away. Zachary lived in constant fear that Bradford would come home someday. Zachary was scared to death of his brother's explosive temper.

"I came here to talk about your precious Angela, not Bradford," Zachary said bitterly.

"Ah, yes. So you want to rehash the same old arguments. Or are these new ones? Zachary, just what do you have against Angela?"

"Personally, nothing. She's a perfectly nice girl, and I wish her well. Only I wish her well elsewhere. Every time she comes home on vacation, the gossip and rumors go on for months, well after she has gone back to school."

"Do you dare to talk to me about these rumors again, when it was *you* who started the gossip in the first place? If you hadn't packed your wife up and moved to the city that first summer Angela was home, then none of these rumors would have started! Your little act of defiance, Zachary, of staying in the city until Angela went back to school, was what led people to believe you were protecting your wife from immorality in this house. You would brave the fever in the city, rather than face the sins that were going on in your home, that's what you led people to believe."

"I'll talk to Crystal, Father, but there is still the matter of the gossip. It's bad enough that our friends are talking about you and Angela behind our backs, but last summer, when she locked herself up in this house with you and wouldn't go anywhere, that made it even worse. Angela isn't even here yet, and already the gossip has started."

"I don't give a damn what people are saying! I've told you that before," Jacob said in a rising voice, beginning to lose his temper.

"Well, the rest of us care. How do you think we feel when we go to the city and people stare at us? They don't even bother to whisper anymore. Do you know what they are saying? That you fancied a piece of white trash and brought her into your home to keep you warm at night. That you had her educated in a fine school so she wouldn't shame you. That you shower her with gifts so she won't leave you for a younger man. And now people pity Robert because he was unfortunate enough to fall in love with a rich man's mistress," Zachary sneered. "Doesn't that bother you in the least?"

"No," Jacob returned angrily, deciding to put Zachary in his place. "But since it bothers you so much, perhaps I should give your brother-in-law my permission to ask Angela to marry him. Robert has already approached me once on the matter."

"You can't be serious!" Zachary was appalled at the thought. "I won't have my best friend marrying the girl you've been sleeping with all these years!"

"Damn you, Zachary!" Jacob stormed, coming to his feet in a burst of fury. "So you believe all those filthy lies too! I thought I explained years ago that—that—"

Jacob brought his hands up over his heart, unable to speak for the stabbing pain in his chest. He fell back in his chair, his face quickly turning white, and was hardly able to breathe.

"Father!" Zachary cried, beside himself with fright. "Father! I'll get Dr. Scarron. I'll ride like hell, Father, only hold on!"

Nineteen

Angela waited anxiously on the dock, sitting on one of the large trunks filled with winter clothes. She had left the steamboat an hour ago, and Jacob should have been here then to meet her. What could be keeping him?

Her stomach rumbled angrily, but she didn't want to spoil her appetite for the dinner Jacob would be treating her to. All the other times when she came home from school, he took her to a fine café before they started for Golden Oaks. Last year, miserable over Bradford, she hadn't been very appreciative, but she would be this year. Her long sadness was over.

A sudden breeze swept a stray curl into her face, and she tucked it under her white bonnet. She was dressed entirely in white, right down to her shoes and silk stockings. She was glad, for it was a very hot afternoon.

The dock was teeming with people, and Angela tried to concentrate on them, but she couldn't. She kept wondering what kind of reception she would receive at Golden Oaks this time. For the past three years, Zachary and Crystal had stayed away from Golden Oaks during most of her visits home. But she was home to stay now, and Hannah had told her last summer that Zachary would never move out of Golden Oaks permanently, so Angela would have Crystal to contend with now. Angela didn't look forward to it.

Why couldn't Crystal accept her after all this time, like her brother Robert did? Angela spoke as well as the older girl did. Angela was much better educated than Crystal, who had deserted school at fourteen. And Angela could hold her own at a social gathering now. She was in all outward respects an equal, so why couldn't Crystal accept her? Would Crystal hold Angela's poor upbringing against her forever?

"Well, fancy this. If it isn't the fine lady. Home from school, are you?"

Angela started, turned quickly, and faced Billy Anderson. Her eyes widened at the sight of him, dressed immaculately in a blue-gray tweed suit. It was seven years since she had last seen him, the day she ran him off at riflepoint. She had often wondered what had happened to Billy. On her frequent trips to the city over the years, escorted either by Robert Lonsdale or Jacob, she had occasionally seen his father, Sam Anderson, but never

Billy. It was as though he had disappeared from Mobile altogether.

"Cat got your tongue, Angela?" he asked with a contemptuous curling of his lips.

"No, I—I'm just surprised to see you," she replied nervously.

He laughed at the fearful look she couldn't hide. "Do I frighten you, Angela? I see you don't carry a rifle around with you anymore."

She moved back from him. "What do you want, Billy?"

"Just a friendly chat," he said in a sarcastic tone. "But then, you never were friendly, were you?" His brown eyes suddenly darkened. "It was a pretty smart move on your part, running' to Maitland Senior about me, havin' him threaten my pa with foreclosure if I didn't leave you alone. Pa sent me up North to live with my uncle, among all them damn Yankees—even while the war was still ragin'! And all because of you, Angela Sherrington!"

There was a bitter hate in his eyes that made her flinch. She could barely catch her breath. "I had nothing to do with that, Billy. I never told him about that day. I hardly even knew Jacob Maitland then."

"You know him well enough now, don't you?"

"What is *that* supposed to mean?"

He ignored her question as his eyes measured her. "You turned out even prettier than I expected. You were a lot smarter than I thought, too.

You set yourself high stakes and went after them." He grinned now. "Can't say I blame you, though. Livin' in that fine mansion, just like a member of the family, sure must beat a tiny house in the city like I offered you. And I suppose it don't matter that Jacob Maitland is old enough to be your father, not as long as he takes care of you in such a high fashion."

"I think this conversation has lasted long enough!" Angela said sharply. She turned to walk away, but he grabbed her arm and swung her back around. "Let go of me, Billy!"

"My pa's done paid off his debts to Jacob Maitland, so there will be no threats this time," he sneered, his fingers biting into her arm. "But it don't make no difference anyway, since I don't answer to my pa any longer. I've made my own way up in New York, thanks to the death of my uncle, who was grateful for my companionship in his last years. Yeah, I'm doin' just fine." He grabbed her other arm and shook her, forcing her to look at him. "I could offer you better now, Angela. Now that you've been schooled to be a lady, I might even marry you."

Angela suddenly became infuriated. She jerked herself free of his grip and glared at him, her eyes glowing a deep blue-violet.

"You *might* even marry me? Well, I have news for you, Billy Anderson!" she snapped. "My answer is the same as it was before! And let me make it clear once and for all. You disgust me!

Never—*never* would I even consider being your mistress. And as for marriage, I would sooner marry a lowly tramp than you! Now since you don't dare do anything to me in front of all these witnesses, I suggest you leave. Jacob will be here at any moment."

He laughed derisively, as if he hadn't even heard her. "You think I'm afraid of that old man? You're right about only one thing, Angela. You're safe enough now, but there'll be another time. I meant what I said the last time we met. I mean to have you. I've thought about you constantly all these years. I hated you at first—I think I do even more now. But that will just make it so much better when I finally make you mine. And I will, Angela. No matter how long it takes, you will answer to me one day. Or you will die first."

He gave her one last long, piercing look, then tipped his hat and walked away.

Angela was deeply shaken. After all these years, would she have to live in fear again? No! She was not alone in the world any longer. She had the Maitlands. Jacob would protect her.

And just then the shiny black carriage that she knew so well pulled up in front of her and she pushed the encounter with Billy Anderson to the back of her mind.

But it was Robert Lonsdale and his sister who stepped out to greet her, not Jacob.

Their solemn faces announced that something

was wrong. She was reminded of the day her father died.

"Where is Jacob?" she cried out, terrified.

"He's had a bad attack, Angela—his heart." Robert broke the news as gently as he could. "But his doctor says he's going to be all right, as long as he takes it easy. He's got to stay in bed until he recovers his strength."

Relief brought tears to her eyes. It wasn't as bad as it might be. But fifty-five years old was too old to be having heart attacks with much chance of surviving them. Dear God, don't let him die! she pleaded silently.

"Don't take it so hard," Crystal said drily. "He's probably gonna be fine, so you needn't worry about losin' your position at Golden Oaks. At least not yet."

Angela gasped. Robert retorted angrily, "There is no call for that, Crystal!"

"I suppose not, but I just couldn't resist," Crystal giggled. "After all, if anything ever did happen to Father Maitland . . ."

She let her words trail behind her as she turned and stepped back into the carriage, leaving Angela staring after her, tears turning to fury.

Twenty

The downtown office of David Welk was tastefully furnished by a mahogany desk and tables, cream-colored chairs, and a sofa. Portraits of Presidents adorned the walls, and a small bar, liberally stocked, stood unobtrusively in a corner of the room.

Behind the large desk was a huge picture window looking out on a garden in full bloom. A summer storm was brewing and a brisk wind played havoc with the delicate flowers, sending leaves and colorful petals scurrying past the window.

Bradford Maitland sat impatiently watching the gathering storm, hoping he could make it back to his hotel before it began. After months without progress, one of Welk's detectives had found Angela. Bradford had rushed here from New York, only to be told that David was out of town, and wouldn't return until that evening. He had arranged to meet David at his office at six o'clock.

As the hour approached seven, Bradford finished his third Bourbon and water, his fingers unconsciously tapping his leg. Lightning struck, signaling the beginning of the storm. He nearly jumped out of his chair when the door finally opened and David, still in his traveling clothes, walked slowly into the room.

"Damn you, David!" Bradford snapped irritably. "Do you think I have nothing better to do than sit around your office and get drunk waiting for you?"

David Welk smiled tiredly, looking much older than his forty years. He removed his hat and coat before sitting down heavily in the chair behind his desk.

"I *was* going to berate you, but you always beat me to it," David sighed, shaking his head. He leaned forward, his brows narrowed. "I think I'll do it anyway. Confound you, Bradford! Must you always conduct your business with me after normal working hours? Here I reach home just in time for dinner, only to find that I have to meet you here. If you're not taking me away from my family, then you're summoning me in the middle of the night!"

"I pay you to be available, so don't expect any apology," Bradford retorted.

David threw up his arms in exasperation. "Far be it for me to expect Bradford Maitland to conform to normal working hours! Or to conform to anything else, for that matter."

Bradford finally relaxed and grinned. "Some of my best deals have been concluded after midnight. And I might add, in more amusing surroundings than offices. And now that we have dispensed with the amenities," he said, and smiled, hearing David's "humph." "Where is she?"

"You do get to the point rather quickly, don't you?"

"You know how long I've waited for this information," Bradford replied, still smiling. "Out with it."

"The news . . . isn't what you're expecting, Bradford," David said, uncomfortable now. "I'm afraid I sent word to you a bit prematurely."

Bradford sat up rigidly. "You did find the girl? Don't tell me you've lost her!"

"Well, yes—and no. What I mean is, we found a girl that fit her description. She's married and living in Maine now. She lived here during the time in question, and her name is Angela, just like your girl—she's even the right age."

"What's the problem then?"

"She just isn't the right one. She's a nice girl."

"So was mine, damnit!" Bradford growled angrily. "Just because she—"

"You don't understand, Bradford," David said quickly. "The girl we found is the daughter of a minister. She was strictly raised."

"What difference does that make? I told you my Angela was not a whore or a thief. That business about the vest was all a mistake."

"I know, I know. But this girl has a three-year-old daughter. We checked to make sure the child was really hers. And you did say your girl was a virgin when you met her."

"All right." Bradford sighed. "So I made this trip for nothing."

"I am sorry, Bradford," David apologized. "I did send you a telegram just as soon as I knew we had gone off on the wrong trail again. Apparently it didn't reach you in time."

"Unfortunately, no," Bradford remarked, dejected. He had been in such high spirits. "Have you nothing encouraging to report?"

"I'm afraid not, Bradford."

"A new lead?" Bradford continued hopefully. "Something—anything?"

David squirmed uneasily. He respected Bradford Maitland, for he was a genius when it came to business. But he felt Bradford had lost his balance where the elusive Angela was concerned.

"David, I have to find her."

"Give it up, Bradford. The girl can hardly be worth all this time and effort—and expense."

"She's worth it," Bradford said wistfully. His eyes were far away as he remembered the soft curves, the hypnotic violet eyes, the delicate beauty, the sunny smile. "She's more than worth it."

Wishing he had more encouragement to offer, David said, "There was a student at the school who fit the girl's description, but she was from the South and you did say at the time not to bother with that lead, since your Angela couldn't possibly have been southern. And the Barkley woman explained that there were no Smiths at the school that year. It's time to give it up."

"No."

"Very well, Bradford," David sighed. "If you want to continue supporting the detectives I've hired—well, that's up to you. I've given you my advice, and that's all I can do. But one last word: Don't keep your hopes up. Too much time has passed. There just aren't any clues left to follow."

"There's that one we passed up. If it's all you have, then start looking in the South."

"As you wish," David replied, and stood up, ending the meeting.

Returning to his hotel, Bradford found the desk clerk eager to see him. "This telegram just arrived for you, sir," the man smiled.

"Thank you," Bradford replied, looking at the piece of paper with annoyance, assuming it was the belated telegram from David Welk. But the message was not what he expected.

YOUR FATHER HAD HEART ATTACK. CRITICAL.
COME QUICKLY. DR. SCARRON.

Twenty-one

Three weeks after Jacob Maitland's attack, Hannah met Angela in the hall outside his bedroom. "Is the master sleepin', child?" Hannah whispered as Angela closed the door to Jacob's room.

"Yes, but I think we should call Dr. Scarron back," Angela said with deep concern.

"What happened?" Hannah asked, her eyes wide. "Has he gotten worse?"

"I don't know," Angela replied, her violet eyes filled with anxious worry. "He ate well tonight, and then he fell asleep. But after a few minutes passed, he started talking as if he were delirious."

"Oh, Missy," Hannah laughed, vastly relieved. "That's nothin' to be worried about. Master Jacob talks in his sleep. Always has."

"Are you sure?"

"Yessum. Don't you recall that's how my Luke

found out about Master Bradford fightin' for the North? And I heard him myself one day long ago, when he was asleep on the sofa in his study."

On her way to the kitchen, Angela thought about what Jacob had said in his sleep. Jacob had called out her mother's name three times; nothing else, just Charissa. She thought he had mistaken her for her mother. But after what Hannah had told her, she didn't think so. Jacob was dreaming about Charissa Sherrington. But why?

Just then, Crystal came into the kitchen, surprising Angela. "So there you are, Angela. I've been lookin' everywhere for you."

Angela's curiosity was quickly aroused, for Crystal always did her best to avoid her. "Can it be you yearn for my company?" she asked.

Crystal put on a false smile. "Why, yes, as a matter of fact, I've been meanin' to have a little talk with you." Seating herself across from Angela, she said without preamble, "I don't think you should spend so much time with my brother. People are beginnin' to talk."

"What are the rumors now, or should I fear to ask?"

"Well—never mind," Crystal replied irritably, her false smile fading away. "It's just that Robert can't possibly find a suitable wife when he wastes—when he spends so much time with you."

"Shouldn't you be speaking to Robert about this?" Angela asked, her patience thin.

Crystal got up and poured a cup of hot chocolate for herself, then sat down again. "Believe me, I have. But Robert just won't listen to reason. It's time he settled down and started a family."

"This is none of my business, Crystal."

"Of course it's your business!" Crystal snapped. "You're the one he wants to marry! But surely you can see that's impossible."

"Are you saying Robert wants to marry me?"

"He says he's in love with you. He's already asked Jacob."

"How long have you known that Robert felt this way about me?" Angela asked.

She didn't understand it. Robert had made countless advances, and she enjoyed holding him off with teasing banter. But she had never dreamed he was serious.

"Why, it's been three years now at least. He's been waitin' for you to finish up your four years of schoolin'," Crystal replied. "You mean you honestly didn't know how he felt?"

"No, I didn't. I wish you had told me about it sooner, so I could have discouraged him. Damn!" Angela exclaimed, forgetting herself.

Crystal's blue eyes rounded even more. "You don't want to marry him?"

"I don't love him, Crystal, so I couldn't possibly marry him." But she did like Robert and deeply regretted that she might hurt him.

"That's wonderful, I mean—well, never mind. Robert will get over it. A ball is what we need— just the thing to help Robert forget his silly infatuation. It's been too long since the Maitlands have given a ball."

"You had one just two years ago," Angela reminded her.

"Yes, but it wasn't half as grand as it should have been. Folks were just gettin' back on their feet then, still feelin' losses from the war. And of course, Jacob didn't want to do it up too fancy, 'cause it would of reminded folks here about that the war didn't hurt him none. But things are better now. What do you think?"

"About a ball, or about how things are now?" Angela teased.

"You know what I mean. Arrangin' a ball would give us lots to do," Crystal returned, excited over the thought of showing herself off in a splendid new ball gown.

"I suppose it would."

"It will be an excellent chance for Robert to meet someone else. And, of course, you too. You don't meet enough young men, not with Robert and Jacob always monopolizin' your time. Don't worry about Robert. A ball is just the thing. There's nothin' like a new love to make you forget the old one."

Angela smiled. She was in the unfortunate position of knowing better. When you love deeply enough, you don't fall easily in love with another. Oh, yes, Angela knew that all too well.

The next day, Robert proposed and Angela said no as gently as she could. He seemed to take the rejection with his usual good humor, but his eyes held more than a hint of pain. Angela hoped he would find another love quickly.

Sadly, ironically, she understood his pain but could not tell him why she did.

Twenty-two

Bradford Maitland paid his bill and left the Mobile hotel. In the short time since his arrival yesterday, he had received more stunned looks than he could possibly have expected. What was the matter with these people? Had they expected him to stay away forever?

Well, maybe, with his return, the subject of gossip would change from what he had heard last night. Could he really believe what people were saying about his father and the young girl who was supposed to be his mistress? No wonder the old man had had an attack!

The streets weren't crowded for midmorning, and Bradford found it easy to hire an open barouche to take him out to Golden Oaks. He leaned back in the carriage and relaxed, letting the burning sun bake him. He realized suddenly how much he hated New York and the life he had been leading. Working only in the afternoons, drinking and gambling the nights away, going from one forgettable affair to another. He missed the morning sun on his face, the burning southern sun, not that cold sun of the North. He missed riding through open fields. But mostly, he missed his father.

It'd been seven years since Bradford walked into his home, late that night in '62, after leaving Crystal. Seven long years. At thirty, he had proved his ability to run the Maitland empire, though that had not been his intention before the War. Then, he wanted only to marry Crystal and take her to the Texas frontier. But the war and his brother had killed those dreams, or most of them.

He was still going to the Maitland ranch in Texas. Soon, in fact, but he had to see his father first, and just hope that Zachary and Crystal would stay out of his way.

Arriving yesterday, he'd gone directly to Doc Scarron for a full report. He left the good doctor's house with the burden of anxiety lifted from him. His father would be all right.

He frowned. Did he hate Crystal now, or did he still love her? He doubted there was any love left, but the bitterness was still there. That sweet southern belle had professed her love for him so strongly that she was willing to give herself to him before their marriage. Why had he played the chivalrous gentleman? He should have taken her. Perhaps it would be easier to forget her if he had spent just one night with her.

Bradford came back to the present as the barouche rolled under the giant live oaks lining the long driveway. He smiled. The tall white mansion was the same, still a part of the old world, unchanged, unaffected by the war. But inside would be different. Time had not stood still for the occupants of Golden Oaks. How many of the old servants still remained? Was Robert Lonsdale still a constant guest? Did Zachary and Crystal have children? How many? Bradford wished now that he had not asked his father to refrain from mentioning anything about home in his letters.

Bradford paid the driver and left his trunks on the front gallery. He entered the house without bothering to knock, then stood motionless in the wide hallway. The only sounds he heard were the indistinct clanging of pots coming from the kitchen.

Bradford started up the stairs, to his father's room. He hoped his father hadn't changed too much. The attack might have taken a toll on him.

"Master Zachary, what you doin' back from the city so soon? Is anythin' wrong?"

Bradford turned on the stairs to see Hannah standing in the doorway to the dining room, a wet towel in her hands. The expression on her face hurt him.

"Don't look so surprised, Hannah. I take it no

one expected me to set foot in this house again, including you."

"Yessuh—I—I mean, no, sir," she stammered, her brown eyes like huge saucers.

"Well, don't tell anyone I'm here, Hannah, because I only came to see Father. Is he in his room?"

She nodded slowly and Bradford continued up the stairs, leaving her staring after him. He knocked on his father's door and waited for an answer, then entered the sun-drenched room.

They stared at each other for long moments without speaking. Bradford was pleased to find his father looking so well. That young girl he's taken up with must be good for him, Bradford thought with amusement.

"It's been a long time, son. Too damn long!" Jacob said gruffly. Misted eyes showed his joy. "It's a fine thing when my ill health is the only thing that will bring you home.

"But that's one way to get you home where you belong. I know I don't have much more time left to me, and I want to see peace between my children before I die. It can't be done if you aren't here."

"It can't be done at all, Father. And besides, I'm only staying tonight," Bradford said reluctantly, watching some of the gleam leave Jacob's eyes. "And even this is too long to expect tempers not to flare. Is Zachary living here?"

"Yes."

"Then there is no point in even discussing it. I came only to see you, not my brother and his wife. Now, what caused the attack, anyway? Dr. Scarron didn't say."

"I can only blame myself," Jacob replied, annoyed by his own shortcomings. "Zachary and I were arguing about Angela again, and I lost my temper. I should have known better. Doc's warned me enough times not to get upset."

"Her name is Angela, eh? It's surprising how many girls have that name," Bradford commented to himself drily. "What's the matter with Zachary? Is he too straitlaced to accept your mistress living in this house?"

"For God's sake, Bradford! So you've heard that filthy gossip? And right away, you believe it's true!"

"There is nothing wrong with keeping a young mistress, as long as no one is being hurt by it," Bradford replied. "It's done all the time."

"Damnit, Bradford, I expected better from you!" Jacob's tone rose dangerously.

"Hey, calm down!" his son soothed, alarmed now. "I only wanted you to know that I don't sit in judgment on the way you live your life. You're a widower and no one expects you to be celibate. But if that's not the way it is with you and the girl, then how is it?"

"I'm sorry I lost my temper, but—"

"Well, you should be!" Bradford scolded.

"Didn't you just get through telling me you can't do that anymore?"

"I know, I know. But I've lived with that gossip for four years now, and though I don't give a damn what people think about me, it's not fair to Angela. Even Zachary believes it, and *he* was the damn fool who started it to begin with!"

"I don't understand."

"How could you, when you refused to let me write you anything about the goings-on here?"

Bradford sighed. *"Touché.* I'm sorry."

"Well, first let me explain about Angela. When William Sherrington died four years ago, Angela was left alone to fend for herself. I have—"

"Wait a minute!" Bradford said with open surprise. "Are you talking about the scrawny little girl whose father farmed on your land?"

"That's right. I have known Angela since she was born. Her mother, Charissa, and I were childhood friends. Charissa's parents, the Stewarts, were friends of the family's when we lived in Springfield. At any rate, because of the family connections, I felt responsible for Angela. Also, because I like the girl. Can you understand?"

"Oh, of course," Bradford lied.

He knew all about Charissa. He painfully recalled all the nights his own mother cried on his shoulder about the other woman in Jacob's life. They thought they were so clever, his father and Charissa Stewart. They were so sure no one knew of their affair. But Samantha Maitland knew, had known from the beginning. She told no one except Bradford. To him she had poured out her shame and grief.

He hated his father for a long time afterward, and hated especially the woman who had caused his mother so much heartache, and who caused Jacob Maitland to pack up his whole family and move to Alabama, just so he could be near her. But finally, Charissa Stewart, then married to William Sherrington, disappeared. His mother was happy again. And as the years passed, Bradford forgave his father.

Bradford didn't care now if his father had a dozen women, for Samantha Maitland was dead. But Bradford couldn't believe his father would take as his mistress, the daughter of his old lover. *That* was inconceivable.

Jacob was saying, "I brought Angela into my home four years ago, not out of charity, but to make her an equal member of this family. I had her educated. She couldn't even write her name. She's an intelligent young woman, and graduated with honors this year. I would give Angela anything she wants, though she asks me for nothing. She helped her father work that farm for most of her life. She is a kind and gentle young woman, though a trifle spirited at times. She's twenty-one now, and quite beautiful." Jacob smiled warmly. "In fact, I have known only one woman who matched her beauty, and that was her mother."

"I take it there is more to tell?" Bradford changed the subject.

"It's Zachary and Crystal. They've both disliked Angela from the start, and they haven't made her life pleasant. They resent her because I've taken her in and treated her like a daughter. I always wanted a daughter," he said reflectively before he continued. "Your old friend Robert, now, is in love with Angela, or so he says, and wants to marry her."

"Well, good for Robert."

"I'm not so sure it would be a good idea," Jacob said quickly. "I've tried to discourage Robert because he's—well, the boy just doesn't show enough sense of responsibility. No, I don't think it would be a good idea for them to marry. Zachary now is appalled at the idea, and I'm sure he will do his best to put a stop to it if Angela agrees to marry Robert. As I said earlier, Zachary is more or less the cause of the gossip. Every time Angela has come home from school, even for Christmas holidays, Zachary has packed his wife off to the city, giving the impression that he is protecting Crystal from his father's immorality. He said he was only doing what his wife wanted, because she didn't want to stay under the same roof with Angela, but I'm not so sure now. Not after I learned he actually believes Angela *is* my mistress."

"That's a hell of a predicament," Bradford remarked, shaking his head. "Can't you make some kind of announcement, setting the matter straight?"

"No matter what I said, there would still be talk. You know that."

"Well," Bradford said with a mischievous gleam in his eyes, "I could take Angela to the city with me tomorrow when I leave. One passionate kiss in a public place for everyone to see, that ought to turn the gossip in a different direction. But that wouldn't be good for my reputation. You see, Father, I'm engaged. And Candise Taylor will make as good a wife as any."

"But do you love her?"

"No. I've looked for love long enough with no luck. I can't go on looking forever. And if I ever do fall in love, I suppose I could always make the woman my mistress." He refrained from saying, "Like father, like son."

"I don't like it, Bradford."

Bradford raised a brow. "What? That I would take a mistress, or that I'm marrying Candise Taylor?"

"I had hoped you would marry for love," Jacob replied sadly. "I didn't, and I always regretted it."

Bradford felt the anger of the past churning once again. "Then why did you marry Mother?" he asked bitterly.

"At my father's insistence," Jacob answered, his voice heavy with remembrance. "He was a man who enjoyed manipulating others' lives, especially mine. At the time, I had no involvements, so I gave in. But you must know your mother's and my marriage was not an ideal one. It is for that very reason that I have never insisted you marry."

"And now that I have decided to marry, my choice being one I thought would please you, you're not really happy about it, are you?"

"If you were happy about it, then so would I be. But you've already admitted you don't love Candise Taylor."

Bradford sighed. "Other than Crystal, there was one other girl I loved and could have been happy with, but she disappeared from my life without a trace. I've given up hope of ever finding her, though I'm still trying." He rose and began pacing. "But I can't wait forever."

"For God's sake, Bradford, you're only thirty!"

"Yes, but should I continue to wait to find the right girl, when chances are I may never find her? And Candise is a lovely woman. She's quiet, shy—we should get along quite well. And who knows, I may grow to love her."

Just then there was a knock at the door and at Jacob's answer, Robert Lonsdale came into the room in an agitated state. He didn't pay any attention to Bradford, who quickly brought a hand up so it half covered his face. Robert directed his attention to Jacob.

"I thought you would like to know, sir, that she

refused me." Robert paced the room as he spoke.

"What are you talking about, my boy?" Jacob asked, though the answer was obvious.

"Angela! She turned me down. She said she doesn't love me, that she loves another. I don't mean to be disrespectful, sir, but it's you, isn't it? She's in love with you, because you've been so kind to her."

"Don't be ridiculous, Robert," Jacob replied in a patient voice. "Angela is like a daughter to me."

"Who else could it be but you?"

"Someone she met at school, most likely."

"Well, no matter who Angela thinks she is in love with, I'm not givin' up!"

"It would be best if you did, Robert, if Angela isn't inclined toward you."

"You'll forgive me, sir, but I can't give up so easily," Robert said emphatically. "I want no other woman but Angela!"

"Does she know how upset you are about this?" Jacob asked with concern.

"Of course not! I couldn't tell her."

"Where is Angela now?"

"I left her at Susie Fletcher's house. Susie invited us to stay over for the night. I was too upset to stay, but Angela accepted. She'll be back sometime tomorrow afternoon, I imagine. But I tell you now, sir, that I'm going to marry Angela. And I don't want to hear any more arguments from you, Zachary. We may be the best of friends, but—"

Robert stopped short when Bradford finally turned to face him. At first, Robert's face lit up with pleasure, but then he scowled darkly and stalked from the room without another word. Bradford smiled, for it seemed his old friend was dealing with pride, rather than genuine dislike.

"I don't think he hates you, Bradford, or ever did. Robert, like all of your old friends, just couldn't understand why you joined the Union to fight against them. The war broke many ties—personal ones as well as those of our country. The personal losses may not be reconciled, but the country is better off for it. I think Robert was more embarrassed just now than anything else."

"I hope you're right, Father," Bradford said with a halfhearted smile. "But it looks like our little plan is off now. I'm leaving in the morning, so I won't get a chance to meet Angela again, or take her with me to the city."

"Could you stay longer?" Jacob remarked with a hopeful look.

"You have enough strife in this house as it is. I won't add to it. I'm going to Texas, and looking forward to it. You know our old ranch went to ruin during the war, but it shouldn't take too long to put it back in order. It should be ready in time for my bride. I've left Jim McLaughlin in charge of Maitland business up North, but I'll still make the decisions if you're not up to it."

"Well, if that's what you want, then what can I say? And yes, I want you to continue handling things. I don't want you to get out of touch with the business, for it will all be yours soon enough. I still wish you would stay here a little longer—just a few days, maybe."

Bradford stood up slowly and clasped his father's hand. "I would love to stay with you, honestly, but it's best if I don't face Zachary at all. And I definitely don't want to see Crystal. Where are they, anyway?"

"Zachary took Crystal to the city on a shopping spree. That woman dearly loves to spend my money. They probably won't be back until this evening."

"I guess I'm lucky I didn't run into them there this morning. I will come and have dinner with you tonight, Father, and we can talk more this afternoon. But other than that, I'll stay in my room. I'm sorry it has to be this way."

Twenty-three

Bradford said good-bye to his father, who tried once again to talk him into staying. But there was nothing that could induce him to stay longer at Golden Oaks, for then a confrontation with Zachary would be inevitable. Frankly, Bradford wasn't quite sure how he would react if they came face to face. It was best not to find out.

The summer morning was beautiful, the sky bright blue. Bradford strode to the stables.

"I's all ready to go, Master Brad," Zeke said, standing beside the carriage.

"I have decided to ride one of the stallions into the city, Zeke," Bradford replied buoyantly. "You can follow me in with the carriage."

"Yessuh."

It felt good to be riding the back of a horse once again. That, and his father's improved health, put

Bradford in good spirits. As he set out down the long road, Zeke following slowly, Bradford put Golden Oaks and its occupants behind him and began to think of Texas.

A few miles later, Bradford slowed when he saw the single rider approaching him at a fast pace. The rider was still a long way off. He couldn't quite tell if it was a boy or a girl astride the gray mare because the rider wore long trousers and a white ruffled shirt with billowing sleeves. But soon he saw that the hair was that of a woman, long curls flying wildly in the wind, with the morning sun lighting the brown hair to a rusty red.

With hair like that, Bradford decided, the rider must be a young girl. But as the distance shortened and he could make out the shapely curves, he realized that she was a grown woman. But what on earth was she doing dressed like a man?

She closed the distance between them quickly, and suddenly his face lit up with joy and disbelief. As she rode past him, she looked over at him, then pulled her horse to an abrupt halt, almost throwing herself from the saddle. She turned to look at him over her shoulder and he could see that she was just as stunned as he was. But then suddenly, unbelievably, she dug her heels into her horse and took off.

Bradford gave chase, catching up to her in moments. He grabbed hold of her reins and brought both their mounts to a halt.

"It *is* you!" Bradford cried. "Why didn't you stop?"

Without waiting for an answer, Bradford jumped down from his horse and pulled her off the gray mare and into his arms. He held her against him, saying nothing more, molding her body to his, remembering the feel of her, remembering the countless nights he'd dreamed of her. He had begun to believe she'd never really existed. But she did, and she was here.

After several moments, he asked quietly, "Did Jim McLaughlin bring you here?"

"W—who?" she stammered.

He did not sense her fear. "My lawyer. I told him that when you were found, he was to bring you to me directly, no matter where I was. It certainly took long enough to find you, Angel."

Angela realized quickly that he didn't know why she was here or who she was. Relief made her almost dizzy. But why was he so happy to see her? He had failed to show up that summer to meet her.

"Why did you bother looking for me? You made it clear you had had your fling and wanted nothing more to do with me," Angela said bitterly.

"What are you talking about?" Bradford was shocked. "You disappeared."

"I did no such thing. I waited for you for a

week after school let out for summer. But you never came."

He grabbed her to him again, holding her tightly.

"Christ, Angel, we've made one hell of a mess of things. I thought you had run away. When the flowers I sent you were returned, I came back to South Hadley to see what was wrong. I went to your school, but there was no record of Angela Smith."

"I—"

Oh, God, what could she say? *Of course there was no record of Angela Smith. Angela Smith doesn't exist.*

"What is it, Angel? Tell me what happened to make us waste so much time apart."

Zeke approached and halted the carriage beside them before Angela could think of anything to say.

"Missy Angela, what you doin' dressed like that? What happened to that pretty red dress you was wearin' yesterday?"

Angela stepped back warily as Bradford looked from her to Zeke, then very slowly, back to her. Understanding registered on his face and his eyes grew lighter and lighter until they seemed to burn straight through her.

Angela panicked. She turned to Zeke quickly, trying to think of something to stop Bradford's growing anger.

"Someone took a pair of scissors to my dress last night while I was sleeping, Zeke. It was probably one of the Fletchers' servants, but I didn't want to stay there any longer to find out. And Susie's dresses were too small, so her brother Joel let me use his clothes. But don't say anything about this, Zeke. Jacob would only get upset and—"

"All right, Angela Sherrington!" Bradford's voice cut through her chatter. "You wait here, Zeke. And *you!*" He dug his fingers into her arm. "*You* come with me!"

Bradford pulled her behind him into the woods beside the road, leaving Zeke staring after them, with consternation showing plainly on his face. When they were well out of sight and hearing, Bradford stopped and jerked her around to face him.

"Why?" Bradford raged. His eyes flamed. "Why the hell did you follow me into Maudie's that day and then not tell me who you were?"

"You—you didn't recognize me. You thought I—"

"To hell with what I thought!" he stormed wildly. "What was I supposed to think? You knew who I was all along, didn't you?"

"Yes."

"Then why did you let me pay for you, make love to you, and take your blessed virginity? Why?"

"Bradford, you're hurting me." Angela tried to pull away from him, but he only held her tighter, making her cry out in pain.

"I've spent thousands of dollars searching for you, when all the time you were safe in your school. You were there all along, weren't you? No wonder there were no records of an Angela Smith. Why did you lie to me? Why the hell couldn't you tell me who you were?"

"Bradford, stop it! You couldn't possibly understand!" Angela cried, tears streaming down her cheeks.

"Then tell me!" he demanded furiously. "You knew I wanted you. I would have given you anything you wanted, but I can see now that my father beat me to it." He pushed her away from him in disgust. "That's it, isn't it? You had your fun with father and son, didn't you?"

"It wasn't like that at all!" Angela answered brokenly.

"Damn you, I want the truth! You let me make love to you and I have to know why!"

"I—I can't tell you."

"You will tell me! Are you a whore? How many other men have there been since me?"

"No one—oh, God, there has been no one else!" She was sobbing now.

"Then why me?"

"You—you hate me now, Bradford, so I can't tell you why. I just can't!"

She twisted free and ran, then stumbled

through the trees until she reached the road. Sobbing uncontrollably now, she mounted her horse and rode off in the direction of Golden Oaks. Dear God, he hated her now, just as she had always feared.

Twenty-four

Angela spent the rest of the day in her room, most of the time crying her heart out.

It was pointless to think of what might have been. He hated her. She had only made him angrier by refusing to explain. But how could she tell him she loved him, when he thought the worst of her? How could she tell him that was why she let him make love to her? He would never believe that. He would have laughed if she had told him the simple truth.

Jacob came to see her in the afternoon, for she had told Hannah that she wasn't feeling well. He told her about Bradford's visit, and that he couldn't talk his son into staying longer.

Was it better this way? she wondered silently. She had been terrified to face Bradford again. And now he was on his way to Texas.

Toward evening, Eulalia came into the room,

full of gossip. "Lordy, this house sure is in a ruckus 'cause of Master Brad's visit last night. The others are all mad 'cause he was here and they didn't even know it. Come and gone, just like that." Eulalia giggled as she laid out a green taffeta dress, with gold-embroidered trimming along the high neckline and hem.

"I won't be needing that dress. I'm not going down to supper tonight."

"Yes you is. This is Master Jacob's first night back at the head of the table, and you know very well you ought to be there for it."

"Yes, of course. I just wasn't thinking." Angela sighed. She let Eulalia take over.

She and Eulalia got along very well, considering that they argued ceaselessly. Eulalia was sure she knew what was best for Angela. Eulalia was right most of the time, but Angela couldn't let Eulalia know that. Doing so would spoil their little battles, and they so enjoyed battling.

Awhile later, Angela descended the stairs and walked into the dining room to join Crystal and Zachary, who were already there. Robert arrived shortly after that, but Jacob was not there.

"You certainly took your time comin' down, Angela," Crystal said impatiently.

"That's enough, Crystal," Zachary warned. "Father isn't even here yet, so it's not as if Angela has held up the meal. And please remember what we talked about, will you?"

"Have you forgotten what I told you, Zachary

Maitland?" Crystal asked saucily. "I will not be a hyprocrite just because of your father's threats."

"Father doesn't make threats lightly, Crystal," Zachary returned. "So you had best take my advice and curb your tongue, if you know what's good for you."

"Don't you threaten me!" Crystal snapped, her blue eyes icy. "I'll say what I please, when I please, even if it *is* about her!"

Robert slammed his fist down on the table. "Why don't you both shut up! And stop talkin' about Angela as if she weren't even here!" he shouted.

"Please keep your voice down, Robert," Zachary pleaded. "This is really none of your business."

"I would rather not be the cause of any more bickering tonight," Angela sighed. Looking directly at Crystal, she said firmly, "We all know where we stand, but this is Jacob's first day out of bed and it should be a pleasant one."

"Did I hear my name mentioned?" Jacob grinned as he walked into the room.

"We were just talking about your health, Jacob," Angela remarked quickly. "You know, you really should have stayed in bed another day, as the doctor suggested."

"Nonsense, I feel fine," Jacob returned. "In fact, I couldn't be happier."

"What has happiness to do with your health?" Crystal asked, bored.

"Everything," Jacob chuckled.

"You're happy because of Bradford's visit?" Zachary said sarcastically.

"Yes, you could say that."

"Did—did he say anything about me?" Zachary ventured timidly. "Did he say how he feels now?"

"Why don't you ask him yourself?"

More than one gasp was heard in the room when Bradford appeared in the doorway, a lazy, relaxed smile on his lips. Calm now, his eyes were a clear golden-brown. He gazed openly at each person in the room.

The silence became oppressive. Zachary had turned deathly white. Crystal seethed with anger. Robert just stared at the table, avoiding Bradford's eyes altogether. Jacob was the only one happy to see his older son.

The serving girls started bringing in the food then, and Bradford took a seat at the end of the table, without another word. The silence lasted until Crystal nervously brought up the subject of the ball. Jacob gave his assent, leaving all the arrangements to the women. Crystal carried the meal with her discussion of preparations. She seemed very tense and repeated herself several times. But by the time dessert was served, she was all talked out.

Bradford said nothing all during dinner. Angela stole occasional timid glances at him. Usually she found him staring coldly at Zachary and

Crystal. They avoided looking at Bradford, and neither of them said a single word to him. Robert was also unusually quiet, but he watched with an amused grin, waiting.

"Well, Robert," Bradford finally spoke, directing his full attention to his old friend, "have you nothing to say? Not even a simple 'go to hell'?"

"Bradford!" Jacob exclaimed.

"I'm only trying to clear the air, Father, and I have to start somewhere," Bradford explained. "I'm sure the ladies will forgive my language."

"I'm glad you're back, Bradford," Robert began, grinning fully now. "I've had a guilty conscience for a long time because I misunderstood you. If you'll allow me to, I'd like to apologize for all the things I called you when you weren't even here to defend yourself."

Bradford chuckled. "I can imagine all the names I've been called. But has 'traitor,' at least, been removed from your list?"

"Yes," Robert grinned. "You merely followed your beliefs. What else can a man do?"

"Indeed. Only some men don't go so far," Bradford mused thoughtfully, staring at the table. Then he raised his eyes again and smiled. "You haven't changed at all, Robert. I see this old house still appeals to you more than your own. But then, you're a member of the family now, aren't you?"

Robert cleared his throat. "I guess so."

Bradford laughed at the hesitant answer. Then he turned his attention to Zachary, and the laughter quickly disappeared.

"Have you nothing to say, brother?"

"I love her, Bradford," Zachary replied in a ragged voice. "What more can I say?"

"Of course. All's fair in love and war, eh?" Bradford asked in an icy voice, his lips drawn tight. "And what about you, Crystal? Not even a hello for the man you were *supposed* to marry?"

"Why of course, Bradford. Hello," Crystal said with a charming smile that vanished quickly.

"So much for greetings," Bradford commented drily. He looked at Angela, and his eyes returned to their golden-brown. "Well, you certainly have changed from the scrawny kid I met seven years ago, Angel."

"Her name is Angela," Crystal snapped.

"Yes—I know," Bradford replied smoothly without looking at Crystal.

Angela wanted to run from the room, but Jacob would never understand. She was so nervous that the heat was pouring off her. She pulled her gold coin out from under her dress, and held it pressed in her palm, praying for the courage it had once given her. Why was Bradford doing this? Why was he here, instead of on his way to Texas? And why, for heaven's sake, did she feel so deathly afraid?

"That's an unusual trinket," Bradford contin-

ued, watching her reaction closely. "I met a beautiful young woman once who had a necklace just
like it. Where did you get yours, Angel?"

Eulalia, who was quietly clearing dishes, giggled at Bradford's deliberate use of the name Angel, but the others in the room were clearly
annoyed, including Jacob.

"A man on a black horse gave me the coin
when I was eleven," Angela answered apprehensively. "He—he splashed mud on my dress and
gave me the coin to buy a new one."

"That must have been a pretty picture," Crystal
remarked.

Bradford ignored Crystal's remark and continued. "So you kept the coin instead of buying a
new dress. Why?"

"Does it matter why?" Angela asked defensively. "I just didn't care about dresses at that
age."

"But you never spent the coin for something
else," Bradford pressed her further. "Why not?"

Angela felt like the walls were closing in on her.
She stood up, unable to take any more.

"May I be excused, Jacob? I'm really not feeling
very well tonight."

"Of course, my dear. Should I send for Dr. Scarron?" he asked worriedly.

"No—no, I'll be all right in the morning."

She left the room quickly, without bidding anyone good-night, and ran upstairs. She threw her-

self on her bed and gave in to the tears she had
held back all evening.

Why had Bradford come back? He had made
everything so much worse.

Twenty-five

Angela had wondered for so long why Bradford never came home. Now she knew why—he was in love with Crystal. He had loved her before the war and he still did. He was in love with his brother's wife!

Angela got up and paced the floor while she waited for Eulalia to finish in the kitchen and come help her out of her dress. But there was no hurry. Angela would find no rest tonight.

Would he be sleeping in the room across from hers? Would he tell Jacob everything?

And then anger slowly began to take over. He had no right to treat her so cruelly.

When Eulalia finally arrived, Angela was still pacing the floor.

"Sorry I's late, Missy. You been waitin' long?"

"Yes!" Angela snapped, but Eulalia paid her no mind.

"I was helpin' Tilda wash up the kitchen. Didn't know everybody was goin' to their rooms early tonight," Eulalia said as she started unlacing the back of Angela's dress.

"Everybody?"

" 'Ceptin' Master Jacob and Master Brad. They's in the study drinkin' and talkin' business."

Oh, God, Angela groaned inwardly. He *was* going to tell Jacob. She just knew it!

Angela made an effort to calm her jumpy nerves.

"Could you bring me up some water for another bath, Eulalia? It was hot tonight."

Eulalia chuckled knowingly. "Tilda's already got the water boilin'. You wasn't the only one had cause to sweat tonight, Missy," she remarked and then scurried out of the room.

An hour later, Angela stepped into the large tub of rose-scented water and attempted to relax. She tried to keep her mind blank and just listened to the cheerful tune Eulalia was humming while she laid out Angela's nightdress and turned down the bed. But then the door opened, startling them both.

"You gots the wrong room, Master Brad!" Eulalia shrieked in surprise, before coming to stand in front of the tub to try and hide Angela from Bradford's view.

"What's your name, girl?" he asked from where he stood in the doorway.

"Eulalia."

"Well, Eulalia, why don't you scoot on out of here?"

"You can't come in here! Master Jacob will have himself a fit!"

"He isn't going to know, Eulalia," Bradford said in a lazy voice. "It would upset my father, and I wouldn't like that."

Eulalia turned around to face Angela. "Why don't you scream or somethin', Missy, so's he'll go away?"

"Oh, for God's sake!" Bradford exclaimed impatiently and stepped into the room. He took Eulalia's arm and escorted her firmly to the door.

"It's all right, Eulalia. Don't worry. He only wants to talk to me," Angela called out before Bradford shut the door and locked it.

Angela sank lower into the tub. Fear churned in the pit of her stomach. But she was also furious. How dared he compromise her by coming in here?

"What do you want, Bradford?"

He moved to stand behind her as he replied, "I want to talk. Or, rather, you're going to do the talking."

"I can't. I told you that already. Now get out of my room before I do as Eulalia suggested and scream!"

"You won't scream, but you will talk, Angel," he said gently, and ran a finger along the back of her neck.

Goose bumps spread down her arms and back.

"Don't, Bradford, please!" she cried, remembering instantly what his touch did to her. Anger dissolved, leaving only fear. It was not fear of his anger, but of the strange power he had over her body.

"Why? You didn't mind my touching you in Springfield," he reminded her.

"That was different. You didn't know who I was then," she answered nervously.

"What the hell difference does that make?" he demanded.

"Bradford, please! Let me finish my bath and get dressed first, then we can talk."

"No! And don't tell me you're embarrassed in your natural condition, because I won't believe it," he said cruelly.

"Why did you come back?" Angela cried in desperation.

"Because of you," he answered simply and came around to the side of the tub. "Don't you ever take this necklace off?" he asked, lifting the gold chain from the water.

"No!" she snapped and grabbed it out of his hand.

"Why did you keep it, Angela?"

"It's none of your business, Bradford, and it doesn't matter anyway," she answered.

"It matters because I gave it to you." He smiled at her surprise. "When you explained how you got the coin, I remembered. Did you think I wouldn't?"

"It happened ten years ago," she said, lowering her eyes. "I didn't expect you to remember."

"And my vest, do you still have that too?" Bradford asked, his brow raised in ironic humor.

"It's in the bottom drawer of the dresser if you want it back," she replied reluctantly.

"I don't want the vest back, Angel. What I want is some answers."

He reached down and lifted her out of the tub and quickly carried her to the bed. He started to remove his clothing while Angela grabbed her nightdress to cover herself.

"Bradford, don't!" she pleaded earnestly. "Please don't do this!"

"Why not? You were willing enough in our little hideaway. I wanted you then, and I want you now."

"Not like this!" she cried. "Not in anger!"

"I melted your anger once, remember?" he asked brusquely and fell down on top of her, pulling her nightdress out from between them. "Now you try melting mine."

Angela was torn between desire and misery, and her tears spilled freely. His body was pressed hard against hers.

"Tell me why you did it, Angela. Why did you give yourself to me that first time?" he asked in a soft whisper as his fingers traced circles around her taut breasts.

"Why must you torture me like this?" Her eyes were shimmering violet-blue pools when she opened them to look at him. "Isn't it enough that you hate me now?"

"I don't hate you, Angel," he said tenderly. "I admit that I was furious this morning, but that doesn't mean I hate you. I just want to know why you did what you did. You gave me your virginity and I want to know why. I think you used me for some purpose you're not telling me about."

"You're lying, just so I'll tell you what you want to know! But I can't, Bradford," she said in a pitiful voice. "I can't because you would never believe me."

"What do I have to do?" he growled angrily, losing his patience. "Do I have to beat it out of you?"

Angela's eyes opened wide. "All right!" she sobbed. "I love you, damnit, I love you!"

Bradford's gentle laughter washed over her. "That's what I suspected, Angel, but I had to hear it."

Twenty-six

Angela awoke with a sudden start, half expecting to find Bradford in bed beside her, but she was alone. Had it been just a dream? It was too wonderful to be real. She remembered it all clearly, telling Bradford she loved him, hearing his happy laughter when she did. He had made love to her then, gently, just like the first time. Afterward they had talked. She explained everything to him, telling him how an eleven-year-old girl had fallen in love, and how that love continued, growing stronger through the years. She told him what her feelings were that day in Springfield, how she had wanted her one day of happiness, not caring what it would cost her. He listened intently, asking only a few questions.

And then he had told her how he'd searched for her, about his countless trips. He said he had thought about her constantly, dreamed about her, hoped for the day he would find her again and could make her his.

"And now that I've found you, I'll never let you go, Angel. Never," Bradford had said, words that made her the happiest woman in the world. They made love again, joyfully and passionately this time.

They talked all through the night, learning about each other, regretting the time lost to them. And then Angela fell asleep in Bradford's arms. Or had she been asleep all along? Could it really all have happened as she remembered it?

"Lordy, Missy, I's never knowed you to sleep this late before. It's almost one, and everybody's done had lunch already," Hannah said as she came into the darkened room.

"Goodness! Why didn't Eulalia come to wake me this morning?" Angela asked with wide eyes.

Hannah chuckled gleefully. "Master Bradford went and chased her off—chased me off too. Said he kept you up late last night talkin' about old times, and you was to sleep till you woke by yourself."

"Did he really say that?" Angela asked excitedly.

"Yessum, that's just what he said."

"Oh, Hannah, I love you!" Angela cried and threw her arms around the older woman.

"I loves you too, child, you knows that. And I can see you's as happy as a babe bein' born.

That's good, that's sure good. 'Bout time your wishes come true."

"Oh, they have, Hannah, they certainly have! Where is Bradford now? Is he downstairs?"

"He's in the dinin' room, sippin' coffee," Hannah replied as she went to open the curtains to the day. "He's waitin' for you to come down, so's he can keep you company while you eat."

"Why didn't you say so?" Angela cried as she dashed to her large wardrobe and quickly picked out a gown of glossy cream-colored cotton.

"Slow down, child. That man ain't gonna run away." Hannah laughed again.

For a change, Angela wore her gold coin on the outside of her dress, and she put on a pair of dangling gold earrings to match. But she wasn't about to waste any more time by pinning up her hair, so she just tied it back with a piece of velvet ribbon, letting the russet waves hang in loose curls down her back.

Angela ran down the stairs in haste, slowing to a dignified walk just before she entered the dining room. She stood breathless, growing weak from the warm smile Bradford gave her. He stood up and went to her, then took her in his arms and kissed her. He pressed her closer to him, squeezing the breath from her with his powerful arms. And then his lips left hers, and he loosened his hold. But he did not release her from his arms.

"Damned if I haven't found myself missing

you already, Angel," Bradford laughed. He held her with one arm and tilted her face up to his, then kissed her again, only softly this time. "I find myself wanting to be with you every minute. I hated leaving you this morning, but I suppose it would have been awkward if I'd been found in your room."

"Hannah would have understood. She's always known how I felt about you."

Angela recalled all the times she used to ask Hannah about Bradford. She understood now why the older woman never wanted to talk about him. She had known that Angela loved him, but that he was engaged to Crystal. Sweet Hannah.

"Eulalia, on the other hand," Angela continued with a smile, "would probably have been quite shocked."

"Well, after I announce that we're going to be married, maybe that uppity maid of yours will look the other way when she finds me in your room."

"Married?" Angela gasped. Married to Bradford!

"For God's sake, Angela, don't look so surprised!" Bradford chuckled. "What did you think I meant when I told you I'd never let you go?"

"I—I didn't think you would want to marry me," she stammered.

"And why not? I'm not going to hide you, Angel."

"But I thought you still loved Crystal. From the

way you talked last night at dinner, I was sure of it."

Bradford sighed deeply, but his eyes were warm and golden as they caressed her face. "I did love Crystal once, but that was a long time ago, Angela. She killed that love when she married my brother. Crystal was part of my youth, and it took me a long time to get over her. But you are my future, and I want to love you and make you happy for the rest of your life. Will you let me do that? Will you marry me and let the whole world know that you are mine?"

"Oh, Bradford, yes! Yes!" she cried, tears of joy stinging her eyes as she threw her arms around his neck and squeezed him tightly.

"Then I will make the announcement tonight at dinner. And there will be no long engagement, my beauty. A week or two will be long enough."

"No!" she spoke sharply, surprising him with the sudden alarm in her voice.

"Very well, I'll marry you tomorrow," Bradford grinned. "But Father is going to be disappointed that he couldn't plan a big wedding."

"No, I didn't mean that, Bradford. I meant we can't tell anyone yet."

"For heaven's sake, why not?" he asked in a confused voice. But then his eyes brightened dangerously and his fingers tightened automatically on her waist. "You weren't lying to me last night, were you?"

"Oh, Bradford, no!" she quickly reassured him, and was relieved to see the flame disappear from his eyes. "I love you with every breath I take. Whatever you want, then that's what I want too."

"Then why don't you want me to make the announcement tonight?" he asked.

"Your family won't understand, Bradford. In their eyes you have known me for only one day."

"They know we met seven years ago."

"You were a man then, but I was only a girl of fourteen. Though that meeting meant the world to me, your family would never believe you fell in love with me then. You still loved Crystal at that time and were planning to return to her. With no other meeting between then and now, your family would not understand."

"Ah, but there was another meeting, Angel," Bradford murmured deeply, the corners of his mouth turning up in a devilish grin as he pulled her closer to him.

"Bradford!"

He laughed shortly. "I suppose we must keep that enchanted encounter to ourselves, mustn't we?" he teased. Then his voice changed to a deep, husky whisper. "Even I was beginning to doubt that I had you all to myself for that week in December—until yesterday. Yesterday, my life began again."

"As did my life, my beloved," Angela returned, joy filling her heart near to bursting. "But you do understand why we should wait before telling anyone, don't you?"

"No," he said flatly. "I'll just tell the members of my straitlaced family that I met you in Springfield when you first started school. I'll say that I visited you often over the years, that I fell in love with you, but that you, with your thirst for knowledge, wanted to finish school before we married. And now that you've done that, I have come to claim you for my wife. Though it is not all the truth, it is believable. Will you not agree to that?"

"But your father will be hurt. He will wonder why I never once mentioned these visits to him, or told him that I loved you. He will wonder why you never wrote to tell him about us. And if what you tell the family is to be believed, then why have you stayed away from Golden Oaks these last four years when I have been here each summer? They will all wonder. Your story will cause Jacob to be very upset."

"Angela, that story I concocted would be for Zachary and Crystal's benefit, not my father's. He's not that gullible."

Her eyes widened. "You're not going to tell Jacob the truth, are you?"

Bradford sighed. "Why do you have to search for flaws, woman? It would have been better if you had stayed the illiterate farm girl. Then you would marry me tomorrow."

"Then we would never have met again, and I would have died an old maid, loving you to my grave."

"Perish the thought, Angel," he grinned. "You will be my wife, have no doubt of that. And we will wait, as you suggest, but no more than a month. In a month the family will know that I have fallen hopelessly in love with you. But in truth, it took only one day—the day you gave your innocence to me."

"Did you really love me then?" she asked, her eyes limpid pools of violet as she gazed up at him.

"Yes, only I didn't know it until yesterday. I thought I only wanted you in lust, but it is so much more than that. You are going to be the mother of my sons, the mistress of my lands, the keeper of my heart. You are the woman who has wiped all others from my mind. I want to grow old with you and love you forever, Angela."

"A happier woman has never lived," Angela whispered, and brushed her lips against his, only to be caught and held in a fiery kiss that brought to the surface all the wonders of the night before.

"I will make the announcement the day after Crystal's ball, and we will be married the following week. But, dear God, tell me how I am to endure this wait. You tempt me to my very soul. I haven't the will to withstand you, Angel."

"You didn't feel the need to last night," she teased him lovingly.

"But that isn't proper, Angela. We will have to restrain ourselves now. So how am I to endure these many nights, wanting you beside me in my bed, but knowing I must wait?"

Angela's ire was aroused. "Honestly, Bradford, you men really can be ridiculous. It's all right to sleep with a woman, but once you propose to her, she's taboo? Is that it?"

He was shamefaced. "Something like that."

"Well this woman isn't going to wait, Bradford," she told him sternly. "My bed is yours."

"Are you serious?"

Her expression softened. "My love is not ruled by convention," she murmured huskily, hugging him closely. "My first seventeen years taught me not to be ashamed of wanting."

He looked at her curiously, his thick black brows almost meeting over his golden-brown eyes. "Do you really mean that, do you love me enough to spare me long nights of suffering?"

"My love has no bounds, but I meant every word I said. I could not bear to be kept from you just because society decrees it. In my heart, we are married already. And I would give everything I possess to be able to wake up in your arms each morning for the rest of my life."

"But what about your maid? Perhaps it would be best if you came to my room instead. I haven't taken a manservant yet, and there really isn't a need for one."

"No, I would have to lie to Eulalia and I don't

like lying. It is best if I tell her everything." Angela laughed gaily then. "She can't really be that shocked, for she meets young Todd, one of the field hands, each night. Besides, she has a great love for your father. She would cut out her tongue before she would upset him."

"But is she loyal to you?"

"I think so. But if we are found out, then Jacob will insist you do the right thing, and we will just be married that much sooner. But if you would rather suffer, my love, then far be it for me to cut short your misery," Angela said with a cunning grin.

"You are a witch," he laughed, "and an angel, rolled into one. When I would try to be a gentleman, you let me follow my will and have my way."

"Because your will is my will," she murmured.

"Thank God that all women are not timid, frightened creatures."

Hannah's gleeful chuckle caused Bradford to release Angela.

"I was sure you would be done eatin' by now. You too busy talkin' about the past again to tell Tilda to bring on the food?" Hannah asked with a knowing look.

"Not the past, Hannah. The future—and what a glorious future it's going to be," Bradford answered easily.

There was only one problem, and that was Candise Taylor. He had to break their engagement. He was not looking forward to that. He had wasted two years of her life, keeping her waiting for him. And now he had to tell her that he was in love with another woman.

Twenty-seven

Golden Oaks was a different house with Bradford Maitland living in it. Jacob was overcome by good spirits. Even Crystal was no longer quite so hard to live with.

No one questioned Bradford about his reasons for staying at Golden Oaks instead of going on to Texas. Each of the family had reasons for not broaching the subject, so each day came and went with no one knowing when he would go.

But Angela knew. There would be a honeymoon after the wedding, which would take them across the sea to a land Angela had only read about. It was Bradford's choice and they had discussed it at length while lying in each other's arms. They would travel to England, to a large estate there that Jacob owned.

They would stay a month or two in England and then return to America, to Texas.

* * *

The days passed quickly for Angela. She lived in a state of continual bliss, wondering if it were real when she was alone, and knowing it was when Bradford took her in his arms and made love to her. The first week, Bradford let the family know that he was interested in Angela. He paid a good deal of attention to her, drawing her into conversation at the dining table, teaching her to play poker. In the mornings, he took her riding over the Maitland lands, lands rich with sugarcane and cotton once again. The invitations to the ball were engraved and sent out that first week, and acceptances began pouring in.

The second week, Bradford began taking Angela to dine in the city, deliberately excluding anyone else from his invitations. The family took note of this, especially Robert.

Two weeks before the ball, Jim McLaughlin arrived from New York on business, and was invited to stay. A day later, Golden Oaks received a visitor all the way from Texas.

Angela stood in the morning-room doorway studying the visitor curiously. The man towered at least half a foot over Bradford, making Bradford's tall frame seem small by comparison. The man's complexion was bronzed by long hours under the hot sun. His golden hair was parted in the middle, like Bradford's, but was much longer, falling clear to his wide shoulders. He wore buckskins.

"Well, Bradford, I'd recognize you anywhere,

but I can see you don't remember me. Can't say I blame you. It's been almost fifteen years since we raced across the plains together."

Bradford wrinkled his brow for a moment, but then exclaimed, "Grant Marlowe! Well, I'll be—you were only ten years old when I came back to Alabama."

"Yeah, and you only fifteen. But it looks like I'm the only one who's changed much. Started growin' and it just seemed like I'd never stop."

Bradford looked his old friend up and down and laughed heartily. "Looks like you've put on a few feet since then. That height must come in handy, though. I'll wager there isn't a man in Texas who would want to tangle with you."

"That's true enough, but it's a hindrance too. Can't find no filly out West who ain't scared to death I'll crush her little bones in bed."

Bradford cleared his throat and indicated Angela's presence. When Grant followed his gaze his face turned red, the color showing through his deeply tanned skin.

"For—forgive me, ma'am," Grant stammered, rubbing his hands nervously against his thighs. "I was so glad to see Brad here that I didn't see you standin' there."

Angela smiled sweetly while she stared into the dark green eyes. "That's quite all right, sir, really."

"Angela, this is Grant Marlowe, a good friend of mine from way back," Bradford said. "Angela is a ward of my father's. And the gentleman lagging at the stairs over there is an old friend of the family, as well as my sister-in-law's brother. Come here, Robert."

Robert came forward and shook Grant's hand, but Grant paid him scant attention. His sea-green eyes were drawn back to Angela. Both Robert and Bradford noticed.

"What brings you here, Grant?" Bradford asked, leading them into the morning room. "I was expecting your father. Is he here with you?"

"No, that's why I came. Pa and I both got through the war without a scratch. Then, a week after we returned to Texas, he was done in by a rattler."

"I'm sorry to hear that. Phil Marlowe was one of the best men I ever knew. I needed him on the ranch," Bradford sighed.

"That's what I figured," Grant replied. "I was foreman on a small spread near Fort Worth when I heard you were lookin' for Pa. I figured old Jacob was finally ready to fix up the JB again, so I quit and come here to see if he could use me. I'd rather work for your pa any day."

"I'm sure Father will be glad to hear that, but he's retired from all our business interests now. If you took on the job, you would be working for me."

"That suits me even better," Grant grinned.

"Good. There's a lot to be done, and you'll be in

complete charge until I get there. That will be about four or five months from now. Do you think you can get the ranch in order by then?"

"I'll give it my best try," Grant replied eagerly. "When do I start?"

"You can head back for Texas in about two weeks," Bradford answered. "We have a lot to discuss in the meantime, and you might as well stay for the ball my sister-in-law is throwing. You may even find a wife to take back with you."

"That'd be worth stayin' for," Grant laughed, his eyes lighting on Angela again.

Bradford took Grant to see his father, leaving Angela and Robert alone in the room.

"Angie, you've been avoidin' me lately, and I have to talk to you."

Just that week Bradford had talked about the way Robert was sulking around the house. They had decided that Robert must be the first to know about them, and Angela insisted she be the one to tell him.

"This is not something you should have to bother with," Bradford had told her. "I will handle it."

Angela lost her temper. "I am the one Robert wants to marry!"

"And *I* am the one you are going to marry!" He came back at her so sharply that Angela caught her breath.

She stared at him heatedly, then pointed a stiff

finger at her door. "Get out of here, Bradford Maitland! We're not married yet, and I'm not so sure we're going to be!"

"What?"

"You heard me!" she shouted. "If you plan to coddle and protect me from every little thing for the rest of my life, then you can just forget it!"

"Fine! Just fine!" he retorted and stalked out of the room.

But he came back after a few minutes, his expression contrite. "Can we at least discuss this?"

"I'm all for discussion, Bradford," Angela said stiffly. "But that's not what you were doing. You were dictating."

"I'm sorry, Angel, but I was with my father when Robert told him that you had turned him down. He said he wouldn't give up."

"I told Robert that I was in love with someone else, but I didn't tell him it was you," she replied, softly now. "When he knows I am going to marry you, he will have to forget about me. But it's up to me to tell him."

He pulled her into his arms then. "You win," he grinned. "But don't think Robert will forget you. No man who loves you could ever forget you."

He squeezed her tightly, then chuckled ruefully, "With two stormy temperaments, I guess we'll have our share of flare-ups. But as long as they end like this, we can't go wrong."

He kissed her, then showed her in the way she

liked best how much he loved her. She recalled the night with a secret smile. Yes, they would undoubtedly have other fights, but as long as they ended so pleasurably all would be well.

Now Robert had finally cornered her and she had to face him.

"What is it, Robert?"

"I don't like all the time you've been spendin' with Bradford," Robert said harshly, coming straight to the point. "And you seem to enjoy all the attention he gives you. I've never seen you so happy before!"

"I thought you would want my happiness, Robert," Angela said in a soft voice.

"I do, but this isn't right! You told me you were in love with another man, and that's why you couldn't marry me—and now this! Does your heart change so quickly? Are you in love with Bradford now?"

Angela sighed. As simply as she could, she told Robert that she'd always loved Bradford. His face grew angry and, when she finished, Robert ran out of the house without a word. A few minutes later, Angela stood by the window and watched Robert's horse gallop down the long row of oaks toward the river road.

Later in the afternoon, another visitor arrived at Golden Oaks to see Bradford. Courtney Harden was a wily man in his midthirties, with reddish-

gold hair and piercing blue eyes. Bradford didn't
like the man and had recently dropped Harden
from one of his business ventures.

Bradford first met Courtney Harden in New
York, where the older man had asked Bradford to
back him in a hotel-restaurant venture. At the
time, Bradford had been preoccupied with other
matters, mainly his search for Angela, and had
agreed to the deal without taking his usual pre-
caution of having Courtney Harden investigated.

Harden, who had found the location for the
hotel-restaurant, was to be in complete charge.
But a few months before coming to Mobile, Bradford was informed that one Courtney Harden
was involved in prostitution and drugs. Rather
than bringing the law into it, Bradford had sent a
message dismissing Harden from his employ.

Now Harden had caught up with Bradford,
and was demanding to be reinstated as mana
ger of the hotel. Bradford informed Courtney
Harden in a very few words that he had two
choices—accept his dismissal, or be arrested. Raging that Bradford would regret his actions, Harden
stormed from the house.

That night, Bradford paced angrily back and forth
across Angela's bedroom floor.

"I never should have hired him!" Bradford
stormed.

"Do you mean Grant?"

"Yes, damnit!" he yelled and turned to her. "I

saw the way he was looking at you, and you weren't exactly indifferent to him! You find him attractive, don't you?"

"Yes, as a matter of fact, I do," she replied with a quick smile. "Grant is very pleasing to look at, but my heart is already taken."

"Is it?"

"You're jealous!" she laughed.

"The hell I am!"

"Bradford, aren't you sure of me yet? For heaven's sake, I have loved you for ten years."

"I can't help remembering the times you have slipped away from me."

She grinned. "If you will remember correctly, I left you only once, and that was because I had to return to school."

She walked slowly to him and wrapped her arms around his neck.

"I'll never leave you again, Bradford," she breathed softly. "It's you I love—no other."

"You've never been with another man, Angela. How do I know your heart won't turn in another man's arms? Another man might please you better than I."

"Now you stop it, Bradford Maitland. You are talking about lust, while I am talking about love," she said sternly, then brought his lips down to hers.

"Ah, but I've found that the two go together so well," he laughed in relief. He picked her up in his arms and carried her quickly to the bed.

On Angela's large bed, there was no room for anger or jealousy, only the seriousness of love. Bradford undressed her slowly, his eyes locked with hers the whole time, so filled with passion that she became excited just watching him. She wanted him to hurry, felt she couldn't wait to have her body covered by his. But Bradford set his own pace. Tonight he seemed to want to savor every nuance of their coming together.

At last their clothes were scattered about the bed, and Bradford drew her into his arms. She tingled everywhere he touched, and he touched her everywhere.

At last he moved to her breasts, cupping one in each hand, kneading them tenderly, his eyes still locked with hers. And then he bent his head and teasingly sucked on one and then the other soft globe.

Angela couldn't bear it anymore. "Bradford!" she gasped. "Are you trying to drive me mad?"

He raised his head and lightly brushed his lips over hers. "Why do you say that, Angel?"

She saw the gleam in his eyes and wanted to scream. Instead she clasped his head in her hands and drew his mouth to hers, letting him know just what she wanted.

Bradford felt her need and delighted in it. The knowledge that she wanted him filled him with such pride and joy that he thought surely he would burst.

He lowered her to the bed, his mouth still covering hers possessively. She opened her legs for him, and his hard member slid smoothly into that moist haven. He worshiped her with his body, drawing out every measure of her passion. She was passionate, wild, shameless in her love, and he loved her all the more for it.

Twenty-eight

Bradford was still determined to keep Angela well out of Grant Marlowe's view. Bradford took her to the city more often now, to the theater and late-night suppers. They went everywhere together, and as Bradford had predicted, the gossip about Angela had now taken a different turn.

Preparations for the ball were nearly completed. The next two days would be filled with cleaning and cooking. A new load of ice would arrive by packet in a few days, to be stored in the cellar beneath the house. Ice cream would be made, and baskets of flowers would be collected from all over the plantation. The ladies were assured that their gowns would be finished in time, and the gentlemen's tailor came to Golden Oaks for a couple of days.

Robert had not been seen since he had run out

of the house the day Grant arrived. Crystal informed the family, without explanation, that he had finally taken an interest in running The Shadows. She doubted they would see very much of Robert in the near future.

The sun rose in a clear sky, predicting fair weather for the Maitland Ball. Throughout the morning and afternoon, the rich aroma of baking filled the lower floor of the house. Mountains of apples and peaches had been peeled and turned into mouth-watering pies. There were French pastries and candies, and large cakes were being frosted and set aside. The ice cream was made and put in the cellar to chill, and soups and gravies were simmering in large pots over the long fireplace in the kitchen. The hams that would be served cold were baked now. The rest of the meats would be roasted later, for the eating wouldn't even begin until midnight.

An anxious excitement filled the air, affecting everyone, including the servants. Angela's excitement had not so much to do with the ball but with what would happen a week from now, when Bradford would make her his wife.

Angela passed through the dining room on her way upstairs, stopping by the long table to inspect the glasses stacked on it. This would be the bar. Liquors were lined up behind the table, champagne and other wines to be brought up later, packed in ice. Seeing that all the glasses were spotless, Angela continued on her way. But as she heard Crystal's voice in the hallway, she stopped.

"You've been avoidin' me, haven't you, Brad?"

"Now what would make you think that?" Bradford asked, a note of humor in his voice.

" 'Cause this is the first time I've found you alone, without that little farm girl trailin' you. You really are payin' that girl too much attention. Are you competin' with your father?"

"You've acquired a vicious tongue over the years, Crystal. But then as I remember, you were pretty cruel seven years ago," Bradford replied.

"Just because a few stubborn words were spoken, you walked out of my life," Crystal pouted. "Was that fair?"

"You walked out of my life when you married my brother!" Bradford reminded her sharply.

"But it's you I've always wanted. Zachary isn't half the man you are."

"You've made your bed, Crystal. I really hope you enjoy sleeping in it," Bradford returned, a slight touch of bitterness in his tone.

"So you're turnin' to that girl? You won't come to me because of her!"

"For God's sake, Crystal, it's long over between us!" Bradford replied brusquely, losing patience. "Even if I had never met Angela, I wouldn't come to you. But I did meet her, and I thank heaven I did. She is like the sun after the storm. If you are unhappy with your marriage, I suggest you look elsewhere. I'm not available."

Angela could hear Crystal running up the curving stairs, and then Angela moved to the door slowly, just in time to see Bradford disappear into the study. She waited a few minutes and then hurried out of the dining room and up the stairs without being seen.

Angela was beaming, for her lingering doubts had been dispelled. Crystal still wanted Bradford, but he didn't want her. Angela wondered if anyone had ever been as happy as she was at that moment.

Twenty-nine

"Angel, hurry up," Bradford called impatiently from outside her door. "The first carriage will be pulling up any minute now."

"She's comin', Master Brad," Hannah called back, sending Bradford on his way downstairs. Then she turned to Eulalia. "You did a real fine job, Eulalia. Miss Crystal will want you to do her hair from now on, after she sees our Missy."

"I told you I'd do her up right. You didn't have to come up here to check on me!" Eulalia snapped saucily.

"I just wanted to see for myself, gal. Now get yourself down to the kitchen and see iffen Tilda needs your help," Hannah said in her bossiest manner.

Hannah chuckled as Eulalia stalked from the room. "That gal's gettin' to be like a mother hen, I swear she is. She always thinks she knows best.

She do a lot of the time, but you can't let her know it."

"I'm going to miss Eulalia when Bradford and I leave. And I'll miss you most of all, Hannah."

"This no time to think about that, child," Hannah replied cheerfully. "You'll be back to visit old Hannah. Now turn 'round and let me see you."

Angela did as she asked and then came to stand before her full-length mirror.

"You sure the angel Master Brad calls you. I ain't never seen no lady as pretty as you, child."

"It's just this gown, Hannah. Anyone would be beautiful wearing this."

"That's what you think."

The gown was exquisite. Of a sheer, deep-red organdy covering dark blue silk, it formed a rich violet color that matched her eyes perfectly. The neckline was extremely low, and trimmed with a thin ribbon of red silk. The gown had tight, fitted sleeves, and layered swirls of material in front that gathered tightly across the hips to form the bustle, in the newest fashion. But Angela had refused to let the seamstress tack on the numerous trailing bows and rosettes and the yards of lace the woman had wanted to add to the bodice and skirt. Angela allowed only the thin silk ribbon to form and line the bustle, and two trailing bows of the same red silk—one at the start of the bustle, and the other at the finish, where the skirt broke away in two straight lines.

At her ears were long dangling garnets, one of many presents from Jacob. The garnet-studded pins that crowned her head and held her hair tightly in place were also gifts from him. Angela wore two short curls dangling from her temples, and nine thick ringlets falling to her neck.

Because of the low neckline, Angela wore only her gold coin around her neck, but it was now in a setting of red garnets. The setting was a gift from Bradford. He had recently had two other settings made for her coin. The other two were gold rings, one with emeralds, the other one plain, with a single dropping diamond. They were round frames for her to place the coin in, each one having one gem larger than the others that hung down to cover the hole she'd carved in the coin ten years ago.

Bradford met Angela at the bottom of the stairs just as the first carriage arrived.

"You look magnificent!" he cried exuberantly. He took her hand, pride glowing in his face.

"Magnificent?"

"Well, you must get tired of hearing me tell you how beautiful you are. There are other words to describe you, Angel, and magnificent is one of them."

She laughed gaily. "As long as you think so, my love, that is all I care about."

"Well, isn't that charmin'," Crystal remarked from behind them, her voice dripping with con-

tempt. "So it's 'my love,' is it? And here I thought
you'd set your trap for my poor brother, Angela,"
Crystal laughed bitterly. "But Bradford is a much
better catch, isn't he? After all, he'll be the heir to
an estate that outshines The Shadows."

Angela kept silent.

Crystal's blue eyes were like ice as she continued. "Of course, marryin' Bradford will insure
that you won't be thrown out on your ear when
Jacob dies, won't it, dear?"

"The lady with the viperous tongue," Bradford
said smoothly, but his eyes were like liquid gold
as they rested on Crystal. "Or perhaps not a lady
at all."

He put his arm about Angela's waist and escorted her into the large ballroom. With the first
guests following them in, the musicians, on a
raised platform in the far corner, began the
evening with a waltz. Bradford should have
stood in the reception line with the rest of his
family, but instead he took Angela in his arms.
They were the first to dance on the newly polished floor.

By the time the waltz was over, eight families
had arrived, with more coming through the
wide double doors. Angela insisted that Bradford join his father, while she went to greet Susie
Fletcher, who was standing with her brother Joel
by the long tables covered with candies and hors
d'oeuvres, and decorated with freshly cut roses.

"Susie, I never did thank you for inviting me to stay at your house last month," Angela said, a little breathless from the dance.

"We really can't blame you, Angela, after what happened," Joel replied.

"Did you ever discover who it was cut up my dress?" Angela asked. She had actually forgotten the matter.

"No," Susie answered quickly, smiling. "Have you and Robert set the date for your weddin' yet?"

"Robert and I aren't getting married," Angela said sharply, startled.

"But you look so happy!" Susie exclaimed.

"I am," Angela laughed. "But not because of Robert. I love another man, Susie."

"But I thought—I mean." Susie looked overjoyed, yet alarmed at the same time. She turned to her brother. "Would you get us some champagne, Joel?"

"Of course," Joel answered, and walked toward the crowded dining room.

"Angela, I'm so sorry!" Susie blurted out as soon as they were alone.

"You have nothing to be sorry for."

"Yes, I do," Susie replied, her pretty face puckered. "When Robert told me he was going to ask you to marry him, I just assumed you would accept. I—I hated you then. I was the one who cut up your dress that night. I'm so sorry, Angela!" Susie was near tears. "It was such a childish thing to do."

"You love Robert, don't you?"

"Yes."

Angela smiled. "We women do strange things when we're in love. Don't worry about the dress, Susie. It was out of fashion anyway. And I wish you luck with Robert, though I don't really think you'll need it. You're the prettiest girl he has to choose from around here."

"Do you really think so?" Susie asked, her brown eyes radiating sudden joy.

"I wouldn't say so if I didn't," Angela assured her. But warmth turned to irritation when Angela saw Crystal coming their way.

"Really, Angela," Crystal said drily as she joined them, "I would think you wouldn't let Brad from your side tonight. Aren't you afraid of losin' him?"

Angela clenched her fists, but she managed a smile. "Having failed once, is his sister-in-law planning on enticing him to her bed again?"

The vivid red that stole into Crystal's face gave Angela ample satisfaction, and she walked away without waiting for a reply. She met Joel on his way back with the champagne.

"Why don't you set those glasses down on the table there and dance with me, Joel Fletcher?" Angela asked boldly, wanting to be out of Crystal's reach. Angela knew the viper would be anxious to retaliate.

"Do you really mean it?" he asked hopefully.

"Has a lady never asked you before? Goodness!" she teased.

Joel set the glasses down quickly and nervously took Angela in his arms. Across the room, Bradford's eyes were like burning cinders.

"Angela looks like she's having a good time," Jacob remarked.

"Yes—she does," Bradford answered curtly.

"What's wrong with you, son?" Jacob asked, concern in his voice.

"Nothing I can't take care of. You'll excuse me, Father?"

"I suppose I'll have to. But I've been meaning to have a long talk with you, Bradford, about your fiancée and—other matters."

"We'll talk tomorrow, Father."

"Very well, then," Jacob replied and turned his attention to his guests.

As soon as the music stopped, Bradford started toward Angela and young Joel. When he reached them he took Angela's hand and pulled her along behind him, leading her out through the first of the double doors and into the garden. Joel stared after them in total bafflement.

"What is the matter, Bradford?" Angela cried. He swung her around to face him, his fingers digging into her shoulders. "You—you are hurting me."

The garden was flooded in moonlight, a soft silver glow all about them.

Bradford loosened his hold, but he didn't release her. "The boy you were dancing with, was he the one whose clothes you came home in that day?"

"Yes, Susie's brother."

"You will not dance with that young man again!" Bradford nearly shouted.

"And why not, might I ask?"

"The boy's in love with you, that's obvious. But you're mine, Angela. I will share you with no one!"

"You're jealous again," Angela said, trying to hold back her laughter. "You're impossible, Bradford. I only danced with Joel so I could get away from Crystal."

The fire left Bradford's eyes as if by magic. "I'm sorry, Angel. I will have to talk to Crystal. I won't have her tongue lashing you anymore. Nobody is going to hurt you."

Angela spoke softly but very firmly. "But you are going to have to trust me more than you do. Just because another man looks at me, that doesn't mean I'm looking back at him. My heart belongs to you."

"I should believe that by now," he replied, his smile apologetic.

"Don't you?" she asked, and brushed her lips gently against his.

"Yes, my love, oh, yes," he groaned, and crushed her small body against his.

It was well over an hour before they walked back into the ballroom.

"If I'm asked, may I dance with other men?" Angela ventured.

"Yes," he grinned, and took her in his arms to claim the dance now in progress. "But not twice with the same man, you understand. It will take a while to tame my jealous temper. Bear with me, Angel."

Toward midnight, the long tables at the front of the room were cleared of hors d'oeuvres, and chairs were set up for the banquet. The soups were brought in, then the salads, followed by large platters of buttered rice, yams, and mountains of golden biscuits. Then came duck, venison, turkey, and hot and cold ham.

After the banquet, Angela danced with several men, most of whom she didn't even know. Mostly, of course, she danced with Bradford. Champagne had gone to her head. And when Grant Marlowe asked her to dance, she found herself giggling.

"I can't believe I've finally found you without a partner," Grant smiled. "I was beginnin' to think I never would."

"Don't be silly. You could've asked me any time." There were those giggles again. Why did he make her laugh?

"I wish they had 'em like you in Texas. Will you marry me, Miss Angela?"

"Now you *are* being silly," Angela replied, laughing.

Grant danced her out into the garden, leading

her to a large, moss-covered oak. Quickly, he pulled Angela closer and kissed her, a passionate kiss that cleared her head.

She pushed against him with all the force she had, but he held her easily. When he did release her, seconds later, Angela fell back several steps, nearly losing her balance.

"You—you shouldn't have done that!" she gasped.

"I just couldn't help myself," he replied lightly.

"Oh, God, Bradford is going to be furious if he finds me out here!"

"Does Brad have some kinda claim on you?" Grant asked, bewildered.

"Yes—he does. Damn! I've got to go back before he finds me gone."

"It's too late for that, ma'am."

"What?"

She spun around to see Bradford running toward them. Before she could say a word, Bradford's fist flew into Grant's face, sending the larger man crashing to the ground. Angela found her voice.

"Stop it! Stop it! He didn't know, Bradford!"

Bradford turned to face her and she stepped away from him. For just a moment, she felt he might kill her.

"How could he know? We haven't told anyone. Do you understand? He had no way of knowing!"

Bradford searched her stricken face and gradu-

ally the flame died. He turned to Grant and extended a hand to help him from the ground.

"I apologize for my fool temper. Will you forgive me?"

"If you'll accept my apology also," Grant
replied as he fingered his jaw tenderly. "If I'd
known you had a claim on the lady, this wouldn't
have happened."

"Apology accepted," Bradford grinned sheepishly. "Now, since you will be leaving in about six
hours, I suggest you call it a night. My soon-to-
be-wife and I have a few things to discuss."

"She's awfully tiny to bear that temper of
yours, Brad," Grant said frankly, his concern for
Angela plain. "You ain't gonna hurt her 'cause of
this, are you?"

"Of course not," Bradford answered with surprise. "This woman's mine. She knows she has
nothing to fear from me. Now get out of here, will
you?"

Grant hesitated, staring at Bradford. From wild
rage to sudden calm—it just wasn't natural. Was
Bradford really as calm as he seemed? Grant said
good-night and walked away reluctantly.

Bradford watched until his young friend walked
back into the ballroom. He could see through the
wide windows and open doors that most of the
guests had departed. His father would be furious
that he had not been there to see them out.

"Come here, you," he commanded, though his
voice was not harsh.

Angela approached him slowly. "You're not mad?" she whispered.

"Not anymore."

She sighed, then shook her head. "Well, I am! You have to trust me, Bradford. I can't worry that every time I look at a man, you're going to whip the daylights out of him. You have *got* to control that temper."

"I know, Angel, and I'm sorry. This is all new to me, Angel. I've never felt such a fierce possessiveness before. But I'll never hurt you because of it. I swear that."

Angela relaxed in his arms, feeling the tension leave them both. They would overcome this jealousy of his. They had to. She would prove to him that there was no reason for jealousy.

Bradford held her tenderly, caressing her back. He glanced up at the sky, now a grayish-pink with the approach of day. He thought briefly of the talk he would have with his father later. He knew what Jacob was concerned about. He would have to tell his father that he couldn't possibly marry Candise now. Then afterward, he would make the formal announcement.

"Tonight we tell the family about us," Bradford continued. "And a week from now, we will be married. After that, no man will doubt that you are mine. But I trust you. I trust you never to leave me, as Crystal did. I trust you to love only me, my Angel, as I love only you."

Thirty

It was nearly one o'clock when Angela awoke, but she had expected to sleep longer. The heavy drapes were closed tightly against the sun. Bradford was not in the room.

After washing and dressing, she was ready to face the day. And what a glorious day it was going to be!

Angela started down the hall, mindful of the guest rooms she passed before reaching the stairs. She and Bradford had to be much more careful since Grant and Bradford's lawyer, Jim McLaughlin, had arrived. But their careful secret meetings would end in a week. Then they would have nothing to hide.

She descended the stairs quickly, but slowed her pace when she heard Bradford's voice raised in anger. He was in the drawing room, but who was he yelling at?

"Is that what you had Tilda's boy wake me for, to tell me this nonsense? Do you think I'm a fool?"

Crystal's shrill laughter sounded. "Why do you find it so hard to believe? Things like this happen all the time."

"It's a lie, Crystal, a vicious lie!" Bradford stormed. "And if you think this trick of yours is going to stop me from marrying Angela, then you are crazy!"

"Then you really do plan to marry her?" Crystal asked, incredulous.

"I told you so last night on the dance floor, when I warned you to leave her alone. Didn't you believe me?"

"Frankly, no," Crystal answered. "I pity you, Bradford. What you want can never be."

"I will not listen to any more of this."

"You'd better!" Crystal insisted. "Surely you didn't believe those excuses your father gave for bringin' her here? Really, Bradford! To make the girl a member of the family for no reason? Because he'd known her since she was born? How gullible are you?"

"He and Angela's mother were childhood friends."

"Exactly!" Crystal exclaimed.

"You've proven nothing! Damn it, Crystal! Must I go to Father to put an end to this?"

"Tell me this," Crystal ventured. "If he had wanted the truth known, then why did he invent so many lies to avoid tellin' it? You musn't say anything. He would be extremely upset if he knew you had discovered his sins. It might cause another attack, and his doctor has warned that another attack will kill him."

"That's very convenient, Crystal," Bradford said drily. "So I can't confront Father with your lies. But that doesn't mean I believe a word you've said."

"Be sensible, Bradford. It's a matter of record that your father bought Golden Oaks almost twenty-two years ago. And shortly after that, one Charissa Sherrington gave birth to Angela. It's obvious that Jacob followed that woman to Alabama. Why else would he buy the land that her newly acquired husband farmed on?"

"This is all conjecture, Crystal," Bradford replied wearily. "It doesn't prove a thing."

"All right, then. Listen to this. I didn't want to admit to searchin' through your father's desk, but you force me to show you what I found there. This is a letter written by Charissa Sherrington. It proves everything. I'll read it to you. You will listen to this, because you know you have to. 'My dearest Jacob,' the letter begins.

I know you must be searching for me, and I'm sorry I left without saying good-bye, but I thought it best. I always knew that you could never leave your wife, for it would mean giving up your sons, and they need you. Even knowing this, I still can't help loving you, Jacob. If only you had realized your love for me before you married her! But I have said that many times before, haven't I?

You don't have to worry about me, Jacob, or about the child I am carrying. I know you said you would give the child everything you would give your other children, but that is not enough, my dearest. You cannot admit to being the father, and I want my child to have a father. For that reason, I have married.

I met my husband only yesterday, when he boarded the coach I was traveling in. He seems to be a kindly man. I know you will think I should have waited until I could find a man I could love. But I will never love anyone but you, so it doesn't matter.

William Sherrington wanted a wife, and I needed a husband quickly. It would be believed that he is the father of my child. The marriage will be a convenient one, and William has promised to raise my child as his own.

He sharecrops on a small farm in Alabama, and that is where we are going. I am telling you this because you have a right to know where your child will be. I will leave instructions with a lawyer in Mobile to contact you in case the child should ever be left in need.

I ask you please not to follow me, Jacob, for no good can come of it. Farewell, my dearest.

"And it is signed, 'Charissa Sherrington,' " Crystal finished triumphantly.

He was so deeply stricken that he failed to watch Crystal's face carefully. Had he done so, he would have realized that she was lying. Crystal lied whenever it suited her, and had he kept his wits about him, Bradford would have remembered that. But he was in agony, and failed to see that special gleam in her eye.

"Damn you to hell, Crystal!"

Angela turned slowly and walked up the stairs in a trance. Her eyes were wide, but unseeing. Something tore at her chest. She was barely able to breathe.

She reached her room without being aware of it, and found herself sitting on the edge of her bed. Her eyes burned for want of tears that wouldn't come.

Dear God, I'm in love with my half brother! My half brother! I have loved him for ten years—half my life. And God forgive me, I can't stop it. I still love him!

Without thinking, Angela got up from the bed and started packing her clothes in the two trunks she had used for school. She quickly packed everything she owned. There was no reason to leave anything behind, for she could never come back to this house.

With her trunks filled and locked, Angela left her room. She encountered no one on her way to the stables, where she found Zeke pitching hay to the horses. He looked up and smiled at her.

"Zeke, I want you to go to my room and bring down the two trunks you will find there. And do it quietly. The rest of the family is still sleeping."

"Is you goin' somewhere, Missy?" he asked, scratching his head. "I ain't been told—"

"Just to the city, Zeke," she interrupted him with a weak smile. "I've put on a little weight lately and just about all my dresses need to be altered. I might as well get it done with."

"Yessum," he said and strolled off toward the house.

She was in an agony of suspense as she waited for Zeke. At last, he returned with the second trunk and they left for the city.

But where was she going? Where in this world was there a place for her? Maybe she could find her mother, Angela thought wildly. Yes, she would find her mother and live with her! Why, she even knew someone who was going West. Grant Marlowe. She would pay him to take her with him.

Angela turned back for a last look at Golden Oaks. The huge white mansion gleamed in the midday sun. And then Zeke turned onto the river road and she couldn't see it any longer.

She refused to let herself think of Bradford, but as she rode farther away from Golden Oaks, she knew she would never see Jacob again. And that was when her heart began to break.

* * *

Bradford burst into his father's room with a greater fury than he meant to show. It was not Jacob he wanted to strangle, but Crystal.

He had realized that he could not accept anything she said. She was lying, she had to be. She had made up that letter herself! She must have!

"You wanted to talk to me about Candise, Father, and I'm here to tell you I can't marry her."

Jacob was silent, knowing something was terribly wrong with his son.

"I didn't think you would," Jacob said at last. "I have the distinct impression that your interest lies elsewhere."

"Damn right it does," Bradford said belligerently. "I'm going to marry Angela next week. What do you say to that?"

"I couldn't be more pleased."

"What?"

Jacob grinned. "Did you think I would object? I have always hoped you and Angela would marry someday, but because of the difference in your ages, I was afraid you would marry before she even grew up. Object? My boy, I couldn't be happier."

Bradford sat down slowly and began to laugh. Suddenly, he couldn't stop laughing. *Damn* Crystal *anyway*. The little bitch should have known her lying scheme would be quickly disproved. Jacob could not allow him to marry Angela if she were his daughter. But Jacob was delighted. The last laugh would be on Crystal, next week, when he walked Angela down the aisle and made her his forever. He was so happy that his anger disappeared almost entirely.

Thirty-one

Zeke halted the carriage in front of Madame Tardieu's little shop. After he carted her trunks inside, she sent him on his way, telling him she would hire a carriage later on to bring her home, since she didn't know how long she would be. She hated lying again, but there was nothing else she could do.

Madame Tardieu, the little Frenchwoman who created such lovely gowns for the Maitland women, came out of a back room and greeted Angela cheerfully. "Mademoiselle Sherrington, I trust the ball last night was a splendid success?"

"Yes, very much so," Angela answered uneasily.

"Good, good. But what is this?" Madame Tardieu asked, noticing the trunks on the floor. "Have you purchased material somewhere else for me to work with?"

"No, *madame*," Angela assured her. "I—I had planned to have some of my dresses altered, but I have changed my mind. Fashions change so quickly. I think I would rather have a complete new wardrobe."

"Ah, *oui*, this new bustle. It requires so much more material. Will you select the materials now? I have a new shipment of silks from Paris."

"Not just yet, Madame Tardieu. I will take my old dresses to the church first, so they can be given to the poor. And I have one or two errands. I will return shortly," Angela replied.

She regretted having to lie again. Why did one lie always have to lead to another and another?

"You must be excited to have a wedding so soon after the ball," the Frenchwoman continued as she walked Angela to the door.

Angela caught her breath. No one had known there was to be a wedding.

"Where did you hear of this?"

Madame Tardieu laughed in delight. "Ah, but it is the talk of the town. News of this sort travels quickly. But it is too bad the lovely bride could not have arrived in time for the ball last night."

Angela stared uncomprehendingly.

"You did not know? Mademoiselle Taylor arrived this morning with her papa. Ah, Monsieur Maitland must be so pleased to have his son marry the daughter of his best friend. I understand they have been engaged for a very long time."

Angela let the words sink in slowly. Candise Taylor and Jacob's son? But Jacob had only one unmarried son. Angela's eyes flashed with sudden awful understanding. Bradford had proposed to her, made love to her, when all the while he was engaged to marry the daughter of his father's best friend.

"You will need a new gown for the wedding," Madame Tardieu was saying. "Perhaps a light green? It will be lovely with your hair."

"No!" Angela snapped, then took hold of herself. "Blue, or maybe pink. But now I really must go."

"Of course. We will decide later."

"Yes," Angela answered quickly. "Later."

Standing outside the dress shop, Angela's whole body shook with outrage. Bradford had wanted only a convenient bed partner while he waited for his fiancée to arrive! And Angela had been too willing to oblige him.

She refused to let herself think about it any longer, but hurriedly found a carriage. She knew that Grant Marlowe would be leaving that afternoon on a ship bound for Louisiana. Finding the ship and then its captain, she learned that Grant was already aboard. It was not difficult to find Grant. What was difficult was convincing him to escort her West.

They stood by the rail watching the last of the cargo being loaded. Grant was unaware that her trunks were already on board and that she had paid for her passage.

"You have to understand, Miss Angela, that I'm travelin' to Texas alone. It'd be different if others were comin' along, with wagons and the like. No—I just can't do it."

"I would be no trouble, Grant. I'm not asking for your protection. I just need a guide."

"And who'd protect you then if not me?"

"I can take care of myself," she replied with a tilt of her chin.

He looked down at her with amusement, a disbelieving grin on his lips. "You're talkin' about Texas, ma'am. It's a wild land, full of Indians, Mexican bandits, and outlaws who wouldn't think twice about killin' a woman. And like I said, I'm travelin' alone. Takin' a wagon along for a lady's comfort would set me back at least a month and I can't afford to lose that much time."

"I wouldn't need a wagon. If you can ride horseback, then so can I," Angela said.

He looked at her curiously for a moment, the sun reflecting in his eyes, making them shining green pools. "Why do you want to go West so badly?"

She had anticipated the question. "I want to find my mother."

"Is she in Texas?"

"I have reason to believe she is," Angela answered.

"You mean you're not sure?"

"All I know is that she traveled West twenty

years ago. But I intend to comb the country until I find her."

"As I understand it, Brad will be comin' to Texas in four or five months. Why don't you wait until he brings you?" Grant ventured. "Or, better yet, have him hire someone to find your mother for you."

Angela cleared her throat and lowered her head. "I—I think you should know that I have decided not to marry Bradford. We—aren't—suited."

Grant wrinkled his brow. "Brad didn't hurt you last night, did he? I mean, have you changed your mind about him 'cause of what happened in the garden?"

"No," she replied quickly, avoiding his eyes. "No, of course not. My reasons have nothing to do with you."

"I don't understand. Last night you swore your love for Brad."

"I can't deny I love him," Angela said in a weak voice. It was true. She would always love him. "But I can't marry him."

"So you're really runnin' away from Brad?"

"You might say that."

"He'll follow you."

"He won't come after me, I'm sure of that," Angela said simply, trying to hold back tears. "When he finds that I have gone, he'll know why, and he'll know it's best. So—will you take me with you?"

"On one condition," he answered earnestly. "And that is that I take you as my wife."

"You can't be serious!" she exclaimed, but saw quickly that he was.

"I asked you to marry me last night and I'm askin' you again now."

"I can't marry you, Grant. I've told you I love Bradford," she said ruefully.

"But you say you can't marry him either. You just don't make sense, Miss Angela."

"I will pay you to take me," she said.

"I gave you my condition, ma'am, and that's the only way I'll agree to take you with me. You're just too pretty to travel alone with, and I'm not made of steel."

"Grant, please—"

"The answer is no, but with regrets."

He tipped his hat and walked away, leaving her standing alone at the rail. But she would make him change his mind. She had to.

Thirty-two

It was nearing dusk as the two riders wearily approached the outskirts of Nacogdoches.

"You'll be able to get passage on a stagecoach there, and then I want nothin' more to do with you," Grant grumbled. How had he let himself be talked into taking her this far?

Grant tied their horses in front of the only building with a sign reading "Hotel." They went inside and Grant pounded on the front desk until a short little old man with gray whiskers came running from a back room.

"Alright, I'm comin'. Hol' your horses," the little man called in a crackly voice.

"When's the next stage out?" Grant asked impatiently.

"Jest missed it, sonny. Left today at noon."

"When is the next stage due?"

"Not fer a week. Kin put you an' the missus up,

though," the man replied, smiling at Angela with an admiring eye. "Got a nice room facin' the street kin let you have real cheap."

"You can give the lady that room, and find another for me for the night," Grant said, then turned to face Angela. "Looks like you'll have a week's wait. I'll be movin' on in the morning."

"But—"

"We agreed I'd take you this far. I've done it."

His abruptness and the realization that she was on her own again threw her. "Thank you, Mr. Marlowe, and good-bye," she said with equal abruptness, then turned and followed the old man up the stairs, leaving Grant staring after her with an angry scowl. With a growing temper, he turned and stormed from the hotel in the direction of the nearest saloon.

It was quite early in the morning when Grant pounded on Angela's door, then barged into her room without waiting for an answer. She was sitting up in the large double bed, fully alert.

"May I ask why you need to present yourself at this hour?" she asked coldly.

"I'm leavin' now, ma'am." His courtesy held more than a touch of sarcasm.

Grant's harsh attitude was a defense against his desire for Angela. He wanted her, but she loved Brad.

"I believe we said good-bye last evening, didn't we?" she said archly.

"You did. And now I will," he replied and crossed to her bed in two quick strides.

He bent down, grabbed hold of her shoulders, and covered her lips forcefully with his own. The harshness left him and he became increasingly tender. Slowly, he sat on the edge of the bed and wrapped his arms around her, pressing her gently against him.

Angela did not try to push him away. She did not return his kiss wholeheartedly, but it was a pleasant kiss and she felt secure in his arms. She did not feel the stirrings that Bradford's touch induced, but kissing Grant was rather nice.

She moaned softly for what she could never have again, but Grant mistook misery for desire.

"Angela, say you will marry me," he said deeply, kissing her neck. "You are like a prairie flower—too delicate to touch, but too beautiful to leave behind."

She was deeply moved by his poetic words. And he was such a handsome young man, far more striking than Bradford. He was taller, stronger, and he would probably be a gentle lover.

He would make a fine husband, one she could be proud of. But she didn't love him, nor did *he* speak of love.

"Why do you want to marry me, Grant?" she asked gently.

"I want to make you my wife," he answered simply.

"But why?"

He stared into her eyes, dark pools of violet, near blue in the morning light. "I want you," he said, so quietly it was almost a whisper.

"But you don't love me. And I don't love you," Angela argued.

"What I feel for you is near to love," he returned.

"Be honest with me, Grant," she said in a level voice. "What you want is to make love to me."

"Well, of course!" he said, astonished, flustered by her frankness.

"And if I were to let you make love to me, then there would no longer be the need to marry me. Am I right?"

"If you ain't the damnedest woman I ever met!" he exclaimed, shocked now. He got quickly to his feet. "That ain't the way it's done, Angela."

She laughed at his expression. "Come now, Grant. I thought you Texans threw convention to the winds."

His expression changed abruptly. A sparkling glint appeared in his dark green eyes and he gazed down at her appraisingly. A grin crossed his lips and, without another word, he started unbuttoning his shirt.

Now it was Angela's turn to be startled. "What—what do you think you're doing?"

His grin widened. "I plan to take you up on your offer, ma'am."

"Grant, no!" she gasped. "I was not offering myself to you. I was just trying to explain something. You don't want me as a wife, you just want me in your bed."

"That's true enough," he returned without taking his eyes from her. "I always assumed you fine ladies wanted the two to go together. But you've showed me different."

"Get out of here, Grant Marlowe!" Angela shouted. Apprehension was turning to fear and she started to leave the bed on the opposite side.

Grant caught hold of her arm and jerked her back to the center of the bed. He held her wrists securely against the pillow as he leaned over her, pure rage on his features.

"I've no intention of rapin' you, Angela," he growled. "But in the future, watch what you say to a man. If you weren't a damned virgin, I'd take you here and now!" Then he smiled at the fear in her eyes. "Good-bye, Miss Angela." He released her hands then and left the room without a backward glance.

Angela stared at the closed door for long moments after Grant left the room. She just plain didn't understand Grant Marlowe. His moods changed as quickly as the sky on a windy day.

Well, Grant was gone now and she was on her own. She sighed and left the bed to begin dressing. She had a lot to do today and in the days before the stage came. She wanted to purchase a small weapon that she was determined to keep under her pillow and to wear strapped to her leg during the day. She could not allow herself to be helpless.

And she would begin asking questions about her mother. Perhaps someone in this very town knew of her. Yes, she had a lot to do.

Thirty-three

The first knock on Angela's door was so light that she didn't hear it. The second knock was like thunder and she bolted upright, completely awake, leaving behind her troubled dream.

With wide, startled eyes, Angela glanced quickly about the darkened room. A continuous hammering began and she jumped from the bed, pulling the sheet with her, and struck a match to light the candle on the bedside table. But before she could get it lit, her door crashed open.

Angela stood paralyzed, the sheet clutched against herself. There was only a dim light coming from the outside hall.

The intruder stumbled into the room and then suddenly fell to the floor. Angela could see only his large frame silhouetted in the dark. He clumsily struggled to his feet and she ran to the bed

and searched frantically under the pillow until
her hand touched the little derringer she had purchased only that afternoon.

With the slim weapon firmly in her hand, Angela gained her courage. "S-stay where you are or
I'll have to shoot you." Her words did not sound
as brave as she had wanted them to.

"What?"

The voice was all too familiar, and with the
sudden recognition, Angela exploded into rage,
so furious that she slipped back into her old
speech.

"Grant Marlowe! Just what in hellfire do you
think you're doin' bustin' in here? I oughta shoot
you just for the scare you gimme!"

"Damn—I knocked—first!" he slurred. "Whyn't
you answer?"

"You didn't gimme a chance to! And you're
drunk!" she yelled, further enraged.

"Yes, ma'am—I'm drunk," he replied. "With—
with good reason."

He sounded like a proud little boy. Relief finally taking over, Angela began to laugh. She
placed the gun down carefully on the table by the
bed, wrapped the sheet firmly about herself, then
leaned over to light the candle.

Grant shielded his eyes from the sudden light,
then squinted at her from the middle of the room
where he swayed. She moved past him to the door
and closed it quietly, then leaned back against it.

"Now tell me what you thought you were do-

ing, busting into my room in the middle of the
night?"

"I tol' you I—I knocked first. I got worried
when you didn't answer—"

"Never mind, Grant," she cut him off. "Just tell
me what you're doing here. I thought you'd left
for the ranch this morning."

"I did."

She sighed. He was having trouble keeping his
balance, so she helped him to the chair by her
bed. He collapsed gratefully into it.

She stood looking down at him like a scolding
mother. "If you left this morning, then why did
you come back?"

"To see—you."

"Why?"

"Was drinkin' on the way. Got—to thinkin'—
had to try once more," he said, holding up a finger to make himself clear.

"Try what once more?" she asked, becoming
exasperated.

He smiled boyishly. "To get you to marry me.
Couldn't leave—you here alone."

"Oh, Grant! Honestly!" she said, shaking her
head. "What am I going to do with you?"

"Marry me."

She sat down on the edge of the bed and looked
at him with gentle eyes. "Grant, the answer is still
no. I do not intend to marry you or any other
man—ever."

"But you need someone," Grant replied after her words had sunk in.

"I do not *need* any man!" she yelled defiantly. "I am capable of taking care of myself!"

Hoping to change the subject, she asked, "Did you get yourself a room before you stormed up here?"

"No," he replied with a sheepish grin.

She sighed. "Very well. Since you're in no condition to go anywhere right now, you can stay here. I'll go down to see about getting another room for myself for the rest of the night."

He grabbed her hand and held it. "Angela, stay here with me. I won't—"

"No, Grant," she replied firmly and started to tug on his arm. "Now come on and I'll help you into bed."

He let her pull him the few feet to the bed. Then she helped him out of his heavy jacket and shirt, and managed to yank off his boots. When she pulled the cover up over him, he grabbed her hand again and looked at her with yearning.

"One kiss—before you go," he ventured, holding her hand to his cheek.

"If that's what it takes to make you go to sleep," she replied.

She sat down on the edge of the bed and leaned over to kiss him. She felt his arms wrap around her and press her closer to him, but she didn't pull away. The kiss was pleasant.

Angela didn't hear when the door to her room slowly opened. Nor did she sense the presence of the man who stood in the doorway, watching her for a long moment. But she did hear the door when it closed, and she pulled away from Grant's embrace to look in that direction.

"What's the matter?" he asked.

She looked back at him and smiled. "Nothing. I thought I heard something, but I guess I was mistaken." She tucked the covers about his neck and smoothed the hair on his forehead. "Now go to sleep, Grant. I'll see you in the morning."

Thirty-four

Bradford Maitland returned to Mobile to learn that his father was dead.

A dock worker, a congenial man who assumed Bradford already knew, relayed the news by way of condolence as Bradford stepped off the packet. The torment of the last few weeks became even more bitter because he had not been there when his father died. There was deep sorrow and a smoldering rage as well inside Bradford as he rode out to Golden Oaks.

It was midmorning, but the mansion was eerily quiet when he entered it. His eyes were a golden blaze of yellow as he scanned the hall to find that all the doors were open, except one. He went directly to his father's study and opened the door with such force that it slammed back against the wall, knocking loose a large picture that fell to the floor with a crash.

Zachary Maitland jumped to his feet. He had been sitting at his father's desk, and he stepped quickly behind the chair, as though the desk and chair would afford him protection. There was sheer terror on his handsome face as he watched his brother walk slowly into the study.

"How did it happen?" Bradford's words were slow and even.

"It was his heart, Brad," Zachary replied appeasingly, his eyes wide. "Nothing could be done."

"How did it happen?" Bradford repeated his question, his voice raised slightly.

"It was another attack!" Zachary shouted now, as if he were defending his life.

And indeed he was. For, at that moment, Bradford felt an overwhelming desire to kill someone, and he didn't much care who it was. He crossed to Zachary swiftly and hooked his hands into his brother's coat lapels.

"*You* caused the first attack!" Bradford said with calculating fury, watching Zachary's eyes grow huge in surprise and fear. "Now, brother, you will tell me what caused the attack that took his life!"

"It—it just happened!" Zachary stuttered. "There was nothing anyone—"

"Do you think I am an idiot?" Bradford cut in. "You will tell me the truth—*now*—or by God I'll beat it out of you!"

"All right—all right, Bradford!" Zachary cried,

his face losing its color. "But it was an accident—I
swear it! How were we to know that Father was
at the top of the stairs—that he could hear us arguing?"

"We?"

"Crystal and—and me. Father was supposed to
be taking a nap, as Dr. Scarron suggested he do
each afternoon since—since—well, you know.
You were here."

"Yes, I quite remember how upset Father became over his *ward's* disappearance," Bradford
remarked distastefully.

He released his hold on Zachary and walked
slowly over to his father's liquor cabinet.

"All right, Zachary," Bradford said as he filled a
tall glass with straight Bourbon. "I want to hear
all of it now, and it had damn well better be the
truth."

Zachary stood frozen to the spot. He cleared his
throat nervously. "Well, as I said, Crystal and I
were having an argument. We had been in the
drawing room, but somehow we ended up in the
hall—I followed her—yes—because she said she
had no more to say and was going to her room,
but—I stopped her in the hall. We didn't know
Father was at the top of the stairs—that he could
hear."

"You're trying my patience, Zachary!" Bradford interrupted. "Husbands and wives argue occasionally. What has that to do with Father's
attack?"

"It was what we were arguing about, Bradford. Or rather—who we were arguing about," Zachary replied in a weak voice, avoiding his brother's cold regard.

Bradford drained his glass as if it were filled with spring water. But the fiery liquid seemed to add a brighter fire to his eyes as they bore into Zachary's.

"I presume you mean Angela?" Bradford asked, though he knew the answer.

"Yes, it was about Angela. Crystal showed me that letter she found—Charissa Sherrington's letter. She told me she'd read it to you, but needn't have gone to the trouble, since Angela ran off with Grant Marlowe. She said Angela had been *your* mistress after she'd tired of Robert, and that's why you went after her. Crystal threw all this in my face to explain why she wouldn't let me—why she wouldn't conceive children in this house—a house of incest."

"My God!" Bradford exclaimed, his body going rigid. "And Father heard all this?"

"Yes. We heard him collapse then. He—"

"Did he fall down the stairs?" Bradford interrupted.

"No, but he was dead when we reached him."

"So Crystal's jealousy and hate killed my father!" Bradford's voice was only a whisper, but filled with such intensity that Zachary trembled.

"For God's sake, Bradford! It was an accident. Don't you think I regret it? And Crystal does too!

I—I beat her that night. It was something I should have done a long time ago. She has stayed to her room ever since, except for the funeral."

"Which was when?"

"A week ago," Zachary replied, his eyes downcast. "We couldn't wait. We didn't know when you would return."

A tense silence fell between them. Bradford stood by the liquor cabinet, the empty glass still clenched in his hand. His hard gaze no longer rested on his brother, but on his father's desk. Zachary could only guess at half the murderous thoughts that filled his mind.

Zachary finally spoke again, unable to bear the ominous quiet. "Father's will hasn't been read yet." When Bradford didn't look at him, he went on quickly. "Jim McLaughlin is executor. Seems Father made a new will the day Jim arrived here. It wasn't necessary for you to be present, but we all agreed to wait until you came back."

"How thoughtful," Bradford remarked coldly and started for the door. Without once looking back at his brother, he continued, "Have it done with this afternoon. I'm not staying in this house any longer than I have to." And then he was gone, leaving Zachary giddy with relief, but still trembling.

Thirty-five

Jim McLaughlin cleared his throat and looked slowly around the room to be sure that all who had been summoned were present. He was wishing that Jacob Maitland had not made him executor.

Bradford, especially, would not be happy with some of the conditions of the will. Jacob had asserted his power even beyond death.

Two of Jacob's beneficiaries would not be present today. His mistress would not force herself on his grieving family. And Angela Sherrington had disappeared.

Jim sighed. He would have to find Miss Sherrington before his job would be over with. He hoped Bradford had been successful in discovering her whereabouts on his trip West. He would have to talk to him about that later.

"If there are no objections, I will begin," Jim began.

"First, I would like to say that this last will and testament is wholly legal." He read:

I, Jacob Maitland, being of sound and disposing mind and memory, and not acting under duress, coercion, or undue influence of any person whomsoever, do make and declare this instrument as my last will and testament, hereby revoking all wills and codicils previously made by me.

First: I direct that all debts owed me shall not be canceled with my death, but shall henceforth be owed to my son, Bradford Maitland.

Second: To certain colleges that I . . .

Bradford let his mind wander while Jim McLaughlin read off the colleges, charities and institutions, employees, friends, and the like. Bradford thought of the brief hour he had spent with Candise and Robert, listening to the details of the funeral and their account of Jacob's death. Zachary had apparently not told them the real cause of his father's death.

Bradford had already decided to turn over Golden Oaks and the plantation to Zachary, if indeed his father had left that decision to him. He never wanted to see Golden Oaks again. Too many recent memories were here, memories that only fueled his rage. He didn't know exactly what he would do now. He wanted to go to Texas, to the ranch he loved, but that was impossible now.

Tenth: To my housekeeper, Hannah, who has been a loyal and trusted servant, I bequeath the sum of five thousand dollars, and the two acres of land known as Willow Farm, to which she may retire at any time henceforth, or retain her position at Goldens Oaks for as long as she wishes.

Bradford smiled at Hannah's stunned expression. Father was always generous with those who served him.

Eleventh: I bequeath the sum of five hundred thousand dollars to Zachary Maitland, and an additional twenty thousand dollars to be allocated each year for the remainder of his life, and the Hotel Rush located in London, England, and to any legitimate offspring that he shall sire, the sum of five thousand dollars each year for female offspring; the sum of ten thousand dollars each year for male offspring, to be kept in trust until said offspring become of age.
Twelfth: I bequeath the sum of five thousand dollars to Crystal Maitland, to be allocated each year for the remainder of her life, with the stipulation that she bear a legitimate offspring within two years after my death.

Bradford smiled when he heard Crystal gasp. He noted that Zachary was smiling, too. Crystal would now have to submit to her husband in bed—rather like a paid whore, Bradford thought with dry humor.

He realized suddenly that he no longer hated Zachary, but pitied him. Bradford was thankful now that Zachary had taken the conniving bitch off his hands. To think he had actually loved Crystal once!

He smiled again as Jim continued, leaving ten thousand dollars a year to the widow Caden, his father's faithful mistress, and a like sum to Robert Lonsdale, who had been almost a third son. But everything turned red in his mind when Angela Sherrington's name was pronounced. He didn't hear Jim's words, or Hannah's gleeful chuckle at the back of the room, or Crystal's second loud gasp. Bradford heard none of this as the picture of Angela flashed across his mind, a loose sheet wrapped around her naked body, Grant's arms about her, her lips clinging to his. Bitch! Whore! Had they just finished making love, or were they just about to? It didn't matter. He should have killed them both as he had wanted to when he opened the door and found them in bed together.

What had she said once? "You are going to have to trust me more than you do, Bradford," and "I'll never leave you again. It's you I love—no other." The lying slut! Bradford Maitland would never trust another woman as long as he lived.

"Well, Bradford, it's all yours now. How does it feel to be a millionaire?"

Bradford glanced up, Jim McLaughlin's question breaking into his thoughts. He saw that they were alone in the study now. The reading of his father's will was over.

"It feels no different than it's always felt," Bradford replied, bored. "It's a waste of money to have so much of it."

Jim McLaughlin couldn't complain about his own state of affairs. Being one of Maitland Enterprises' most important lawyers, his yearly income was substantial. He was well on the way to becoming a millionaire himself.

"At any rate," Jim continued in his business voice, "I have here a copy of your father's will, as well as a detailed list of all his holdings. No doubt you are already aware of all that Maitland Enterprises encompasses, having been in control of your father's interests for many years now. But your father believed that land was wealth and he acquired quite a bit of it over the years. As a matter of fact, you now own properties all over the world."

"Properties that I will probably never even see," Bradford said.

"Does that really matter?" Jim asked. "Most of these properties bring in sizable incomes, and they provide jobs for many. You have hardly taken an attitude your father would approve of."

"I suppose I haven't," Bradford replied. "But I find there is no longer any challenge in making money, when I already have more than enough of it. What if I should give it all away and make my own fortune?"

"I'm afraid you can't do that," Jim said firmly. "As it states in your father's will, all of his holdings must remain in the family. They can be sold, of course, but not given away. And if you choose to relinquish your inheritance, then it will all go to Zachary."

Bradford gritted his teeth. No, it would not go to Zachary, not as long as Crystal was his wife. He would have to resign himself to being in complete control of the Maitland millions, just as his father had wished.

"What are your plans now, Bradford?"

"I suppose my only course is to leave for New York tomorrow morning. I might as well get back into the business," Bradford said reluctantly.

"So you no longer plan to control things from Texas?" Jim ventured.

"No!" Bradford replied quickly and a bit harshly, his eyes suddenly turning amber.

Jim eyed the brooding young man carefully. Something was definitely troubling Bradford, and he was in no mood to be questioned about it. Jim had expected Bradford to fly into a rage when he heard the conditions of his inheritance. But

Bradford hadn't appeared to be listening.

"Well, I will be returning to New York myself, just as soon as I can find Miss Sherrington," Jim said as he stood up from behind Jacob's desk. "Did you have any luck discovering her whereabouts?"

Bradford did not answer immediately. He was trying hard to keep his raging temper in check. When he finally spoke, he couldn't hide the bitterness in his voice.

"I last saw Miss Sherrington in Nacogdoches, but I have reason to believe you will be able to find her at the JB ranch. She will undoubtedly be there with her current lover, my foreman, Grant Marlowe."

Jim was speechless. Miss Sherrington and Bradford had seemed quite attached not long ago. That was shocking in itself because he knew of Bradford's engagement to Candise Taylor.

"Here are the papers I spoke of earlier," Jim said, coming around the desk to hand them to Bradford. "There is also a personal letter from your father that he asked me to give you after the will was read. I will leave you alone to read it. We will see each other again before you leave, I'm sure."

Bradford waited until Jim had left the room before he opened his father's letter. He read it slowly, the words on each page jumping up at him like little demons. It was impossible that his father could be asking him to do the one thing he could never do. It was also hypocritical of him. He always said he would not force his wishes on his children.

Now Bradford had a deeper sorrow to bear, for he would not, he *could* not possibly fulfill his father's last wish. Jacob was asking too much.

This room where his father had spent so much time over the past twenty-two years seemed to hold Jacob's presence. Bradford stared fixedly at the desk and the empty chair behind it—*empty*. Uncaring, his control dissolved and a tear slid down his cheek, followed by another.

It was a long time before Bradford left the study.

Thirty-six

 Under the torrid western sun, the stage-coach bounced along the hard dirt, each bump hitting the passengers harder than the one before. The cramped interior was stifling, the journey apparently endless.

The passengers, all strangers, seemed content to remain that way, except for one inordinately cheerful woman who was traveling with her husband, an austere-looking minister who was sound asleep beside her. The middle-aged woman, who introduced herself as Aggie Bauer, was plump and dressed in heavy black traveling clothes. She seemed not to mind the oppressive heat, the jolting ride, or the fact that nobody spoke to her.

Mrs. Bauer's ceaseless chattering went unheeded as she explained the best way to grow a garden in this arid land. Angela listened with only half of her mind, while the other half wondered where her journey would end, if it ever did.

After saying her final good-bye to Grant Marlowe, she had gone on to Crockett, and then to Midway, staying a week in each one, asking questions and learning absolutely nothing. She would reach another town tomorrow morning, but would it be any different there? Was there really any hope of finding her mother? Twenty years was a long time. Her mother might have married and changed her name, or gone on to California or Mexico. And there was always the dread possibility that Charissa Sherrington was dead.

The man on Angela's left made her quite nervous, a gun strapped to his leg pressing against her skirt. She had seen many such men recently. Would she ever get used to them? They were called gunmen or cowboys, these dangerous-looking men who openly sported guns and engaged in brawls.

Angela had seen one such fight in the middle of town on the open street. It wasn't a traditional duel of the civilized South. Instead of the opponents walking away from one another to turn at the count of ten, two men approached each other slowly, until one man found the nerve to draw his gun. No doubt the man next to Angela had killed many men in gunfights.

The young woman on Angela's right was Spanish with a white lace mantilla draped over her head and shoulders. Her traveling companion, sitting across from her next to the minister's wife, was a tall, fierce-looking woman with a thin frame.

Angela stared at the chaperon now in puzzlement, watching the older woman's face turn white as she stared out of the window. Suddenly the coach pulled up.

"Well, why on earth are we stopping in the middle of nowhere?" Mrs. Bauer asked, leaning over her husband to glance out the window. Gasping, she exclaimed in a frightened voice, "It's a holdup! Good Lord, we're going to be robbed!"

"Calm down, now. Calm down," the minister spoke firmly, fully awake now. He stared solemnly at the other passengers. "You'd best hide your valuables if you want to keep them."

"We'll be lucky if we keep our lives!" his wife screamed. She turned to the man beside Angela and demanded, "Why don't you do something? You have a gun—use it!"

He shook his head. "I ain't no fool, ma'am. The driver chose to give up without a fight, so I suggest we do the same thing."

At that moment the door was flung open and a stocky man with a bandanna over the lower half of his face stuck his head inside. He pointed his gun at each of the passengers in turn.

"You—with the gun. Toss it out the window," the bandit ordered, and the man beside Angela did so without hesitating. "Now all of you step outside, and line up beside the coach."

"You there, get down," another man called from outside, and the coach moved slightly as the driver got down from his box.

There were five robbers. Four of them were still sitting on their horses, their weapons drawn and leveled at the passengers. The fifth man, the one who had ordered them all outside, was presently throwing down the trunks and baggage from the top and back of the coach. Then another man dismounted and came forward, putting his gun away as he did so.

The young man who stood before them, hands on his hips, was quite tall, lean, with broad shoulders. Black hair escaped below his wide-brimmed hat, but he was clean-shaven. His gray eyes, oddly, held a touch of humor.

"Your luggage no doubt, holds much of value, but your persons must also be searched," the man said now. His voice carried a slight accent, either Spanish or Mexican. "You will save time and trouble if you will cooperate."

The minister's wife broke into hysterics, clinging to her husband. Angela steeled herself as the young bandit began searching the driver, going slowly through the poor man's pockets. Producing only a few coins, he put them into a small sack hooked to his belt. Then he moved on to the gunman, and then the minister.

The bandit turned to the women, and his eyes
crinkled, as if he were grinning. He went to the
Spanish women first, and spoke sharply to the
duenna in her own language. The older woman
answered harshly and shielded her young ward
with her arms. The young man laughed at this,
but pulled his gun from its holster and pointed it
at the woman, who turned pale and stood rigid.
The bandit ran his free hand over the woman's
skirt, inspecting the hem of her dress for hidden
money. He then spoke to her again, causing her to
shriek. The bandit laughed again and shrugged,
then swiftly ripped open the woman's bodice and
stuck his hand inside for his final, humiliating
search. It produced two gold rings and a locket.

The minister's wife fainted, and the duenna began pounding on the bandit's back as he moved
toward her ward.

Angela nervously moved her hand into the
pocket of her skirt and grasped the small derringer strapped to her thigh. The young bandit
had moved on to Aggie Bauer, who lay unconscious, having fainted against the large coach
wheel. As his wife's bodice was opened and
searched, the minister turned away, thankful that
his wife was unaware.

Angela stiffened as the young man approached
her. He stared for a long moment at her face and
his eyes crinkled again. She might have mistaken
him for Bradford, for he was built similarly and
had the same wavy black hair.

"You will find nothing of worth on my person."
She tried to sound calm, though fear and anger
were tearing at her. "Everything I own is in my
trunks."

"We shall see," he said.

He began to search the pockets of her light
jacket, then inspected the hem of her jacket and
also the hem of her skirt. She stood still for this,
but when he stood up to face her again, the furious look in her eyes made him hesitate.

"You will not be troublesome now, *señorita*. As I
explained to the other ladies, what I must do now
is necessary."

"But I told you I have nothing of value on me!"
Angela returned in a loud voice.

"I must see for myself," he replied, and started
to unbutton her bodice.

"You touch me and I will kill you." She said it
slowly, almost in a whisper.

He noticed the bulge at the side of her skirt and
his eyes narrowed. "Yes, I believe you would,
señorita. But if you do this, then my friends will
shoot you. Are you prepared to die at such a
young age, for such a small thing?"

Angela's courage left her and it showed in her
eyes.

"Come now, *menina*." The man spoke softly so
that only she could hear. "It will be over with
quickly—it will not be so bad. And I will even
leave you your little weapon."

Angela closed her eyes and let him continue to

unbutton her bodice. When she opened her eyes, she found that he was holding her gold coin in his hand.

"You lied, *señorita*."

"I did not lie. The coin has no value. You can see there's a hole in it. Please," she whispered, her eyes pleading, "don't take it."

"It must have value, or you would not want to keep it," he replied, turning the coin over in his hand.

"It has value only to me!" she cried, and jerked the coin out of his hand.

He shrugged and his eyes crinkled again. "Well, let us see what other treasures you have hidden."

He unfastened two more buttons, then slipped his hand inside her bodice. Angela's face brightened with humiliation when his fingers moved slowly under each breast.

She gasped and, without thinking, slapped the man's face. His eyes turned dark. Before she had a chance to regret the impulse, he grabbed her about the waist with one arm and pulled her to him. In the next instant he raised his bandanna and kissed her, then released her just as quickly and covered his face again.

"I have found much of value, *señorita*," he said in a quiet voice, his face close to hers. "Were there not the danger of someone coming this way, then I would stay to explore your other treasures."

Angela fumed with outrage. "You—you—"

"Bandit? Outlaw?" he interrupted with an amused chuckle. "Yes, I am. And since I always do a thorough job, I will take this," he added, yanking the coin from her neck. "To remember you by, violet eyes."

She started to plead again, then understood, looking at him, that there was no point. She watched with a terrible sense of loss as he turned from her and mounted his horse.

Everything she owned was gone. All her clothes and jewels and money, and the precious coin from Bradford.

She knew it was ridiculous, but the coin meant more to her than everything else.

Thirty-seven

Angela sat across from the sheriff's desk, close to tears. "But everything I owned was in my luggage—my jewels, my money!"

"I'm sorry, Miss Sherrington, but there's nothing we can do. Perhaps you have relatives you can send word to," Sheriff Thornton offered.

Angela stared hopelessly at the floor. "There is only my mother," she said, more to herself than to him.

"Then there's no problem, ma'am. We'll just get in touch with your mother and—"

"I wish that were possible, sheriff," Angela interrupted him. "But you see, I don't know where my mother is. That's why I came to Texas—to find her."

Sheriff Thornton shook his head. "I guess you'll be needing a job then. The restaurant at the hotel needs a waitress. If you've had schooling, I might be able to get you a job at the bank. Then once you have a job, I'll talk to Ella about giving you a room at her boardinghouse on credit. Maybe you can save enough to get you where you want to go."

"I don't know, Sheriff Thornton," Angela said, "but I do appreciate your help."

Angela walked slowly down the hall to her room at Ella Crain's boardinghouse. It was a comfortable room, with homemade furnishings, and a large double bed that she could lose herself in each night.

Two weeks in this small town seemed like two years. The other passengers had all been able to draw money from the bank where she now worked, and had gone their ways. How long would she be stuck here? She had thought briefly of sending word to Jacob, to ask him for money. But then she thought better of it. No good could come of it. Even though Jacob loved her, he was obviously ashamed of her. Otherwise he would have acknowledged her as his daughter.

Angela opened the door to her room and then shut it slowly. She leaned back against the door and closed her eyes with a heavy sigh. What did she have to look forward to? Only dinner in the large dining room downstairs. And then back to her room and a restless sleep. When would it be different? Would she stay in this small, dreary town for the rest of her life?

A slight noise made her open her eyes and glance around. She gasped when she saw the man sprawled on her bed.

"Who are you?" she cried as her hand slipped into her pocket to grasp the derringer. "What are you doing in my room?"

The stranger leaned over on an elbow to face her, a wide grin forming on his lips. "You would not shoot me, *señorita*, when I have come here to do you a service?"

"How do you know I have a gun? And—" Angela stopped short and her eyes widened. "You! It *is* you! How dare you!"

"Ah, I dare much, *señorita*. But as I said, I came to do you a service," he answered easily, and sat up on the edge of the bed, his dark gray eyes studying her intently.

Angela stayed where she was, one hand on the doorknob, her other hand holding her gun. "What service do you speak of?"

"You are not frightened of me, eh?" he asked, amusement in his voice.

"Why should I be?" she returned tartly, her chin tilted up. "Your friends are not here to protect you now." As she spoke, she quickly glanced around the room to make sure she was right. She looked back at him with confidence and added, "Before you could draw that gun strapped to your leg, I would shoot you. Don't doubt it."

"I do not doubt it," he said casually. "But relax. I mean you no harm."

"I could shoot you just for being in my room. And believe me, the prospect is quite tempting after what you've done! And I would be justified," she warned. "There are wanted posters out on you, you know."

"Yes, I have seen them," he said with a shrug of his wide shoulders, and stood up to light the candle by the bed. "You described me quite well."

"How—what makes you think I gave the description?" she asked in surprise.

He stood by the bedside table and faced her, a smile playing on his supple lips. "The others did not look at me as you did. They were not aware of me as you were."

"I don't know what you're talking about!"

He laughed then. "Of course you do, *menina*. To you I was not just a bandit, but a man. And to me, you were not just another victim, but a woman, and such a beautiful woman."

Angela's face burned as she remembered how he had touched her. "Get out of here before I scream for help and have you arrested! Or better yet, I *will* shoot you!"

He took a few steps toward her. "You would do that to me after I have risked coming here to return your jewels?"

"My jewels?" She looked at him in complete bewilderment.

"Why not put away your little weapon and

come away from the door, *señorita*? I promise not to surprise you with any tricks." When she stayed rooted to the spot, he chuckled. "You still do not trust me, eh? Look on your dresser, *menina*, and you will see your box of jewels there."

Angela turned her eyes away from him gradually and saw her black velvet jewel box. She forgot about him completely in her haste to inspect the box. She laid her gun down on the dresser and opened the lid gently. Everything was there, all her beautiful jewels, and the three settings from Bradford—everything except her gold coin.

"This is an amusing toy, *señorita*."

Angela turned around quickly to find the outlaw standing close to her, examining her derringer. She gasped, realizing how stupid she had been. She was defenseless now and she watched with wide eyes as he slipped the gun in his pocket. She started to scream, but he grabbed her swiftly and covered her mouth with his hand.

"You must trust me, *menina*, for you have no choice. If you scream, you will bring help, of course. But you will not like what happens. You have your jewels now. They will not believe that an outlaw would return loot out of the goodness of his heart. No, they will think you are my accomplice—for that is what I will tell them."

When he lowered his hand from her mouth, she didn't scream, but glared at him accusingly. "Why *did* you return the jewels?" she asked coldly.

"Why not?"

"But you could have pawned them for money!"

He shrugged, still holding her with one arm. "It is too risky to exchange objects of value for money—too easy to be traced. No, we usually give jewels and the like to our lady friends, in return for—ah, favors."

Angela jerked out of his hold and walked away from him. "Is that what you want from me, a *favor*?"

"And if I asked one of you, would you grant it?"

Angela swung around to face him, her hands on her hips and her eyes flashing angrily. "No!" she replied sharply. "And where is my gold coin? It's not with the other jewels."

He looked puzzled. "But I left it behind, in the pocket of a green jacket. You did not find it yet?"

"No—I—"

She ran for her wardrobe without saying any more. Quickly she found the coin and held it tightly in the palm of her hand. All her anger left her. She turned around, ready to express her thanks, but stopped when she found him only inches from her. He rested his hands on the wardrobe, one arm on each side of her, effectively pinning her there.

"When you are happy, you are even more lovely, *menina*," he said in a soft voice close to her face.

"Stop calling me that!" she retorted. "I don't even know what it means."

He laughed heartily, and she noted again how handsome he was. His face was smooth and clean-shaven. Lights danced in his gray eyes. Though he was an outlaw, he didn't seem a cruel man.

"How did you know those were my jewels, or where to put the coin?" Angela asked.

"The gold rings with the other jewelry were perfect settings for this coin you treasure so much," he answered smoothly. His eyes held hers as he continued, "I decided one meeting was not enough for you and me."

"Well, now that you have seen me again and you have returned my jewels, would you please leave? You were crazy to come here in the first place."

He looked like a little boy, his brow wrinkled in disappointment. "Is this the gratitude I get?"

"I thank you for returning my jewels, but it was because of you that I was forced to seek employment and end my journey. Should I thank you for that, too?"

"Ah, such bitterness from one so lovely." He ran one finger along the side of her cheek. "But you would have had to seek employment eventually, when your money and jewels were exhausted. Am I right?"

"What makes you think that?" she asked, surprise showing on her features.

"If there were anyone to help you, *menina*, then

you would not be here now," he replied. "No, I think you have no one."

"Well, you are wrong, *señor*, for I have very powerful friends," she retorted. "Only I do not wish to impose on them."

"Perhaps you speak the truth, perhaps not," he speculated, lowering his face even closer to hers. "But what does it matter? Now you will continue your journey. Tell me where you go, *menina*, so I can find you again."

Her reply was cut off as his lips covered hers. Though outraged, she found herself caught up by his passion. His hands on her shoulders were like steel, pressing her against him. His kiss was molten fire. She did not think. She yielded.

She didn't know when he carried her to the bed, but she soon found herself there with the dark-haired stranger. By then, nothing mattered but being born again in his touch. And when his hands began to unlace her bodice and his lips followed the trail of his fingers, she could not contain herself any longer.

"Bradford!" she cried out. "Bradford! I love you."

She opened her eyes and found a cold, enraged face above her. His eyes were frightening.

"I'm sorry," she gasped. It was the only thing she could think to say.

"For what?" he asked sharply. "Sorry that you led me to believe something that is not so? Or sorry that I am not Bradford?"

"You don't understand—"

"Yes I do," he said, cutting off her explanation. He leaned over her, his fingers digging into her shoulders. "I could still take you, *menina*. Even though you want someone else, I can make you forget him."

"Don't!" Angela implored, tears brimming. "Please!"

"Why?" he demanded. "Why? You let me think you were willing. And I still want you."

Angela was sobbing now, but whether it was fear or regret, she didn't know. "But I do love another—or did! He was the only . . . Even though it can never be, he must be the only one."

The man swore violently in Spanish and left the bed. Standing beside it, he looked down at her tear-streaked face and said harshly, "You were right, *señorita*. I do not understand." He took her derringer from his pocket and tossed it on the bed beside her. "When I love a woman, she must be with me, not with a man from her memories. So I leave you to your memories, and I wish you whatever pleasure you can find in them. *Adios*."

Thirty-eight

It didn't take Angela long to pack. Soon, wearing a light blue traveling dress and matching brocaded jacket, she sat waiting at the stage depot. There were three others waiting, men in dark suits and derby hats—comically out of place in this barely civilized land.

When the tall, dark-haired man walked in and sat down beside her, Angela stood up immediately, but he rose at the same time and took hold of her elbow. He leaned close.

"If I believed you could get used to a different way of life, I would take you with me to Mexico, to the land I will have back one day, the land that was stolen from my family."

"I wouldn't go with you!" she said firmly.

"I did not say I would ask your permission, *menina*," he replied just as firmly.

Before she could answer, his arms encircled her waist. She tried to move away from him, but he held her too hard. Their battle joined, both were startled by the voice behind Angela.

"Do you give your favors away so freely now, Angela?"

"Grant!" she gasped, whirling to face the angry green eyes. "What—are you doing here?"

"I just arrived on the stage. But maybe you'd rather I hadn't," he said, staring coldly at the bandit.

"Stop being so presumptuous!" Angela snapped. "This is—a friend of mine. We were just saying good-bye."

The bandit laughed softly. "Yes," he agreed, and brought Angela's hand slowly to his lips. "I hope we will meet again one day. Till then, *adios.*"

He walked away quickly. Angela turned to face Grant, ready for the lecture she was sure he would give her. She was shocked when he said, "I've missed you."

What could she say?

"Is that why you came?"

"No," Grant replied, his voice growing somber. "Jim McLaughlin came to the ranch looking for you and asked if I'd help."

"What does he want with me?"

Grant looked down at the floor, his face solemn. "He has some matters to discuss with you. Angela . . . Jacob Maitland is dead."

He helped the stricken young woman out of

the stage depot. In their preoccupation, neither of them noticed the man hiding in the corner behind a newspaper. He had just arrived, and Angela had not seen him.

Billy Anderson's eyes were gleaming. He had succeeded! He had followed Jim McLaughlin all the way from Mobile, knowing the lawyer had business with Angela, sure he would lead Billy to her. The time was not right for what he had in mind, but Billy could be patient. After years of waiting, a little longer wouldn't matter.

An hour later, Angela and Jim McLaughlin sat in a small office at the bank while he read to her from a long document. She tried to listen but the words didn't register. She sat very still in a hard-back chair, staring blankly at the paper in Jim's hands. But what she saw was Jacob, sitting in his study, his eyes lighting up when she arrived to help him with the books. And Jacob in the dining room, Jacob with his slightly graying hair, leaning sideways to whisper something to her. Jacob.

Jacob dead? No, he would still be at Golden Oaks, giving orders. Jacob was too real to be dead. So why was Jim McLaughlin sitting here reading Jacob's will?

"Did you understand all I've read, Angela?" Jim McLaughlin asked kindly.

"What?"

She glanced up, her eyes blank.

"I realize this has been quite a shock to you, Angela," Jim said.

"Let me sum it up for you," he continued. "You will have twelve thousand dollars a year, which you may draw on any bank. And two residences now belong solely to you—a comfortable town house in Massachusetts, and a small estate in England. Aside from these, you may use any residence from the bulk of the estate at your convenience. Should anyone deny you welcome—I assume this to mean Bradford, since he owns these properties now—they will be disinherited. This was a harsh stipulation, but Jacob insisted on it. Beyond all of that, you now own half interest in the JB Ranch, the other half belonging to Bradford. The ranch is quite large, consisting of thousands of acres, and I believe it is now being restored. Once it becomes productive, you will be a very wealthy woman, even more than you already are."

Angela listened in astonishment. Jacob had been extraordinarily generous. She no longer had to worry about money.

"If you'll let me advise you, Angela, it might be a good idea to retire to your ranch for a while. Grant Marlowe will be going back there, so he can escort you. It will give you time to get over the shock of Jacob's death, and to decide what you want to do. There are limitless possibilities. Travel is one, and you won't even have to stay in hotels, because there are Maitland properties all over the world."

"Yes, well, maybe I will go to the ranch for a while," Angela replied.

She would no longer have to travel this wild land in search of her mother. She could hire someone else to do the searching for her.

"Have you understood everything?" Jim asked.

"Yes."

"Well then, there is nothing left for me to do but give you a copy of the will and this letter from Jacob," Jim said, handing the articles to her.

Angela took the letter without surprise, for she had been expecting it, or something like it. She knew what would be in it—Jacob explaining that she was his daughter and how it had all happened. Holding the letter, she suddenly felt Jacob's presence. She shook off the feeling, knowing it was absurd. Jim McLaughlin quietly left the room as she opened the envelope.

My dearest Angela,

I will be dead when you read this letter, and I hope with all my heart that you will not grieve for me. You were a blessing to me in my last years, the daughter I always wanted, and I could not bear it if I caused you any unhappiness.

That is one reason why I could not bring myself to tell you about your mother. I regret having to tell you now that she is dead, and buried on my ranch in Texas.

Angela sat immobile, the letter in her hand. She did not move for a long time.

Her mother was dead, and Jacob had known all along. The tears began. Angela cried hard for her mother. And then, finally, she cried for Jacob.

At last, she continued reading:

I blame myself for her death. It was so tragic—she was so young.

You see, I loved your mother with all my heart. And she loved me. But we realized our love too late, after I was married and had children to care for.

I would have left my wife, but Charissa wouldn't permit it. She would have become my mistress, but I respected her too much to allow that. I regret my decision now, for we argued over it, and Charissa vowed she would go away and marry the first man who asked her.

Your mother was a stubborn woman and she did exactly as she said. I tried desperately to find her after she left Massachusetts, but didn't succeed until a year later. She was married to your father then, and expecting you. I bought Golden Oaks then, for even though we were both married, I couldn't bear to be far from her.

Then, after you were a year old, I had to go to my ranch in Texas. Bradford was staying there and I wanted him at home. Your mother begged me to take her with me. She was unable to bear marriage to a man she hardly knew, and life on a farm was so different from what she knew.

The biggest mistake of my life was to refuse to

take Charissa to Texas with me. But the West was no place for a woman in those years, especially a woman of your mother's gentle breeding.

Believe me, Angela, when I say that I never dreamed she would follow me. She came West unescorted, on a wagon train that was attacked by Indians. She was wounded in the attack, and she died when she reached my ranch.

Her dying wish was that I look after you, though I would have done that without being asked.

Forgive me, Angela, for not telling you this before. I just couldn't bring myself to do so. I was afraid you would blame me for your mother's death, as I have blamed myself.

My fondest dream has always been that you marry my older son. I have seen that you love him, and that he loves you. The two of you will have the life that Charissa and I were denied.

You are so like your mother, Angela. She lives again in you. Be happy, my dear, and don't grieve for us. If there is a heaven, then I am with your mother now.

> *With deepest love,*
> *Jacob*

Angela read the letter again and then again. She wasn't Jacob's daughter after all. She wasn't Bradford's half sister!

But what of the letter Crystal had used to taunt

Bradford? Had she invented that letter? Of course! Crystal would have done anything to get Bradford back, or to hurt Angela.

Still, Bradford *had* been engaged to Candise all the while he professed his love for her. What a bastard he really was!

Just then, Jim McLaughlin knocked on the door and stuck his head in. "Are you ready to leave, Angela?"

Angela and Jim left the small office and met Grant at the hotel. The three of them shared an early dinner and then left the following morning. Jim traveled with them to Dallas, then left them there to return to New York.

Angela had refrained from asking about Bradford and Candise. She didn't want to know whether they were married yet.

She was relieved to learn that Bradford had returned to New York, and had engulfed himself in business affairs. She was fairly sure that he wouldn't be coming to the Texas ranch, so there would be no hurry for her to leave it.

The JB Ranch was only twelve miles outside of Dallas. Angela and Grant rode in a small buckboard through the barren land, flat prairie relieved only by low-lying hills and a few sparse trees. The ranch house was just as Bradford had described it, though fairly run-down. There was the long one-story house itself, a large barn and corrals to the left of it, and a bunkhouse opposite the barn. There were a few large old trees by the

large house, and on the right was a patch of
ground where there had once been a garden.

Grant apologized for the appearance of the
place, explaining that he had had only enough
time to hire a few men, and that most of them
were on the range rounding up the scattered cattle. Two men were repairing the corral and the
barn.

The house needed a great deal of work. Windows were broken, paint had peeled, a side railing off the porch was lying in the dirt. Angela saw
all of this from the outside, and shuddered to
think what the inside looked like. She had her
work cut out for her. But then, she had lots of time
to do it in. And, she realized, she now had something useful to do, hard work that she would enjoy doing, work to keep her from brooding.

Billy Anderson, hidden behind a nearby hill,
turned his horse around. He had seen Angela go
inside the ranch house with the large man. Billy
knew where to find her now. He rode back to
town, sure that he wouldn't have to wait much
longer. His only obstacle now would be finding
her alone.

Thirty-nine

Angela finished the breakfast dishes and sat down at the kitchen table for another cup of strong black coffee. She glanced out of the window above the kitchen sink to see the sun just clearing the mountain range in the far distance. She felt strangely contented, remembering how she used to watch the sun rise on the small farm in Alabama. Her life wasn't all that different now, except that she didn't have any fields to plow, or worries about whether the crop this year would be a good one. The small garden she had started a month before was the only crop here.

Grant had warned her that it was ridiculous to start a garden this late in the season, what with the cold ready to set in in a few months. But she had tried anyway. She wanted fresh vegetables, or those she would jar herself, not the canned stuff she had been forced to buy from Mr. Benson's mercantile store.

The large ranch house looked like a home now. The storeroom was stocked with supplies that would last at least three months, and Angela had started making comforters for the beds. Last week she had ordered the men to scrub down the bunkhouse, which they did only grudgingly. They had flatly refused to let her replace the flour sacks over their windows with curtains.

Most of the hired men were still rounding up cattle out on the range and in the hills. Grant said it would probably be at least another month before the herd was brought in. Then they would be branded and set to graze nearby until it was time to drive them along the Chisholm Trail to Kansas. The drive would take about two months, and the cattle that hadn't died on the way would be shipped East by rail.

Her only company was Grant, and that was only for dinner and only occasionally. Then he would leave and she would go to bed, alone. Grant had mellowed after Angela became the "boss-lady," as he teasingly called her. They no longer fought. Nor did he ask her to marry him again. But Angela liked the change, for Grant was a friend now and she enjoyed his company.

Angela got up and walked to the front door when she heard the horse approach. She stepped out on the porch to see a young woman on a black mustang. The woman was dressed in tight breeches and an open-necked white shirt with a short brown vest. The woman looked familiar, with light auburn hair in a short ponytail, and soft blue eyes. And then Angela's eyes widened.

"Mary Lou?"

The other woman laughed, happily surprised. "Angela, is that really you, honey? Well, I'll be!"

They both laughed and hugged each other. Angela was thrilled to see the only schoolmate she had ever been friendly with. And Mary Lou was equally delighted. Once they were inside and coffee was poured, a swarm of questions followed.

"I'd heard in town that a woman was living out here on the JB," Mary Lou began as soon as they were seated on the long couch, covered now in a pattern of red and yellow autumn leaves. "I just couldn't believe it. There's never been a woman here before, so I had to come see for myself. And now I find it's you of all people! What are you doing here? Did you marry Bradford Maitland after all?"

Angela stiffened, humiliated by remembering what a fool she had been for so many years. "No, Bradford's father died and left half of the ranch to me."

"You own it? That's wonderful—I mean, about the ranch, not about Mr. Maitland."

"You know, I've been so busy fixing up the house, I completely forgot that you lived near here."

"Only ten miles. And my father's spread is fif-

teen miles south of here. But our ranches combined aren't nearly as big as the JB. And goodness, you certainly have changed this place,"
Mary Lou said, looking around her. "I used to
come here when I was a girl, and it didn't look
like this. Of course, it was only Mr. Maitland and
Bradford then, and you know how men can be.
They don't care for comforts the way we do."

"Yes, so I've learned," Angela laughed and explained how she had tried to brighten up the
bunkhouse. "But tell me how you are. You've
been married a couple of years now. Are there
any children yet?"

"No children," Mary Lou returned with a
slight blush. "But my husband, Charles, died last
winter."

"Oh—I'm so sorry."

"Don't be, Angela. There was no love between
us. Charles was a lot older than I, and my father
arranged the marriage. My father wanted the two
ranches to be combined."

"That's terrible!" Angela exclaimed. "To be
married off like that."

"It doesn't matter now," Mary Lou smiled.
"The two ranches are combined, but my father
isn't in charge, because I'm running Charles's
ranch on my own now."

"Good for you," Angela laughed. "You're just
the girl who can do it."

"I like to think so," Mary Lou replied with an
impish grin. "But are you running the JB? I heard

you have men out on the range rounding up the JB cattle that have been running wild since the war."

"That's none of my doing," Angela said. "Bradford hired Grant Marlowe as foreman, and he's in charge of everything."

"Humph! That's just like them, Bradford in particular. They were always know-it-alls, even when they were boys. I remember they'd never let me go riding with them—they said I was too young. But I'd tag along anyhow, just to show them. I see they're still know-it-alls who think a woman can't do anything."

Angela laughed, for she had caught a definite sparkle in Mary Lou's eyes when Grant's name was mentioned.

They continued talking for the rest of the morning, then Mary Lou said she had to go. Angela saw her out to the porch with the promise that Mary Lou would come for dinner on Saturday night and bring her father.

As she watched Mary Lou ride off down the path leading from the house, Angela's eye was caught by the large hard-wood tree some distance by the road, and the grave beneath it. She had discovered the grave the day after her arrival and visited it often whenever no one else was around.

She turned as she saw Grant by the well and started toward him. Grant finished filling a second bucket of water and set it down on the ground. He smiled as she approached. She had her hair tied back with a red bandanna, and was wearing a crisp yellow blouse tucked into a russet skirt. As dark as the skirt was, it still showed dirt stains around the knees from where she'd knelt in her garden. But she still looked as beautiful and fresh as ever, Grant thought wistfully.

"You're gonna end up ruinin' all your pretty clothes, boss-lady, if you don't give up on that fool garden," Grant teased.

Angela looked down at her skirt and smiled. "I guess I'll just have to start wearing breeches again, like I did on my pa's farm."

"I ain't so sure that's a good idea," Grant replied. "I'd like the men to get some work done, not spend their time watchin' you in that damn garden."

"How would it be if I wore baggy shirts?"

"You're gonna do as you damn well please anyway, so why ask me?"

She laughed and pointed to the buckets of water. "Are those for me?"

"Yeah. I thought you'd be wantin' 'em about now, but if you ask me, it's a waste of water."

"You'll change your tune once you get a taste of fresh vegetables on the table. Come spring, I thought I'd widen the area and plant some corn and peas too."

"This is a ranch, not a farm, Angela."

"It never hurts to be self-sufficient."

"Well, it's your land," he shrugged. "Was Mary Lou Markham here?"

Angela nodded. "You knew her before the war, didn't you? Back when your father was foreman here?"

"Yeah. She's turned out right pretty from the girl I remember. Though I see she hasn't changed much. Still a tomboy."

"She's running her own ranch now. That can't be easy."

"She should have gone back to her father when Charles Markham died, instead of tryin' to prove she can run a ranch by herself," he snorted.

"You're so sure of what everyone should do! You're infuriating, Grant!"

He laughed. "Yeah, I've been called names before."

Angela shook her head and watched Grant saunter back to the barn. He really was impossible. But she had grown very fond of him.

With Grant out of sight, Angela turned and walked slowly across the dirt yard to her mother's grave and knelt down beside it. This was a private time for her, one she didn't indulge in often.

"What are you doin' out here, Angela?" Grant spoke from behind her, causing her to jump. "This is twice now I've spotted you by this grave."

"You were here when she died, weren't you, Grant?" she asked in a soft voice, disregarding his question.

Grant stared for a moment at the wooden cross. "Yeah, I was here. I was a kid—five, I think—when old man Maitland buried her there himself. My pa told me about the woman later. He said Jacob took her death real hard."

"Wasn't Bradford here when it happened?"

"Fact is, Jacob had only arrived a few days earlier. He had sent Brad to town to close out his accounts. The old man made Brad take care of all his own responsibilities, even when he was young."

"But he found out about it when he returned?"

"No. For some reason, Jacob didn't want him to know anything about it. They left the next day to return to Alabama. But why all the questions, Angela? You couldn't have known the woman. You must have been just a baby when it happened."

Tears came, and she couldn't stop them. "I knew her," she murmured softly, "for a short time."

"She was your mother, wasn't she?"

"Yes."

Grant's green eyes darkened. "I'm sorry, Angela."

"I'm all right, Grant," Angela said weakly. "I grieved for my mother when I was a child—when I didn't have her with me. All these years, I thought she was alive. I only recently learned that she died here so long ago. I'm so sorry I never knew her."

They were silent for several minutes, and then Angela turned around and started back to the house. In her room, she cried for the lost love of Jacob and Charissa, and for her mother, whom she would not see again.

Forty

The wind howled fiercely against the windows. The sky was a black sheet, as if thick curtains had been drawn against the moon and stars. With the wind came the cold, seeping in through loose boards in the walls.

"Looks like we'll be getting some rain finally," Angela remarked as she poured Grant a second cup of coffee and then went back into the kitchen.

"More like a storm," he replied and picked up his guitar to start a sad, lonely tune. "Hope your little garden can withstand a heavy downpour."

As Grant continued strumming his guitar, she asked, "You will be available for dinner tomorrow night, won't you?"

"That's twice you've asked me that," Grant replied. "What's so special about tomorrow night?"

"Well, you usually go into town with the men

on Saturday night. I just want to be sure you'll be here. I'm having guests."

He looked up at her now, his brow raised. "Oh?"

"Mary Lou and her father will be here," Angela said quickly, hoping he wouldn't object. "You don't mind, do you?"

Grant smiled. "Why should I mind? As a matter of fact, I haven't seen Walter Howard in years. The evenin' ought to be quite interestin'."

"Why do you say that?"

"Have you met Walter Howard?" Grant asked, amused.

"No."

"If he hasn't changed, I think you'll find him a little, uh, difficult. You'll probably hear his views on women before the evenin' is through, and you certainly won't agree with him."

"Another Grant Marlowe, only older, is that what you mean?" she asked.

He laughed heartily. "Now have I ever told you what you should or shouldn't be doin'?"

"You certainly have," she laughed. "In fact, that's about all you ever—"

The door burst open with a gust of wind and Angela looked up into a glowering face.

She could have sworn she was looking into the fires of hell, but the golden blaze belonged to Bradford Maitland, who stood just inside the doorway, his saddle in one hand, his bedroll and saddlebags in the other.

What on earth was he doing here, covered in dust and bedraggled, with a thick stubble of beard covering his face? And why did he look at her as if he wanted to kill her? She had imagined many times their meeting again, but never like this, with the furies of hell showing in his eyes. *She* was the one who had every right to be furious, not he!

Bradford finally looked away from her and dropped his saddle on the floor, making Angela jump. She watched the dust fly off the saddle and the rushing wind catch the dust and scatter it about the room. Bradford then kicked the door shut. With the wind locked outside once again, the room suddenly felt stifling.

With great effort, Angela tore her eyes away from Bradford and looked at Grant. He stood a few paces away from the couch. These two men were friends. Then why then did Grant look so wary? And why didn't Bradford say something?

The strained silence continued as Bradford moved across the room to the kitchen and dumped the rest of his gear on the table there, scattering more trail dust. Angela followed him with her eyes, remembering all the sleepless nights she had spent cursing this man. She wanted to lash out at him now, but she couldn't find the power to speak, or even to move.

Bradford broke the silence, his voice strained and hard as he faced Grant. "I can see that neither of you expected me, but I'm here. It was unfortunate that I had to break up your tender scene. Now I want you to get your things, Grant, and clear out."

"You firin' me, Brad?"

"Of course not. We have a deal," Bradford said harshly. "I have no intention of letting a *woman* break it. Now get your things and move them back into the bunkhouse."

"But that's where my gear has always been!" Grant replied indignantly. "If you've got a bone to pick, Brad, I wish you'd get to it."

"Nothing of the sort. So you've practiced discretion for the lady's sake," Bradford sneered cruelly. "That's very commendable. But I'm tired, so please get the hell out of here and take her with you."

Grant looked quickly at Angela, whose violet eyes were steadily growing darker. Brad had no call to talk about Angela that way.

"You've got it all wrong, Brad," Grant began, his own temper rising. "There's nothin'—"

"Save it!" Bradford cut him off sharply. "Now do I have to throw you out of here, or will you do as you're told?"

"I'm goin', damnit!" Grant shouted angrily, then turned to Angela and lowered his voice. "Maybe you'd better come with me," he offered gently, but he could see that her temper had surfaced too.

"No!" she cried, folding her arms across her

breasts. "This is my house as much as it is his and I'll be damned if I'll leave it!"

"What the hell are you talking about?" Bradford demanded, coming forward to stand between the open shelves that reached from floor to ceiling, serving as a wall to divide the kitchen from the living area.

Angela looked directly at him without flinching. "Jacob left half of this ranch to me. You must know that."

"If I had known, I wouldn't be here!" Bradford stormed.

He cursed himself silently for not paying attention when the will was read, or looking it over when he had the chance. He had assumed Angela would be here, but he was sure he could get rid of her easily. Now what the hell was he going to do?

"I have a copy of the will if you don't believe me," Angela said stiffly.

His eyes met hers again, and she refused to be cowered by the burning rage. She had been frightened of Bradford before, but she would not be intimidated by him anymore.

Bradford finally spoke. "I have my own copy of the will, and I shall read it. If what you say is true, then I will buy you out."

"No thank you," she replied icily. "I happen to like it here."

Bradford was livid. "Do you honestly intend to stay in this house with me?"

"Why shouldn't I?"

"Because you will regret it, Miss Sherrington. I promise you that!"

Bradford turned and stalked down the hall. Soon, she and Grant heard one of the bedroom doors open and then slam shut.

"You better go now, Grant. I'll talk to him in the morning."

"It don't look like the two of you can have a civil conversation. Maybe you better let me talk to him," Grant offered. "Brad seems to have gotten some mighty wrong impressions."

"No, I'll work it out. You just remember to be here on time tomorrow night."

Grant grinned. "Are you sure Bradford will let me in the house?"

"I'm sorry about that, Grant. You were here at my invitation tonight and I should have stood up for you. I assumed Bradford knew I owned half of the ranch, but he didn't. It won't happen again. I can invite anyone I please into this house."

"Then I'll be here tomorrow night. But I advise you to stay clear of Brad for the rest of the night. Let him cool off before you try to explain anything to him."

Angela stared, aghast. "I have nothing to explain!" she snapped. "Bradford Maitland is the one who has explaining to do—if he can!" she added bitterly.

Grant shook his head. "I have a suspicion why

Brad was so riled, but what have you got to be so angry about?"

"Never mind, Grant. Now go on and get some sleep. I have a lot of thinking to do," she replied.

He left then, and she moved about the room turning off all the oil lamps except one. She did not expect to sleep well that night.

Forty-one

Morning dawned bright and sunny, without a trace of yesterday's brooding black clouds. The storm had left behind large puddles throughout the house, caused by holes in the roof.

Angela was beside herself when she discovered the soaked rugs in the main room and the pools of water on the kitchen floor. The rain had even leaked into the storeroom, ruining two sacks of flour and a large barrel of cornmeal she had foolishly left half open the night before.

It took her two hours to clean up the mess and to pull the large living-room rugs out onto the porch to dry over the railing. She was exhausted by the time she finished, having slept very little during the night. It was Saturday, and she had invited Mary Lou and her father to dinner.

Angela dreaded the prospect of seeing Bradford again. She would have to face him eventually. And then what?

Angela reheated the coffee Bradford had made
earlier, then fixed herself a light breakfast. While
she was sitting at the table, he came in through the
kitchen door, stopping abruptly when he saw her.

"Any more of those left?" he asked curtly, indi-
cating the biscuit she was holding.

Angela sighed. He couldn't even offer a civil
morning greeting. She stared at him as he stood
belligerently in the middle of the room. He was
clean-shaven now, and his hair was still damp
from bathing. But the bath had done nothing for
his sour disposition.

"There are only a couple more in the oven, but I
can make you some eggs and hotcakes if you
like."

"Don't bother," Bradford replied, then added
irritably, "And a ranch is no place for those damn
chickens I saw out back."

"I happen to like eggs and roast chicken," she
told him, trying desperately to keep her voice
level.

"Ed Cox raises chickens just for that purpose,"
he retorted.

"I know," she smiled. "That's where I got my
chickens. And I might remind you that I don't
need your permission to keep them."

He grunted and moved to the counter. "What

about this?" he asked, lifting up the towel covering a large loaf of golden cornbread.

"That is for the dressing I'm going to make for
tonight's dinner," Angela replied.

"You can make more cornbread later, can't
you?" he asked impatiently.

"Yes, but—"

Bradford picked up a knife and cut the loaf in
half. She sighed and moved away from the table
to get syrup and more butter. Without a word, she
set the food on the table, then brought him a
steaming cup of strong black coffee.

He sat silently eating at the table with his back
to her. Angela fumed. He was treating her like a
servant. She would be damned if she would go to
any bother for him again. He could eat when she
did, or he could fix his own.

She busied herself at the counter, starting another batch of cornbread.

"Bradford," she began, without turning away
from the counter, "there will be guests for dinner
tonight. I've invited Mary Lou Markham and her
father, Walter Howard. And Grant too. Can I expect you also?"

"Quite the little hostess, aren't you?" he asked
bitterly. "So the runaway sparrow has found a
nest. Just so I'll know, do you have these little
parties every night?"

Angela's back stiffened and she turned around
to face him. He was sitting sideways with the cof-

fee cup in his hands, and looking at her in a contemptuous manner.

"For your information, this is the first time I
have invited guests to dinner."

"Besides Grant," he replied, his voice turning
harsh.

Angela gasped. So that was it! Bradford was
acting like this because of Grant. But that was
ridiculous. He had absolutely no right to be jealous, not when he was engaged.

"Bradford, I invite Grant to have dinner occasionally because we have become friends. There
is nothing between Grant and me."

"I am not a fool, Angela," Bradford said drily
and walked to the door. "Nor do I give a damn
who you keep company with. And as for tonight,
no, I won't be here for your little party. I'm going
into town this afternoon, and since I feel the need
of a good whore, I probably won't be back
tonight." He opened the door, then turned back to
her. "Unless, of course, *you* would like to oblige
me. I pay top dollar for a good whore, and as I remember, you were quite a good one." He chuckled at her shocked face.

Bradford leaned precariously against the long
black bar, staring pensively at the glass of
whiskey before him. He had drunk heavily all
evening while playing cards at a corner table. He
was finally feeling the results of his liquor con-

sumption and had only just quit the game. He had lost more than two hundred dollars. But what the hell, it was only money.

He drained his glass and then bought a full bottle of whiskey from the bartender. He glanced slowly around the smoke-filled room.

Two tawdrily dressed saloon girls had caught his eye earlier, but now he just wasn't inclined. He couldn't deny that he needed a woman. In New York, he had thrown himself into business matters so completely that he hadn't found the time for female company. But he decided just to lose himself in the sweet relief of liquor. He had to drown out the torturous images playing havoc with his mind.

Moving unsteadily, he left the saloon, the bottle of whiskey clutched in his hand. The fresh night air was like a splash of cold water after the stench of smoke and sweat from the crowded saloon. He gained his directions without too much difficulty, and started toward the hotel at the other end of town. The long street seemed deserted, and the din he had just left receded slowly as he walked.

Suddenly a blast of gunfire exploded across the street and Bradford heard a bullet whiz past him. It took him a moment to realize what was happening before he dove for the nearest doorway and crouched into it. He saw a streak of light across the street as another bullet was fired, then another flew from a different gun some yards away from the first. He understood that whoever held those guns were firing at him.

Bradford was instantly reminded of two other recent attacks. He bore a scar from an attack in New York. And not too long after that, he had battled robbers in Springfield. He had come close to losing his life. In fact, now that he thought about it, it seemed the robbers had been more intent on killing him than robbing him.

Could this attack be connected with the other two?

He had no more time to wonder. A bullet embedded itself in the door behind him, inches from his head. He tried to open the door, but it wouldn't budge. The nearest shelter was a plank stairway at the end of the building. There being no other course open, Bradford ran for it quickly, hearing three more shots as he ran.

He crouched down beneath the stairs, cursing himself for not having a gun. He should have known better than to come to town without one. He wondered briefly why his attackers didn't come after him. Maybe they didn't know he was without a gun.

Down the street, people had come out of the saloon to see what the shooting was about. But no one came forward to help. Where the hell was the sheriff, anyway? The men across the street kept up their barrage of gunfire, making it impossible for him to escape. How much longer before they realized he wasn't firing back at them?

Just then one of the men crossed the street. In the dark, Bradford couldn't make out his features. He ducked behind the other side of the building, his new position making Bradford's cover useless. In the next moment the man darted out of his hiding place and fired one shot, then disappeared. In that instant, Bradford felt a searing flame across his skin. His shirt was torn and blood was trickling down his arm, but the bullet only grazed his skin.

A burning rage filled him. How had he let himself be left so helpless? His only chance was to make a run for his hotel, where there was a rifle in his room. He would have to dodge bullets while making a run for the hotel.

Bradford steeled himself to run, his muscles tense, his breathing ragged. He waited until there was a pause in the firing, hoping his assailants were busy reloading. In that moment, he poised himself for flight.

Forty-two

Angela waved good-bye to her guests, waiting on the porch until Mary Lou and her overbearing father had driven off. Angela smiled and breathed deeply of the fresh night air, a pleasant relief after enduring Walter Howard's cigar smoke all evening.

Walter Howard was just as Grant described him—opinionated, raucous of voice. His sunburned skin, large, beaked nose, and jutting chin made Angela wonder where Mary Lou had gotten her delicate features.

Mary Lou seemed to know how to handle her father, which had made the evening bearable. The man thought his ideas were the only ones worth consideration. At first Angela felt her temper rising when the conversation turned to what a woman should or shouldn't be allowed to do on a ranch. But then Grant had whispered to her that he had given her fair warning.

Finally Angela gave up arguing and took Mary Lou's advice: "You just have to smile and ignore Daddy. He's gonna say what he wants to say anyway. Pay him no mind, honey, or he'll never give up."

After a huge meal of roast chicken and dressing with gravy, potato salad, peas, sweetbread, and apple pie, they sat around the fireplace, and Grant entertained them with songs from the trail drives. It was nice while it lasted, but then Grant excused himself early, explaining he had to get up before dawn. Mary Lou and her father stayed a couple more hours. Over coffee, which Walter spiked heavily with whiskey, he spent the rest of the evening extolling Grant's virtues to Mary Lou.

Angela was amused. She knew that Mary Lou didn't need any encouragement. The two of them would make a fine couple, for Mary Lou already had years of experience in handling a man with Grant's temperament. Angela hoped something would come of their flirtation.

Angela stepped back into the house, thinking wistfully of Mary Lou and Grant, and of the courtship they would probably soon begin. Her thoughts led to Bradford . . . and to Candise Taylor. Angela slept fitfully that night.

Bradford sat straight in the saddle, the effects of his hangover wearing off. The night air helped.

What a day, he thought with anguish. Between his retching stomach and his throbbing head, he had spent the whole day in bed. It would take him quite a while to get used to the raw whiskey they served in town.

Bradford glanced silently at his companion, barely making out his features in the moonlight. He had to give his new friend credit for being able to withstand that fiery brew. The man didn't seem to be affected in the least today, and was still as cheerful and smiling as he had been last night, when the two men had met.

The man had saved Bradford's life. He remembered the moment when he prepared to run from his shelter, and the blast of a shotgun. The shotgun had forced a halt to the gunfire directed at him. Another blast followed and Bradford watched in amazement as one of his attackers started running down the street, then quickly ducked into an alley. The other assailant quickly followed.

And then Bradford saw the Mexican sitting on a horse right in the middle of the street. The man just sat there without any cover at all and fired the shotgun.

The stranger nudged his horse over to Bradford. He eyed Bradford with concern.

"You are all right, *amigo?*"

Bradford was still stunned by the close escape.

"I'm fine now, thanks to you," Bradford answered shakily. He finally stood up. "I've only a small nick on my arm."

"Your small nick bleeds a lot," the stranger replied, smiling, showing even white teeth below the bristling black moustache.

"It's nothing."

"You should not go about unprotected, *amigo*," the other man admonished. "Those men, did you know them?"

"I certainly hope not."

"They were trying to rob you then?"

"I don't think so," Bradford replied thoughtfully. "I just lost all of my cash in a poker game. But then, they probably didn't know that."

"It is too bad. If you need a place to bed down, I was on my way to get a room at the hotel. You are welcome to stay with me."

Bradford laughed shortly. "You have already done me the biggest service you could, friend. You saved my life. I insist you let me repay you. Your room at the hotel is on me. The name's Bradford Maitland. Yours?"

"Hank Chavez."

They spent the rest of the night in Bradford's hotel room, getting thoroughly drunk. Bradford felt he couldn't do enough for the man and offered him anything he desired. Hank Chavez refused payment. But since he had business in the area, he accepted Bradford's offer to stay at his ranch.

It was quite late when they reached the ranch, a peaceful setting in the still night. After bedding down their horses in the barn, they approached the house, which was bathed in moonlight and dark inside.

"My, ah—partner—must have gone to bed already," Bradford said quietly as he tried the door and found it locked. "No point in causing a commotion. Are you opposed to climbing through windows?"

"I have left by many a window, but never yet entered by one. It will be a change," Hank Chavez laughed.

After a few moments they were inside the house, moving like cats. Bradford showed Hank to the room across from his and bid him goodnight, then came back to his own and made ready for bed. But having slept most of the day, Bradford lay awake for many hours.

He was troubled by the attack. He had given it more thought and was almost sure now that someone was out to kill him. But who? And why?

Bradford tossed restlessly. Three separate attempts to kill him, all three recently. There would surely be another, and then another. His luck might run out. He had to find out who wanted him dead.

Zachary, of course, had the most to gain. But Zachary had left for London with Crystal. Still, he might have hired someone.

And there was Angela. He had put a damper on her freedom by coming here. Now that he thought about it, the first two attempts had happened before he came here, but after he had met Angela.

Christ! Was she after revenge for what happened in Springfield? Could that be it? Bradford didn't want to believe it—he couldn't.

But who else could there be? He always dealt fairly with business associates. And he made it a point not to gamble with someone who couldn't afford to lose.

His thoughts turned to the woman in the room next to his. Was she really so treacherous?

He got up and tossed on a robe. It took him only moments to reach Angela's room, and he entered it quietly, without waking her. He stood silently by her bed, looking down at her. Angela lay in peaceful slumber, her russet hair spread out in waves around her face. She was wearing a light blue nightgown, with ruffled lace about her neck and at her wrists, and only a loose sheet was draped over her. She was such a beautiful woman, Bradford thought wistfully.

Suddenly rage filled him. He needed to hurt her, to cause her pain as she had hurt him in destroying his love and his trust.

Bradford yanked the sheet away and took off his robe. He sat down on the bed and started to untie the ribbons of her nightgown. She came awake as his fingers brushed against her skin.

Angela's first reaction surprised him. She seemed happy to have him there. But then she remembered what he had said to her as he left.

"So you stayed in town! I guess you couldn't tear yourself away from—from—"

"The town whores?" he finished with a sardonic grin. "I found I didn't need them, not when I have a whore under my own roof."

Angela gasped. Twice now he had called her a whore. But why? And why was he in her room in the middle of the night?

"Bradford, what are you doing in my room? If you came here to insult me, then please leave."

"I haven't insulted you," he said gruffly. "I only spoke the truth. And I'll leave just as soon as I'm finished with you."

She started to sit up, but his hands pushed her back down.

"Bradford, no!" she gasped, her eyes wide with sudden fear.

He clamped his hand over her mouth and she struggled against him. He moved on top of her swiftly and in a desperate attempt to make him stop, she bit his hand.

The pain sobered him. He looked down and groaned, seeing her fear and the tears, like glistening diamonds on her cheeks. He felt sick with revulsion at what he'd tried to do. Irrationally, he blamed Angela for it. He needed to lash out at someone.

"What the hell are you crying for?" His voice was husky. "Can you be feeling remorse over deserting and deceiving me?"

"What are you talking about?" Angela gasped. "I didn't deceive you, *or* desert you!"

"What would you call it then, damn you?" he

raged. "I had already been dealt one shock the day you ran off with Grant Marlowe. My dear sister-in-law was up to her treacherous schemes again. She tried to convince me that you were my half sister! I was going to inform my father of our forthcoming marriage, so I went ahead and did it, waiting for his reaction. The old man was never more pleased in his life, which shot Crystal's lying scheme to hell.

"Then, after I felt my world was right again, you desert me for Grant."

Angela was stricken speechless. She felt relief, regret, and then soaring joy. He had told Jacob he was going to marry *her*, not Candise!

"Bradford, I—"

"Save it!" he cut her off harshly.

"But I never deceived you, Bradford," she said quickly, her eyes brimming with tears again.

"More heartless lies to add to the others?" he replied, his eyes a golden blaze.

"But I'm not lying!"

"What kind of fool do you take me for?" he snarled cruelly.

"Bradford, I love you!" she cried. There, she'd said it, and just then she realized it was true, fully true. "I've never stopped loving you!"

Dear God, how he wanted to believe her! But he would not be drawn into her web again. In his mind's eye, he saw her entwined with Grant, saw it so clearly that his eyes flashed even brighter. His voice was like steel and his fingers dug cruelly into her shoulders. "I believed you once, but I won't make that mistake again!"

She wanted to plead with him. But pride took over. Outrage gripped her.

"What about Candise Taylor, Bradford?" she whispered furiously. "What about the fiancée you had *all the while* you swore you loved me?"

He stared at her for a long moment. She felt a glimmer of satisfaction in his confusion. And then he smiled cruelly.

"You mean my wife? We were married shortly after you disappeared."

She could hardly breathe. Silently, Bradford put on his robe and crossed to the door. Without looking back at her, he said coldly, "I suggest you leave here if you don't want this to happen again."

He was gone. And with him went all the hope that had come to life for a flickering moment.

Forty-three

"Did you sleep well, *amigo?*"

Bradford cast a sideways glance at Hank, who was sitting at the kitchen table with a cup of coffee braced in his hands. Did his friend know what had happened last night? Had he heard anything?

"I slept fine. And you?" Bradford replied, pouring coffee for himself.

Hank laughed. Bradford was getting used to hearing that laugh. "Like a baby, as soon as I hit the pillow. But I am not used to such quiet nights as you have here. It's not like the noisy hotels I am accustomed to."

Angela wasn't up yet, but Bradford told himself he wasn't worried. He didn't care. What would it take to get her out of his system once and for all?

"Your thoughts are far away this morning, eh?" Hank broke the silence.

"Not so very far," Bradford muttered, then grinned. "Tell me, how is it a man of your heritage has a first name like Hank?"

Hank laughed heartily. "My mother was an Anglo. She gave me the name just before she died, not giving my father a chance to object. Out of respect to her, he let me keep the name."

"You don't seem to find your mother's death a tragedy. Does anything ever hurt you?"

Hank shrugged. "You cannot cry over the loss of someone you never knew."

"I suppose you're right," Bradford grinned. "But you, I've noticed, take everything with a smile."

"And why not, *amigo?*" Hank asked. "My grandfather always told me that it is easier to smile than to frown."

"It is a nice philosophy, but not suited to all of us," Bradford remarked slowly.

Just then the door to Angela's room opened and a moment later she appeared in the kitchen. The men were taken aback by her attire. She was wearing breeches, tight against her hips and thighs, and a crisp white blouse that was just as tight, outlining her firm, round breasts.

Bradford sat up stiffly. He wanted to thunder at Angela for the way she was dressed, but he stopped himself. Why the hell should he care? But Hank Chavez was staring at her. And, Bradford noticed, her eyes were riveted to Hank's face.

"What are *you* doing here?" she snapped without thinking, her eyes darkening. He looked just as she remembered, with the addition of a black moustache.

"I might ask the same of you, *menina*," Hank replied, his smile returning.

Bradford jumped up, looking from Angela to Hank and then back to Angela.

"How do you know Hank?"

"We met in Mobile," she said quickly, realizing that she had heard the bandit's name for the first time.

Angela smiled impishly at Bradford. "If you must know, I met this man when he held up the stage I was traveling on."

"You expect me to believe that?" Bradford stormed.

She managed to keep the smile. "As a matter of fact, Bradford, I don't care what you believe," she said coolly.

She walked past them to the stove and poured herself a cup of black coffee, deliberately keeping her back to them. Hank sat grinning silently, relieved that Bradford did not believe the holdup story.

"I'm going for a ride before breakfast," Angela said.

"I would like to join you," Hank said quickly, rising from the table.

Angela finished her coffee and left the kitchen, not waiting for Hank to catch up with her.

The early morning was pleasantly cool. The

sun was shining brightly, but it would be a while yet before it would make itself felt. Winter was approaching.

Hank finally caught up with Angela when she reached the barn, and offered to saddle her horse for her. Since none of the hired hands were nearby, she agreed. She was bursting with questions, but she held back. It would serve no purpose to have an argument here. Bradford might overhear.

With the sleek brown mare saddled, Angela mounted her without Hank's assistance, then waited while he saddled his own horse. But before he finished, Bradford appeared at the front of the barn.

He glared at her. "Just where do you think you're going dressed like that?" he demanded, taking hold of her horse's muzzle.

"I'm going riding," she replied hotly.

"Not like that you're not!"

Angela sat tensely, clutching the short riding crop in her right hand. "You are my partner, Bradford—my *equal* partner. You have no authority over me. I am my own woman—answerable to no one!" she stormed, fury evident in the deep blue-violet appearing in her eyes. "I will do as I please. Is that clear?"

"What you're going to do is get down from that horse!" he growled.

At that point, she lost control of her fury. "You go to hell, Bradford Maitland!" she cried, slashing her riding crop against the horse's flank.

The animal reared once and then bolted out of the barn in a swift gallop. Angela clung desperately to the mare's neck. Her hat flew away from her head, the thin string attached to it cutting into her throat. Only when the horse slowed a little did she look back.

A rider was just leaving the barn, half a mile behind her. Angela relaxed now and slowed her horse even more, giving Hank time to catch up. She rode over a small hill and down to an outcropping of trees on the other side of it. There, she pulled her horse up, out of view of the house and barn, to wait for Hank.

She had quite a few things to say to him, and this was a good place to do it. Dismounting, she tethered her horse to a low branch. She paced fretfully, tense, and still bristling over Bradford's audacity. He had no right to issue orders.

When she heard the other horse approach, she turned around swiftly, glad to have something to occupy her mind instead of Bradford. But it was not Hank who jumped down from his horse and came bounding over.

"I ought to horsewhip you!" Bradford said as he grabbed her shoulders and shook her roughly.

Angela pushed away from him and stumbled backward. She didn't feel quite so reckless out here in the open, alone with him. Suddenly she wanted to crawl away and hide from his anger, but she wouldn't let her feelings betray her.

"How dare you go out like that? Look at you!" he continued storming, his eyes running the length of her body. "That damn getup leaves very little to the imagination. There's no telling who you might run into out here!"

"Unfortunately, I ran into *you!*" she snapped. "Where is Hank?"

His eyes narrowed. "Was it your intention to seduce him out here? Is that why you're dressed like—"

"Stop it, damn you!" Angela screamed. "I didn't even know the man was here when I got dressed to go riding. I can't very well ride in a skirt, unless I pull it all the way up to my thighs. Would you prefer that?" She waited for him to answer. When he didn't, she continued more calmly. "I haven't had a chance yet to get proper riding clothes made. And I can't help the fact that these breeches have shrunk through so many washings. They are the only pair I have right now."

He approached her slowly, but Angela refused to flinch. She stood proudly, inches from him, and boldly met his eyes.

Angela waited for him to strike her. When he didn't, she started trembling. Suddenly she found herself crying.

"You told me you loved me once," she cried. "How can you hurt me so after all we shared together?"

He turned abruptly away. "How dare you bring up the past to me, when it was you who killed our love?"

Her eyes widened with confusion. "For God's sake, what did I do?"

"Damn your whore's heart!" he growled, turning back to her. "Did you really believe I would never find out about you and Grant? How many others have there been, Angela? Is Hank one of your lovers too?"

She was utterly stunned. "Is that what you think? Is that why you hate me?" She threw her hands out to him in an imploring gesture. "There has never been anyone but you! The only man who has ever made love to me is you. *You*. Damn you, Bradford!"

He could not allow himself to believe in her. "Don't play innocent with me, Angela! I said I found out about you and Grant. Do you think I would say that if I were not sure?"

Angela didn't wait to hear more. He was set against her, and she couldn't make him listen. She ran for her horse and quickly mounted it. She turned back to look at Bradford once, her eyes sparkling.

"I'm beginning to find that hate comes easily, indeed," she said bitterly.

She rode away without looking back.

Neither Bradford nor Angela was aware of the man concealed on a faraway bluff, with a spyglass turned on them. The place where he was lying was worn, for he had come to this spot often. He was waiting, waiting for the opportunity he prayed for daily. Angela couldn't always be protected. One day would find her alone on the ranch, with no hired help about and Maitland out of the picture. One day . . .

Forty-four

Angela stood on the porch, leaning against a post, looking up at the star-studded sky. She pulled her shawl closer about her shoulders and felt her teeth begin to chatter. It was very cold outside, but she preferred that to the different kind of cold inside the house with Bradford.

Now she understood why Bradford had been so cruel, why he hated her. He felt that she had betrayed him. And he wouldn't believe her when she denied it.

Condemned, but innocent. She might as well be guilty of his accusations. But no, she just didn't want to bed a man she didn't love.

Angela sighed. Maybe she should leave the ranch.

"You look very unhappy, *menina*."

She started. "Do you have to sneak up on a person?" she snapped.

Hank stood close by her side, the ever-present smile gracing his lips. "If you had not been so lost in your troubles, you would have heard me." He stretched languidly. "It is a beautiful night—and I finally have you alone."

"Where is Bradford?"

"Your partner has retired for the night," Hank said lightly. "I guess he feels it is safe to leave me alone with you now, since he has warned me that you are off limits."

Angela's expression turned incredulous. "Did he really say that?"

Hank laughed. "Those were not his exact words, but he made himself clear. I think that if Bradford did not feel indebted to me, he would have kicked me off this ranch by now. As it is, I am sure he regrets his invitation."

"You make it sound as if he were jealous. I can assure you that is not so."

Hank quirked a slim brow. "What else could cause the blind rage he has been in all day? I have never seen a man so furious over a woman before."

"It's not jealousy, though," Angela replied wistfully, wishing it were. "You see, it's *my* presence that incites Bradford, not yours. He can't stand me, and is doing his best to make me leave."

"Then why don't you?" Hank asked, gently picking up a lock of her hair. "I told you once that I wanted to take you to Mexico with me. Circumstances have changed now, and I am going home to claim what is mine. Mexico is not much different than Texas. Come with me, Angelina."

"As I recall, you said you would take me there whether I protested or not. Am I to fear abduction now?"

"No," he grinned. "But the thought has crossed my mind."

She smiled. "You make it very hard for me to detest you, Hank. But I'm afraid Mexico is not for me. If I went anywhere, it would be to Europe. But what are you doing here anyway? I didn't expect ever to see you again."

"I followed you to this area to return the rest of what I owe you, but I can see now that you have no need of it. This ranch is one of the largest in the area, from what Bradford tells me. You are quite a wealthy woman."

Wealth. Angela looked away. She would rather have the wealth of love than all the money in the world.

"Since I no longer have financial worries, you might as well keep the rest of what you stole," Angela said. "After all, you risked your life for it."

"You are generous, *menina*, but then, you can afford to be," he stated simply, his gray eyes gleaming in the moonlight. "And I will admit the extra money will come in handy. It will be rough going for a while, until my lands start to produce."

She looked back at him and studied him with

shaded eyes. "You told me why you came here, but how did you meet Bradford? And what is this about his being indebted to you?"

"He seems to think I saved his life the other night," Hank replied with a shrug. He related the story. Then, after a long silence, he took her hand and brought it to his lips. "A woman such as you should be happy. Come away with me, Angelina. I offer you my love."

She smiled. "Thank you, Hank, but no. I could not return your love."

"You feel nothing for me?"

"I hardly know you."

"You are being evasive, Angelina," he said pointedly.

She couldn't help but grin. "And you are being persistent."

"Only because I cannot accept your refusal. I will be honest with you and tell you the money was only an excuse to find you again. I have tasted the passion of your kiss, *menina*. I would be a fool if I did not try more than once to win you for myself."

He put his hand behind her neck and started to draw her to him, but Angela braced her hands on his chest to stop him.

"Hank, please."

He hesitated a moment, then let her go, reluctantly. "I will leave in the morning, for my presence here cannot help if Bradford is the man you really want. But I will wait in Dallas for a while. If you do not find your happiness here, *menina*, then come to me. I swear I can make you forget him." And he walked away before she could refuse him again.

Angela sat in the old rocking chair in her room, staring dismally at the shooting flames in the fireplace, fingering her gold coin absently. Life dealt such ironic quirks of fate. Her whole life seemed to revolve around Jacob Maitland. He took her in when she was desolate. He had her schooled. And she loved his son.

Angela went to her bureau and found the letter. She stood with her back to the fire and reread Jacob's letter slowly. Jacob had wanted her and Bradford to marry. They could have been married now if not for Crystal and her scheming. But then, maybe not. Most likely something else would have happened to stop them. It just wasn't meant to be.

And it was certainly too late now. She cried for a long, long time, sitting before the fire.

Forty-five

 Angela reclined against the corral fence, one foot resting on a lower plank as she watched the branding. It had been going on for weeks now, the cattle branding and the breaking in of three hundred or so wild horses. It would all be over today, or so Grant said.

Grant stood beside Angela, calling out orders to the men in the corral. She saw very little of Grant lately. He elected to stay out on the range with the men. She supposed the reason was that Grant preferred to stay away from Bradford and his foul temper.

Dust swirled as another cow was brought down by its horns to await the hot branding iron. Angela turned away and faced the house. Bradford was sitting on the railing at the end of the porch, watching her. He seemed always to be watching her, watching her with brooding eyes.

Ever since she had learned that Grant and Bradford would be going on the trail drive together, she had had bad feelings about the drive. She was sure something terrible was going to happen. It would take at least two months just to reach the boomtown of Ellsworth, Kansas, where the cattle would be shipped East. The men were starting out tomorrow morning. Angela shivered just to think about all the time the two of them would be in each other's company.

Bradford and Angela hardly talked to one another now. Ever since Hank had gone, Bradford had been silent. When they did talk, they were barely civil. She asked herself why she stayed on, but she never answered the question.

Mary Lou visited one afternoon and Angela tried to explain her fears about the cattle drive.

"You see, ever since Bradford came here, things have been very tense between him and Grant. Bradford got it into his head that there was something going on between Grant and me."

"You mean Bradford's jealous of Grant?"

"It's past the point of jealousy," Angela replied forlornly. "Bradford thinks I betrayed him with Grant and he won't forgive either of us."

"Maybe he'll feel different when he learns that Grant and I are going to get married." Mary Lou grinned.

"What?"

"You can't really be surprised," Mary Lou laughed. "Grant's been visiting me regularly ever since Daddy and I were here for dinner that Saturday night. Do you know Grant was waiting for me at my ranch that night? We must've talked till dawn."

Angela leaned back and sighed happily. "No wonder he hasn't been around here lately."

"You don't mind, do you?" Mary Lou asked. "I mean, you're going to be losing a good foreman."

"I think it's wonderful. I secretly hoped you two would get together."

"I hope you'll stop worrying now, Angela. Things are going to work out fine."

No, things wouldn't work out fine. Nothing would ever be fine again, Angela thought bitterly.

The bright moon began to edge over the rim of the mountain range. A young cowboy strummed a tune on his guitar by the campfire, and the soft melody carried through the quiet night to Bradford, some hundred yards away, perched on a large boulder for the first night watch.

Soon the camp grew silent and the night wore on. Bradford pulled a blanket over his shoulders as the chill wind slapped his face. He could no more stop the biting wind than he could stop those violet eyes from haunting him. The eyes seemed to follow him everywhere, day and night.

Only a week had passed and already he missed Angela desperately. He swore silently, cursing himself and cursing her. She had become a part of him, growing under his skin. He couldn't shake her.

"You plannin' on takin' the full watch by yourself?" Grant asked as he came up behind Bradford.

"What?"

"Perkin's came in for his relief and woke me at the same time. Thought maybe you'd fallen asleep."

Bradford grunted but didn't move.

"Here, I brought you some coffee," Grant offered and sat down beside him.

Bradford accepted the coffee, but didn't reply. "Guess now's as good a time as any to tell you I'm quittin' soon as the drive's over."

Bradford looked at him squarely. "I see," he said coldly.

"Ain't you even interested in why I'm quittin'?" Grant questioned.

"No, I guess not."

"Well, I'll tell you anyway, seein' how Mary Lou's plannin' to invite you to the weddin'."

"Wedding?" Bradford was incredulous. "You and Mary Lou Markham?"

"Yeah," Grant grinned. "That little gal's gone and stole my heart."

"What—about Angela?"

"What do you mean?"

Bradford's muscles stiffened and his eyes suddenly burned with an intensity that could surely have melted stone.

"I ought to tear you apart!" Bradford stormed, coming to his feet.

"What the hell's got into you?"

"You steal my girl from me, and then you dump her!"

Grant was thoroughly bewildered. "Hold on, Brad."

Bradford raged, his fists clenched at his sides. "Stand up or I'll lay you flat right where you are!"

"You stubborn bastard," Grant growled, his own temper rising. "So you're still festerin' over a fool idea?"

Bradford grabbed Grant by the front of his jacket and yanked him to his feet. With lightning speed, Bradford's fist slammed into Grant's jaw, sending him sprawling back against the rocks.

Grant fingered his jaw tenderly, but stayed where he had fallen. "You know, Brad, if I didn't know you better, I might take offense at this. But the fact of the matter is, you're a love-sick fool."

"Get up!" Bradford demanded. "I should have done this long ago, when I found out you'd brought Angela to Texas with you."

"It's not as simple as that," Grant began, sitting up slowly. "She asked me to bring her along, but I turned her down. But that little lady's as stubborn as all get out. She followed me—without my knowin' it."

"She followed you?" Bradford asked suspiciously.

"She just wanted an escort, Brad," Grant explained quickly. "She came out here to find her mother. There was never anything between her and me. Not that I didn't give it a try."

Bradford's eyes blazed again.

Grant didn't wait for Bradford to reach him, but bolted forward and caught him. They tumbled down off the boulder and landed in the dirt below. Grant had the advantage of landing on top of Bradford, and when Bradford swung at him and missed, Grant let his fist fall twice.

"Will you listen to me now, damnit, without flyin' off the handle?" Grant demanded, straddling Bradford's chest. "I asked Angela to marry me, but she turned me down. She never explained why she took off from you, and I never pressed her. All she would tell me was she couldn't marry you—even though she still loved you. And she wouldn't marry me because of her love for you. It didn't make sense to me, but that's the truth."

Bradford wiped the blood from his mouth. "You should have thought of a better story than that, Grant. I'm not buying it," he said before knocking Grant off him with a blow to the chin.

The fight was unmatched. Grant was stronger, and had been badly provoked. When it was over, Bradford didn't even have the strength to get up. Grant stood over him, his face bleeding some, though not nearly as badly as Bradford's was bleeding.

"I'm not gonna take this personally, Brad, since
 know it was your fool jealousy that brought it
·n. But you've got nothin' to be jealous about, or
·ver did have. So I asked Angela to marry me.
Vhy the hell shouldn't I? She's a damn beautiful
voman."

Bradford turned over and raised himself gently
·n one elbow, groaning. He spit the blood from
·is mouth, then glared up at Grant through eyes
lready beginning to swell.

"Is that how you enticed her to your bed? With
 proposal of marriage?"

"What the hell are you talkin' about?" Grant
houted, losing his temper all over again. "I've
·ever taken Angela to bed. She's a lady and she
leserves better than what you're accusin' her of."
;rant started to walk away, then stopped. "We
·een friends a long time, Brad. Once you start
hinkin' straight, we'll be friends again. Now, if
ou want to fire me over this—fine. Otherwise,
ll take this herd to Kansas as we agreed. What
lo you say?"

"I told you once I wouldn't fire you over a
voman."

"So you did." Grant grinned and offered Brad-
ord his hand. "Let me help you back to camp.
our cuts need lookin' after."

Forty-six

The afternoon was cold, with dark purple clouds approaching from the north. Angela looked out her bedroom window and frowned.

"It's going to rain before night. I hope I can make it to town before it does."

"Are you sure I can't change your mind, Angela?" Mary Lou asked.

Angela turned away from the window with a sigh and gazed at her friend sitting in the rocker in the corner. "No. But I'm glad you stopped over. You saved me a trip out to your place."

"Can't you at least wait till they get back?" Mary Lou tried again, deep concern in her voice.

"I hope to be in Europe by the time Bradford returns."

"You ought to think about it some more, honey. You know you love him. Give him a chance."

Angela moved to the bed to finish packing. "He won't change, Mary Lou. And he won't listen to reason. You don't know how hard it's been, living here with him, knowing he hates me."

"You're mistaking jealousy for hate," Mary Lou said emphatically.

"It hurts too much to stay."

"He can't stay mad forever."

"Yes he can," Angela returned.

"I still say you're bein' too hasty," Mary Lou ventured once again. "Give him time."

"I'm not strong enough," Angela said, feeling tears begin. "I've been hurt too much already. And he'll only go on hurting me. Besides, there is—something I never told you about Bradford. He's a married man."

"Married!" Mary Lou exclaimed. "I don't believe it."

Angela sighed. "He claimed he was married, then never brought it up again."

"Angela," Mary Lou said urgently, "you don't really want to go, do you?"

"No," Angela smiled. "I've grown to love it here, the land and the people. I'll miss Texas. But I have to leave."

Just then they heard a rider approaching. "Is someone coming to meet you?" Angela asked her friend.

"No."

"Then who could that be?" Angela's curiosity was aroused as she walked to the window.

"That's Decker, a boy who runs errands in town," Mary Lou said from behind Angela. "I wonder what he wants."

The knock sounded before Angela reached the front door. A slim boy stood on the porch. He was holding an envelope.

"A telegram came for Mr. Maitland, ma'am," Decker said.

"Mr. Maitland isn't here, Decker," Angela replied.

Decker grinned. "The telegraph operator knows that, ma'am. But he didn't know what else to do with this, so he had me bring it on out here."

Mary Lou came to the door and handed Decker a coin. "Here, Decker. Miss Sherrington will see that Mr. Maitland gets the message." Mary Lou took the telegram and closed the door.

"Why did you do that?" Angela asked.

Mary Lou held the envelope up and inspected it. "Aren't you even curious?"

"Why should I be?"

"But you're going to open it."

"Of course not. It's for Bradford, not for me."

"Honey, you're Bradford's partner and are supposed to take care of his interests in his absence. Now open this. I'm dying of curiosity. It's from New York."

"New York?" Angela's eyes widened. "All right, then. Give it to me."

Angela opened the telegram and read it. Stunned, she then read it aloud to Mary Lou.

BRADFORD,

TOOK YOUR ADVICE AND MARRIED MY SWEET-HEART WITHOUT FATHER'S PERMISSION. FATHER WASN'T HALF AS MAD AS EXPECTED. ALL WELL. CAN'T THANK YOU ENOUGH.

LOVE,
CANDISE

She dropped the paper and looked at Mary Lou, fury and disbelief turning her violet eyes to sapphire. "I was led to believe she was Bradford's wife!"

"I don't understand."

Angela's eyes sparkled with anger. "Don't you see? Bradford told me he was married just to hurt me. It was just another blade to twist in my heart! I should have realized he was lying."

"So he's not married?"

"No!"

"But that should make you happy, Angela, not furious. Now you can stay here and work things out."

"Not on your life!" Angela stormed. "If I stayed here, I'd be tempted to kill that bastard!"

Mary Lou sighed. "You'll write to me?"

"Of course," Angela replied. "I thought I'd go

on a grand tour first, to keep myself busy. Then I'll probably settle in England. Jacob left me a small estate there. But I'll always keep in touch with you. I'll want to hear all about your wedding."

"I'd best be going then." Mary Lou came forward and hugged her friend. "I'll miss you, honey. But I have a feeling we'll be seeing each other again."

Angela listened to Mary Lou ride off, and then Angela continued packing. An hour later, she had the only hired hand left on the ranch load her things in the buckboard and drive her into town. By the time she checked into a hotel, her temper had cooled and remorse was beginning to take over. She would take the stage the next day, and soon buy passage on a ship bound for England. She didn't really want to go, but she could think of no other solution. She stood staring out her hotel window for a long, long time.

Forty-seven

Threatening clouds hovered and an eerie quiet prevailed as Bradford urged his horse on to greater and greater speed. One of the four riders with him eased ahead of Bradford's horse and pulled in on the reins. The animal slowed gradually, finally coming to a stop. The beast was frothing at the mouth.

"Are you crazy?" Bradford shouted, trying to jerk the reins away from the other man.

"Take it easy, Mr. Maitland," the sheriff said as he dismounted. "You come to me for help and you're gonna take my advice whether you want to or not."

"But I've wasted enough time as it is," Bradford returned, desperation creeping into his voice.

"Well, go on then—if you want to get yourself *and* the lady killed!"

Bradford slumped forward. "What do you suggest then?"

"Tell me again about the old drunk. You said he came to you at the bar, and he called you by name?"

"Yes. He said he'd been paid a dollar to deliver a message to me, that I was to return alone to my ranch immediately if I ever wanted to see my partner alive again."

"Those were the exact words?"

"Yes."

"And who gave him the message?"

"A couple of strangers, two men he'd never seen before."

The sheriff took off his hat and wiped his forehead with the back of his hand. He looked up at the brooding gray clouds overhead and smiled, then turned back to Bradford.

"Those storm clouds are a blessing. Time is important and they'll make it darker all that much sooner, 'specially if the storm breaks."

"Get to the point, sheriff," Bradford replied irritably and dismounted.

They moved away from their three riding companions. "All right, now. Whoever it is at your ranch, we gotta assume they're after you, and not your lady partner."

"I'm not arguing that point."

"We also gotta figure they're in your house with Miss Sherrington," the sheriff continued. "If we just go ridin' in there, they got all the advantage. They're in a position to make any demands they want, since they're holdin' the lady."

"*We* are not going to ride in there, sheriff—I am!" Bradford pronounced adamantly. "The message said specifically that I was to come alone."

"I agree with you," the sheriff returned. "I'm not inclined to endanger the lady's life. But if you want to save your own skin, then you'll wait till dark."

"Dammit, sheriff! They said to get out there immediately!" Bradford exclaimed.

"Look, Mr. Maitland. You said it was an old drunk gave you the message, that you couldn't even understand him at first."

"Yes."

"Well then, they have to take a delay into consideration, considerin' who they picked to deliver the message. They'll wait. And you can see by the sky that it'll be dark very soon."

"All I see is that Angela's in danger," Bradford replied tensely, his eyes burning. "She must be scared out of her wits by now."

"But she'll be alive. Now, what you gotta do if you want to get through this with the least risk to your own life, is to sneak in there after dark. We're about a half mile from your ranch, I'd say. We'll move in closer when you're ready to go. And just as soon as I hear any shootin', then me and the boys here will come on in."

"Fair enough," Bradford said, and they moved back to wait with the others.

* * *

Bradford lay flat in Angela's garden, thankful for
the small cover it gave him. Large drops of rain
started to fall, but then stopped. He scanned the
yard, but could see nothing in the darkness surrounding him. The house was also in darkness.

Taking a deep breath, he dashed for the side of
the house. He pressed his back against the wall
and then moved slowly toward his bedroom window.

Without wasting a moment, he slipped through
his window, praying he would find no one waiting for him. But the room was empty, the door
closed.

It was pitch black inside, making it impossible
for him to see even a foot in front of him. He crept
toward the door, careful not to bump into anything. The house was deathly still.

Bradford carried in his hand the colt .45 given
him by the sheriff. Bradford held it up against
himself now as he edged the door open and
looked out. The house was dark and he could
hear nothing.

"I advise you to throw down whatever weapon
you have, Mr. Maitland, and come on in here with
your hands raised. Otherwise, your partner dies."

Bradford couldn't tell who the man was, only
that he was in the living room. Bradford dropped
his gun on the floor and came forward, his hands
above his head.

The front of the house was still in darkness, but

Bradford could make out a man's shadow by the fireplace. Scanning the area quickly, Bradford saw another form in the kitchen.

"All right, you can get some light in here now, Logan," the man by the fireplace called. "And bring the rope."

When a lamp was brought to the living room, Bradford recognized the man with flaming red hair immediately. He wore a heavy jacket over dark blue pants and shirt, and a gun belt strapped to his legs. The gun was in his hand, leveled at Bradford's chest.

"Courtney Harden," Bradford said, lowering his hands.

"Looks like you have more enemies than just me," Harden laughed, looking closely at Bradford's face. "Who beat you up? I'd like to congratulate the fellow."

"What do you want, Harden?"

"I suppose you thought you'd never see me again, eh, Bradford?"

"To tell the truth, I didn't think about it much one way or the other."

"No, of course you wouldn't. The only thing on your mind is adding to your already abundant riches. Never mind the little people you step on along the way."

"Just what is it you want, Harden?" Bradford asked impatiently.

"I know this is going to be hard for the likes of you to understand, but some people just don't like getting stepped on. That's why I'm going to kill you."

"For dismissing you?" Bradford laughed.

Courtney came forward. "That hotel-restaurant was *my* idea, not yours! I worked for years on that setup before I ever came to you with it. You cost me my contacts, my girls. You left me with nothing!"

"I'll admit you might have a grievance with me, Harden, but—isn't murder a little extreme?"

"That's your opinion," Courtney replied with a cold smile. "I've got nothing to lose."

"So you were the one responsible for the other attempts on my life."

"Yes. When you escaped unharmed in New York, and then again in Springfield, I decided to give you the chance to make amends. That's why I came to see you in Mobile. But you weren't agreeable. Then I tried once more to hire it done, but that damned Mexican came to your rescue. So, to get the job done, I'll have to do it myself. It's all worked out very well. There won't be anyone to connect me with your death."

Bradford stiffened. "Where is—my partner? Do you intend to kill her too?"

Courtney Harden's laughter was genuine. "I knew my message about your partner would do the trick. I've seen the lady in town before and I've got to hand it to you, Bradford. She's the most beautiful woman I've ever seen. It was quite a nice arrangement you had here."

"Answer my question, Harden!" Bradford growled, and started toward him. "If you've touched her, I'll—"

Courtney raised his gun, leveling it at Bradford's head. "You're not in a position to do much of anything, my friend." He motioned and Logan came forward. "Bring a chair and let's get this over with."

Logan brought one of the kitchen chairs and placed it beside Bradford. Logan was not a very large man, with graying brown hair and wary eyes. He was no match for Bradford and neither was Courtney. When Logan reached for him, Bradford sent the smaller man sprawling to the floor.

"That wasn't wise, Bradford," Courtney said calmly, secure because he was armed. "If you want your lady partner to survive this, I suggest you be obliging and let Logan do his job."

"But if she has seen you—" Bradford began.

"She hasn't, I assure you. So I have no reason to kill the young woman, unless you give me trouble."

It was against Bradford's nature to give up, but he had to think of Angela's safety. So when Logan approached him again, Bradford let himself be tied to the chair with the rope.

"I had almost hoped you would give me reason to put a few bullets in you, Bradford, but the lady must mean a great deal to you. It's really too bad that I'm not a forgiving man."

"Where is Angela?"

"That's what is so beautiful about all this, Brad," Courtney grinned. "You see, she's not here. And I have no idea where she is. I fully expected her to be here, but when I arrived, the place was deserted. There was no sign of clothes or anything else that might have belonged to the lady. Fortunately for me, you didn't know that. Otherwise you wouldn't have come."

"You bastard!"

"Yes, I am that," Courtney chuckled. "I'm a sonofabitch too. But I will live out my days knowing that you will not. Now I must end this conversation, however much I have enjoyed talking to you. We really must get on with this before the storm breaks and puts out the fire."

Bradford's blood chilled. "Fire?"

Now Courtney's eyes lit up grotesquely. "Didn't I tell you? That's how you're going to die."

Logan got the lamp from the kitchen and handed it to Courtney and they crossed to the door. Courtney looked slowly around the room, then rested his exultant gaze on Bradford once again.

"It was a nice place you had here—once," he said before he threw the lamp down in the middle of the floor. "I'll surely see you in hell someday, Bradford Maitland," he cried.

The fire spread rapidly across the floor. In just

seconds the closed door was aflame, then the curtains. In minutes the whole house would be a blazing inferno. Bradford watched, stunned, as the flames danced closer and closer.

Forty-eight

Angela returned to her hotel room after an early dinner. The room was quite luxurious, but that wasn't surprising. In many ways, Dallas was a sophisticated city.

A large brass bed dominated the room. There was also a quaint gold velvet love seat with matching chair beside it, and a walnut writing desk. A fire was burning in the marble fireplace, taking away the chill that accompanied the brooding weather. Portraits of eighteenth-century royalty covered most of the green-and-gold wallpaper.

Angela sat down at the desk and gathered pen and paper. She only just started a letter to Jim McLaughlin when there was a knock at the door.

"Who is it?"

Hearing no answer, she got up and walked to the door. She opened it and saw a slim young man standing there grinning and she paled.

"Hello, Angela."

"Billy Anderson." Her voice was a hoarse whisper.

"Aren't you gonna invite me in?" Billy asked pleasantly.

Angela shook off her shock. "Certainly not! What is it you want, Billy?"

"To talk."

"We have nothing to talk about."

She started to close the door, but he shoved it open violently, sending her into the middle of the room. Suddenly the door was closed and Billy was leaning back against it.

"How dare you?" she stormed. "Get out of here, Billy, before I call the manager!"

"I don't think you'll call anyone, Angela," he replied as he pulled a gun from the inside of his fawn-colored coat.

Sudden fear crept through her. She stared at the gun, much like her own little derringer, and wished to God hers were on her instead of packed in her luggage. She looked at her luggage, on the bed where she had left it, but couldn't see much hope there. Both cases were closed.

Billy grinned wickedly. "I told you the day would come, didn't I, Angela? It took a long time, but the rewards will be worth the wait."

Angela tried to ignore the icy fear that clutched her. "What do you want, Billy?"

"I haven't quite decided yet. For a long time

now, I just wanted to kill you. Does that surprise you?"

Angela was stunned. This couldn't be happening.

"Aren't you gonna ask me why I wanted to kill you?" She could only nod slowly. "I've always wanted you, Angela, but even when you were nothin' but poor white trash I wasn't good enough for you. When I began to get somewhere, you still wouldn't have me. You've obsessed my mind, Angela. But now that I've seen you again, I think I'll let you live after all. There are ways to make you mine, and mine alone."

She finally found her voice, though it came out as a cracked whisper. "You—you can't be serious."

"Of course, you will have to become my wife," he continued as if he hadn't heard her. "But that will only be a title, for the sake of appearance. No, you're gonna suffer for the years you have made me suffer. You will be my slave, but only you and I will know it. Oh, I have such wonderful plans for you, Angela."

She stared at him with wide violet-blue eyes. He was crazy, truly crazy!

"What you want is impossible," she said, as evenly as she could. "I would never consent to marry you."

"Really?" Billy asked with a raised brow and a grin on his lips.

He sauntered forward, waving his gun dangerously in the air. When he reached her, he stuck the gun between her breasts, and with his other hand, took a handful of her hair and pulled her painfully against him. Still holding her by the hair, he jerked her head back and brought his lips down over hers. She gagged at the smell of sour whiskey and tobacco on his breath, and tried to push away.

He released her hair and grabbed her arm with the hand that held the gun, pulling her arm cruelly behind her back. She was unable to move without pain tearing through her shoulder.

With his free hand he grabbed her breast, his fingers digging into her excruciatingly. She cried out.

Billy laughed.

"This will be even more enjoyable than I thought," he rasped. "I'll have you grovelin' at my feet before I'm finished with you."

He released her and she stumbled back. She grasped her throbbing arm, feeling tears of pain beginning to surface. But she fought them. She would be damned before she would let Billy Anderson see her cry.

She watched him warily as he moved around the room, taking in the surroundings. "You live pretty high on the hog, don't you? I guess I can get used to that. And I see you were plannin' a trip."

"Yes, I was."

"Looks like I got to you just in time, then," he

remarked and moved back to her. "But even if you had gone, I would have found you again, just like I did this time."

"How did you find me?" she asked, stalling for time.

He laughed. "I knew about the inheritance Maitland left you, and followed that lawyer here. I've been waitin' here all this time, just for the right moment. And when I saw you come into town today and check in here, I knew the time had come. Now get that luggage off the bed," he commanded, picking up a lock of her hair. "We'll be usin' it now."

Angela suddenly saw her chance. "I have to unpack something first," she said quickly.

"There will be time for that later," he replied. "Just move it for now."

Her body went rigid when she saw her only hope vanish. "Move it yourself!" she snapped. "I will not—"

He backhanded her, sending her tumbling to the floor. Then he yanked her to her feet and pushed her toward the bed. "You'd better learn now that you'll do what I say, Angela. I'm not opposed to dealin' out punishment if you don't. In fact, I'd enjoy that as much as takin' you to bed."

Angela had no doubt that he would take pleasure in beating her to death. She considered screaming for help, but cast that idea aside, sure that he would shoot her. She could think of no way to save herself, at least not yet. But if she could just get that gun away from him . . .

She lugged the heavy trunks off the bed and waited for his next move. A rumble of thunder sounded in the distance and, at that moment, there was a knock.

Angela ran for the door. But she was jerked to a halt before she got halfway there, and Billy's arms circled around her, squeezing the breath from her.

"Whoever it is, get rid of them!" Billy whispered urgently, the short barrel of his gun touching her jaw. "Do you understand me?"

She nodded slowly.

"Who is it?" she called out tremulously.

The only answer was another knock, much louder this time. Then the handle of the door was tried, but Billy had locked it.

"What do you want?" she called.

"I'm not about to talk through the door, Angela," was the reply.

"It's Bradford!" she gasped.

Billy swung her around to face him. "That's impossible! I saw him leave for Kansas myself!"

"You saw him?"

"Yes. I wanted to be sure he was gone so I went out on the range and watched him leave. He has no business bein' back here so soon!"

"Angela, will you open this door, or shall I break it down?" Bradford called.

"Get rid of him—or I will!" Billy said meaningfully.

Angela understood well enough. She had to make Bradford leave, but how?

"I'll get rid of him, but let me handle it, Billy," she said firmly.

When Billy released his hold on her, she smoothed her hair back and crossed to the door slowly. Opening the door just wide enough to peek through, she took a deep breath and looked up. The sight of him turned her face ashen.

"What happened to you?" she gasped, completely forgetting Billy. Bradford was covered in black soot from head to foot.

"What took you so long to answer the door?" he asked gruffly.

"I'm busy, Bradford," she replied, Billy's presence frightening her once again.

"What are you doing here?"

"I don't think that's any of your business," she answered abruptly, hoping he would be angry enough to leave.

"Everything you do is my business."

"Not anymore," she returned sharply. "Please leave."

Without replying, he suddenly pushed his way into the room and confronted Billy.

Billy instantly sensed the fury of the larger man and backed away, his gun hidden in his hand.

Angela cleared her throat nervously. "I told you I was busy, Bradford."

"Who is this?" Bradford asked furiously, turning the smoldering golden gaze on her.

"A friend of mine," she replied, growing more desperate by the moment. She had to get Bradford to leave. "Just like Grant was a friend. *Now* will you go away?"

Bradford turned on his heel and stormed from the room, slamming the door. She sighed in relief. At least Bradford was safe now.

"You handled that very nicely." Billy grinned, relaxing. "Who was Grant? One of your lovers?"

"You wanted me to get rid of him!" Angela hissed. "Well, what does it matter how I did it? He's gone, isn't he?"

"Yes," Billy replied with a savage grin. "And now for the rewards I've waited so long for."

Bradford stood at the top of the stairs, staring ahead without seeing. What she had said couldn't be true, not after what Grant had told him. Which of them would he believe? Would he—could he— trust Angela after all they'd been through?

Angela unfastened her skirt and let it fall to her feet, her eyes glued to the small gun pointed at her.

"You're learnin' to follow orders very well, Angela," Billy said, a cruel gleam in his eyes. "Now spread yourself out on the bed like a good little whore. And just remember, if you cry out, I'll make you wish you were dead before I—"

At that moment the door burst open.

Angela screamed. "Bradford, he has a gun!" But before she could finish the sentence, Billy fired at Bradford.

Angela stared in horror, expecting to watch Bradford fall. But he kept charging forward, like a bull. Billy was terrified. His one bullet was gone. He tried to dodge Bradford's reach, but he was too late.

The men fell to the floor together. Angela turned her back on the scene, sickened by the sounds of bones crunching. She grabbed the cover from the bed and wrapped it around her, then faced the men again. Billy was no longer struggling. He had fallen unconscious. But that did not stop Bradford from hammering away at him.

"Bradford, that's *enough*! He can't feel it anymore."

Bradford did not answer. He continued to deliver blow after blow to the body under him.

"You're killing him!" Angela screamed.

Bradford stopped suddenly and looked at her. Without a word he took hold of the back of Billy's coat and dragged him out of the room and down the hall. She heard Billy's body falling down the stairs. If the beating hadn't killed Billy, the fall easily could.

"You didn't kill him, did you?" she whispered when Bradford returned.

"No, but it will be a long time before he'll be able to move again," Bradford replied. "And then I will see to it that he is shipped across the continent."

"How did you know I needed you?" Suddenly she felt overwhelmingly shy. She held the bedspread around herself tightly.

"You told me," he answered gently, keeping his distance from her. "It was something you said."

"I don't understand."

"It can wait. You need some rest, and so do I. We will talk tomorrow."

She watched him go, perplexed. Did he pity her now? Well, pity was the last thing she wanted from Bradford Maitland. She would leave tomorrow, as she had planned.

"*Amigo*, is that your mess at the bottom of the stairs?"

Bradford turned from his doorway to see Hank coming down the hall.

"What the hell are you doing here?"

Hank grinned. "This is a free country, is it not? Or do you own Dallas?"

"You were supposed to be on your way to Mexico," Bradford reminded him stiffly.

"So I was," Hank shrugged. "But with a little luck, I will not have to go alone. I have been waiting for a certain lady to join me."

"Anyone I know?" Bradford asked drily.

Hank laughed. "I believe you know her very well, *amigo*. The lady is your partner."

Bradford went rigid. "Is that why she's here?"

"She is here?" Hank asked, surprised. "Where?"

"Wait a minute! Is Angela here to meet you or not?"

"No," Hank replied. "I have not seen her since I left your ranch."

Bradford's eyes blazed. "I warned you to stay away from her!"

"By what right?" Hank demanded. "She is only your partner. Does that give you the right to speak for her? No, *amigo*. She is a woman without a man, and I would be a fool not to try to make her mine."

Bradford grabbed Hank's shirt front and shoved him up against the wall. "I'm warning you—"

Bradford stopped when he felt the barrel of a gun pressed against his belly. He let go of Hank, bristling at the man's amused grin.

"Is this how it will always be for you, *amigo*? The man at the bottom of the stairs, you beat him senseless. But the bruises on your face are old. Was that another fight over the woman? And now you wish to tear me apart too, eh?" Hank shook his head. "You will let no one else have her, but you do not claim her for yourself. What is wrong with you?"

Bradford did not have the energy to pretend. "I don't know if she'll still have me."

Hank put his gun away. "If she knows you love her, then she'll have you. It's you she loves. I wish you had not come to your senses, *amigo*, for then you might have driven her to me. But now . . . there is nothing for me here. *Adios.*"

Grinning at his bigheartedness, Hank loped down the hall and out of sight. Now there would be no coming back for her. He was certain of that.

Forty-nine

Angela spent two full days in bed. The storm raged outside as she lay watching it.

Against her protests, Bradford sent for the doctor, who ordered strict bed rest. She gave in, needing the time to settle her nerves, time to think, after her ordeal.

She hadn't seen Bradford and they had yet to have their talk. She had learned of the fire and rejoiced that Bradford was safe. Fury and terror had given him the strength to break free of the ropes and escape the flaming house.

Mary Lou came to visit in the afternoon of the second day. She talked of pleasant things, but she was unable to cheer her friend.

After Mary Lou left, Angela stood by the window, staring out at the darkness, listening to the rain. The room was pleasantly warm, with logs blazing in the fireplace. She slipped out of her robe and laid it over the chair by the window. She didn't hear Bradford enter the room, and she jumped when he said, "Where are you going, Angela?"

She turned and found him staring at the trunks at the foot of her bed.

She moved over to the trunks and closed the lids without looking at him. "I thought I'd go to Europe. I plan to leave tomorrow."

"I had the impression you liked it here," Bradford returned, his voice almost a whisper. At least she had not said she was going to Mexico.

Her eyes were filled with unconcealed longing. "I do, Bradford, but I've been here long enough. I'd like to go places I've never been," she said lightly and crossed to stand by the fire, the light behind her making her nightgown almost transparent. "You know, you never told me why you came back here. Or how your face was bruised."

Bradford fingered his jaw self-consciously.

"Grant and I finally had it out," he answered uneasily.

"Does he look as bad as you do?" she asked, whirling around.

Bradford leaned against the side of the bed, a weak grin on his lips. "No, he got the better of me this time, and I deserved every bit of it."

"Yes, you did," she replied.

"Grant told me what I was too pigheaded to listen to before."

Angela began to feel faint. "Which was... what?"

"That you didn't come out here because of him—and that he never made love to you."

"Why didn't you believe *me* when I told you the same thing?"

"Because I saw the two of you in bed, Angela, in Nacogdoches. You were kissing Grant, with only a damn sheet wrapped around you. I went there to bring you back to Golden Oaks, but when I opened the door to your room and saw the two of you like that, I assumed the worst. What else was I supposed to think? I still don't understand how you could be in a position like that unless you were lovers."

She listened to him quietly and then said, "Grant came to my room drunk. He busted in on me before I could get dressed. And since he was too drunk to stand up, I put him to bed. He had come to ask me to marry him, but I refused. He pleaded for the kiss before I left, and I saw no harm in that. Then I got another room for myself for the night. That is the whole story."

Bradford crossed the room to stand before her. "I realize how wrong I have been, Angela. But why did you leave Golden Oaks without a single word? My God, do you know how I felt? And then I thought you had run away to be with Grant. It nearly destroyed me. Why did you do it?"

"I was in the hall that morning when Crystal

read you the letter. I heard it all, Bradford. I believed it wholly. I believed you were my half brother. I knew I had to leave, because seeing you again would have hurt too much. I continued to believe the lie until Jim McLaughlin found me and gave me a letter from Jacob."

"But why have you never told me all this?"

"Because you never gave me a *chance*."

Everything was clear to him now. Everything except one question. Had he killed her love with cruel treatment?

"I know how *I* felt when Crystal claimed that you were my half sister. The world suddenly became black and empty. Did you feel the same way?" he asked her gently, his eyes shaded. For once, he was thinking of her and not of himself.

"Yes. Even when I went to town and found out that your fiancée had just arrived. It almost didn't matter, because I thought I could never have you anyway."

Bradford groaned. He had forgotten about his lie, and wished now that his pride had not goaded him into hurting Angela with it.

He cleared his throat and said sheepishly, "I'm not married, Angela."

"I know," she grinned. "Candise sent a telegram while you were gone, explaining that she had married on your advice."

"I would have told you about her," Bradford rushed ahead. "I only asked her to marry me to please my father, and she agreed to please hers, even though she loved another man. But then I found you, and I knew what happiness could be. She arrived the day you left Golden Oaks, and I broke our engagement before I came after you. She was as relieved to break it off as I was."

"So you told me you had married just to hurt me?"

"I . . . well, I wanted to show you I didn't care. But I guess I did want to hurt you—to make you suffer as I was suffering—because I thought you didn't love me." He tilted her chin and searched her eyes. "Why were you leaving Texas, Angel?"

"Because I couldn't bear to live with your hate anymore."

He took her face in his hands. "I love you, Angela."

Her eyes filled with tears. "Please don't say that, Bradford. Not unless you mean it."

He smiled. "I can't blame you for doubting me. I convinced myself that I hated you, and I guess I convinced you too. But it was only because I loved you so much. I just couldn't stand it, loving you as much as I do, and not having you love me any longer."

"I never stopped loving you, Bradford."

Very gently, he brought her close to him. "It's not easy for a stubborn fool like me to beg forgiveness. I know I've treated you badly. So many things I said and did were calculated to hurt you, to show you that you meant nothing to me. I've cursed myself a thousand times for my cruelty.

My damnable jealousy has made us both suffer.
Can you ever forgive me, Angel? I know I have
no right even to ask."

"I already have," she answered softly. Her eyes
were sparkling.

Bradford picked her up then and kissed her
hungrily. "I'll never mistrust you again, Angela,"
he whispered huskily. "I swear it! I know my
faults. I know that whenever I see another man
looking at you my temper will flare. I can't help
that. But I won't let it come between us ever
again. Oh, Angel, it's only because I love you so
damn much!"

His eyes were a golden brown as he carried her
to the bed. He was thinking with pride, *this
woman's mine!*

The storm continued all through the night, but
neither Angela nor Bradford heard it.

Epilogue

On a glorious winter morning not long after, Angela and Bradford were married in a small Dallas church.

Angela's thoughts were with Jacob. His fondest dream was her own, and their dreams had come true. *I have not lost him, Jacob. I have him now and forever.*

And it was true.

Please look for
Johanna Lindsey's
newest bestseller

THE PURSUIT

Available Now Wherever Books are Sold

And now enjoy an excerpt!

Kimberly MacGregor waved the letter in her hand to gain her husband's attention as he entered her sitting room. "Megan has written again," she told him. "She has invitations piling up, too many as usual, but in this case that's ideal. Let her pick and choose the best ones. She's sounding really excited about this. Want to read the letter?"

"Nay."

That answer was too abrupt and a bit disgruntled-sounding for a man of Lachlan MacGregor's easy temperament.

"You aren't having second thoughts about letting Melissa go to London, are you?"

"Aye."

"Lachlan!"

His disgruntled tone was now accompanied by a matching look. "I dinna like asking the Duke and Duchess o' Wrothston for favors."

Kimberly relaxed. She should have known. Lachlan might get along famously with Devlin St. James when he and his wife Megan came to visit them at Kregora Castle, or vice versa, but it wasn't always that way. They had in fact met under bizarre circumstances which didn't account for Lachlan's remark about favors.

"This was Megan's idea, so there's no favor involved," she reminded him. "As soon as she heard that all of Melissa's beaux were being frightened off by my over-protective brothers, she suggested Meli come to England where the MacFearsons are unknown. You agreed it was a good idea. I agreed it was an excellent idea. And Meli is looking forward to it. So don't be having second thoughts now."

"I assumed she'd be staying at Wrothston, as we do when we visit them in England, no' in London town," he grumbled. "The lass has been tae Wrothston enough tae be comfortable and feel right at home. London's no' the same, and she'll be nervous enough—"

"Nervous?" Kimberly interrupted. "Our daughter is excited about this trip, she's not the least bit nervous. If anyone's nervous it's you, and you and I aren't even going until later in the summer. Is that it, then? You're letting your worry for her override your better judgment?"

"Nay, I just dinna want her feeling she has tae find a husband afore she comes home. That's tae much pressure tae be putting on her at her young age. You have assured her—?"

"Yes, yes, I've assured her she can be an old maid if she'd like."

"Och, this isna funny, Kimber."

She tsked at him. "You're the one making too much out of it. Most young girls her age go through this; I did myself. Now I might have been nervous about it, but Meli really isn't. She plans to have fun, to make some new friends, to be awed by such a big town as London is, and she even figures she'll probably find a husband while she's at it. But that's not at the top of her to-do list by any means. She thought we wanted her to make a concerted effort to get affianced, but I've assured her if she does, that's fine, and if she doesn't, that's fine, too. Maybe you should tell her the same before she leaves, so she can just relax and let what happens happen. Now have we covered all your last minute doubts?"

"Nay, 'tis still a huge undertaking tae be putting on the duchess on our behalf."

"Would you like us to go as well for the whole summer instead of just a few weeks as we planned?"

He looked appalled. Just as she expected. "You said that wouldna be necessary."

"Nor is it. We covered Megan's willingness already. And furthermore, she isn't planning any events herself; she merely has invitations lined up that she was no doubt going to accept anyway. Besides, she adores Meli and is an old hand at this sort of thing. She sponsored me, didn't she? And had a hand in matching you and I to wedded bliss."

That made him grin. "Is that what we've been having, darlin'? Wedded bliss?"

She quirked a golden brow at him and asked, "You don't think so?"

He pulled her to her feet, then meshed her hips to his. "I'd be calling it heaven m'self."

"Would you now?" She grinned back at him, then made a face. "Bah, you're not going to get out of this subject that easily. Why are you really having doubts? And no more of these lame reasons that don't wash."

He sighed. "I had the hope remaining that our lass would end up wi' a fine Scot brave enough tae ignore the legend and trounce any o' your sixteen brothers that think tae bully him."

"What an unkind thought," she said, and smacked his shoulder before she moved away from him. "I love my brothers—"

"I know you do, Kimber, and I even tolerate them m'self, but you canna deny they deserve a trouncing or two for scaring off all o' Meli's suitors. If we didna have friends in England willing tae sponser her for a season there, the poor lass could end up permanently unwed, and I want m' daughter tae be as happy in wedlock as I've made you."

She chuckled. "Listen to that bragging."

"True nonetheless," he said with complete confidence.

"Perhaps," she allowed with a teasing grin, but then grew serious again. "As for Meli and her future happiness, is the nationality of the man she loses her heart to really of importance to you? And before you answer, keep in mind that if you say yes, your English wife will be insulted."

He laughed. "Half English wife, though one could wish yer Scottish half didna come from the MacFearson himself."

She ignored the reference to her father this time. "Answer me."

"Nay, darlin', the hope was no' that her husband be Scottish exactly, was more that he just hail from closer tae home than England is. I'm no' looking forward tae our lass moving far away is all," he ended with another sigh.

She moved closer again to cup his cheeks in her hands. "You knew that would be possible."

"Aye."

"You also knew that her prospects in our neighborhood were very slim. We don't exactly live close to any towns up here, and the other clans nearby don't have any sons of an age appropriate for our lass. And being the MacGregor's daughter limits her choices even further."

"Aye, I ken that as well."

"So this is all just a father bemoaning the loss of his only daughter in marriage, even before she's married?" she asked in exasperation.

He nodded with a sheepish look. She decided not to scold him for such silliness but said instead, "Lach, I'll be just as unhappy to see her go, but we knew from the day she was born that she would be leaving us one day to start her own family, and even then we didn't expect her to start that family near Kregora Castle. Granted, we weren't thinking as far as England, but still—"

Kimberly amazed even herself when she suddenly burst into tears. Lachlan gathered her close and made all the soothing sounds appropriate to providing comfort. She finally pushed away from him, annoyed with herself.

"Don't ask why that happened," she mumbled.

He grinned at her. "I'm sorry, Kimber. I didna mean tae refresh all your own misgivings."

"You didn't. Unlike you, I'm delighted Meli has this opportunity for a season in London. I just"— she paused for a sigh of her own—"just had the same hope as you still lurking, though I thought I had given up on that long ago. And it is pointless. Even those few young lads who did come to call on her live miles away, which is probably why you weren't all that displeased when my brothers ran them off."

"Miles away is no distance a' tall up here; they just didna impress me too much is all, and rightly so as it turned out. Look how quickly they turned tail when your brothers started in on them. That last one made his excuses after one wee warning from Ian Two that he'd be displeased if his niece was e'er made unhappy."

"I think it was because he had a fistful of the poor boy's shirt when he said it."

They both laughed for a moment, remembering how quickly the suitor had fled. He'd practically run for the door the moment after he'd made his excuses. The laughter eased their misgivings.

"Och, well, this trip canna be avoided I suppose," Lachlan conceded.

"No, it can't."

"Speaking o' which, is Meli done wi' her packing?"

"She's not leaving for three more days, plenty of time to finish that up. She's gone to see my father and probably will be spending the night. Actually, I think her intent was to assure my brothers that she forgave them for ruining her prospects here at home—a few of them have been quite gloomy over that if you didn't know. She was also going to assure them that when the right man for her comes along, she'll know it herself, so they needn't worry on that account."

"She actually thinks saying so will assure them of anything?"

"Well, she's hoping," Kimberly grinned. "My brothers can be reasoned with—some of the time."

Read the further adventures of a woman
brave enough to stand up to
her sixteen protective uncles in

THE PURSUIT

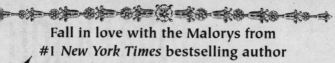

#1 *NEW YORK TIMES*
BESTSELLING AUTHOR

JOHANNA LINDSEY